DIVIDED MINDS

War of the Worlds within

SANJAY KOPPIKAR

™
Sapna
Ink

Sapna Ink.

Published by Sapna Group.
Sapna Book House (P) Ltd.
3rd main road, Gandhinagar,
Bangalore – 560009, India.

ISBN: 978-93-86116-37-6

Printed in India SIP- 031

Sapna Ink is an imprint of the Sapna Group,

Dedicated to
all scientists trying to make our lives
better through
Nano Technologies.

PROLOGUE

Five days of no connectivity from the outside world. I get all the time to sit and think of what I should be writing next. But this time things were different. I was going through a writer's block and nothing was coming to my mind. There was no topic. But I was confident that if I relaxed and gave myself space, something would pop. I would get my story out here on this vast sea voyage.

Just then, I felt a warm pat on my back. I turned to see retired Army General AK Singh smiling at me. In a conference some years ago, we'd ended up on the same table. We'd bonded over a shared love of stories of courage, dedication, passion, war, and even love. It was sad that he did not write but I thought that his being here was actually rather perfect for me!

'What's cooking? Is this another of your story writing journeys you told me about?' he asked.

'Yes and no, General', I laughed. 'This time, I am in search of a story. And I am so glad to find you here!'

'Any time, my boy! Any time. But what are you planning to write?' he asked as we slowly moved towards the nearest lounge chair on the deck.

'Frankly, I don't know yet. May be I'll write about the toughest war that you have ever fought. I have you now for next 5 days!' I said with a sly smile.

But to my surprise, he didn't react. In fact he seemed lost in thought. I wasn't sure if he'd even heard me. Then, quite suddenly he stood up and waved at someone who was just coming up on the deck. A woman in her late twenties, may be. Very attractive, to say the least. She waved back at the General and started walking towards us.

'You asked me for a war story. I'll throw in a love story as well,' he said. I blinked, wondering what he could mean.

As she approached us, General said, 'There you go, you have your story! Where is Doctor Saheb?'

'Ah! I don't know what Singh Sir has told you! I certainly don't have any story!' the lady who was dressed in a simple but beautiful salwar kameez said. Her tone implied anger but I had to look at her a little more carefully to see that she wasn't really angry. True to my assumption, she smiled quickly and then continued, 'Doctor saheb is sleeping. You know him. He worked like a madman for the three days and nights just so he could come on this cruise! And now he'll spend it sleeping'. Both of them laughed out loudly.

The General introduced us to each other. Her name was Dr. Payal and she had a brilliant smile.

'Payal, Sanjay is a good friend and an author. He was looking for a good story. I thought maybe your story would fit in quite well. What do you think?'

'Are you serious?' she asked, her eyes growing big.

'Yes, I am. It has to come out. At least as a story. And why not? Let us see if he likes it. Then, it could be his call to write it or not,' the General explained. Well, I was surely intrigued by now.

It took a little more persuasion but she finally gave in. We settled in the corner of the shaded deck on comfortable lounge chairs, looking out at the beautiful cerulean sea with glasses of drinks in our hands.

Payal started hesitantly.

CHAPTER - 1

We were late.

Gautam and I entered the auditorium, holding hands and I was desperately hoping that no one would notice our tardiness when just then, the speaker on the dais threw a question to the audience.

'What is love?'

We looked at each other amused. Did we come to the right auditorium? We were doctors, particularly post graduate students in various specializations, so what did love have to do with us?

As we tried to make our way in as discreetly as possible, I spotted Archana, my room-mate from the hostel, sitting near the dais, and she turned around at the same moment to glance at the door, probably wondering where we were. She'd reserved a couple of seats for us. Since it was right up in front of the dais, it was rather impossible not to come under the attention of the speaker, who looked at the two of us, and continued with his question, that no one had ventured to answer.

'What is love? Is it holding hands?' People behind us, sniggered and I quickly let go of Gautam's hand although everyone in college knew that he'd been my boyfriend for years now. I wasn't amused at coming under the spotlight for romantic reasons.

Somewhere around the last year of our MBBS we had grown really close. Close enough to be branded the 'cutest couple' in our class and while Gautam certainly enjoyed the attention, I didn't.

I slid into my seat, my head down and watched Gautam do the same, from the corner of my eye. He winked at me swiftly and I glared at him before focusing my attention to the speaker on the dais.

The speaker, Dr. Amit Deshpande was a well-known personality who visited our hospital a couple of times every year to give lectures on fields that he was researching. I had been waiting for him to return to our hospital for a lecture because I'd only heard and read about him and I was quite keen to see all the fuss about him firsthand.

'What is love? Is it the sweat that pops up on your forehead when you see your sweetheart in front of you? Is it when your heart starts beating faster? What is it?', he continued, eyes passing over everyone.

Everyone seemed a little wary of replying to what was certainly a trick question. Sensing that no one was keen to answer Dr. Amit smiled and shrugged.

'Okay, I'm surprised at the lack of response. I thought Doctors would have come up with one answer at least! If you look at it from a biological perspective, love is like a mammalian drive, similar to hunger or thirst. However, psychology sees love as more of a social and cultural phenomenon. But we're all doctors here although I am the only one without any patients!' Some people tittered nervously as he continued.

'Certainly love is influenced by hormones, neurotrophins, and pheromones. For example, passionate love is intense longing, and is often accompanied by physiological arousal.' He paused.

Archana nudged me and whispered, 'Passionate love, hmm?' I nudged her back exasperatedly, although my eyes were trained on Dr. Amit.

'And arousal is a physiological and psychological state of being awake or reactive to stimuli. It involves the activation of the reticular activating system in the brain stem, the autonomic nervous system and the endocrine system, leading to increased heart rate and blood pressure and a condition of sensory alertness, mobility and readiness to respond,' he rattled out, and we listened to him in rapt attention.

Tapping his own head lightly, he continued, 'In other words, we all know that the pinkish-beige thing that resides here, which we inanely refer to as grey matter, has neurons. And we know that a neuron is an electrically excitable cell that processes and transmits information through electrical and chemical signals.'

'Now let's revisit our question. Love can be defined as electrical pulses that are sent from the brain to the body and that results in particular reactions such as the heart racing, or sometimes sweating, or the mouth getting dry. All these are reactions that can be explained biologically because it all eventually comes from the brain, right?'

Some of the doctors in the front nodded. I was a little skeptical about this cut and dried explanation of love but then it did make sense in a way. Well, it was logical and so it had to make sense.

'So,' he continued, 'Love is nothing but some random messages sent from the brain to the body to react in certain ways. But the brain is not aware of what it is doing. The brain cannot decipher these messages to tell us in exact words, what we are feeling. But what if your body is able to play a more active role in helping your brain decipher these messages? What if a part of your body that is malfunctioning can tell your brain about the problem so that it can be fixed in time?'

I blinked rapidly trying to understand what he was saying. But before I could formulate my thoughts, he went on.

'Everyone knows that electronics and medicine are tied up intimately. From monitoring machines to pacemakers to body scans and almost every aspect of health care, electronics have played a vital role so far. There has been so much development in this field that at present, electronics has taken over a really active role when it comes to treatment. But what I'm talking of is the future, because we are standing at the threshold of something big and important.'

He paused and looked around and signaled to a couple of boys standing in the corner. They brought something that looked like equipment on a trolley and placed it at the center of the stage. He, then continued speaking.

'The research in the field of medical electronics is at a point where there are many exciting possibilities. There are so many more ways in which lives can be changed with what we are learning and developing. '

'I would like to show something that is going to blow your mind. I need volunteers, though.' He looked around expectantly.

Gautam, mischievously lifted my arm, as I struggled to let go. It was too late, and he had already seen me. Nodding, he said, 'Yes, please come'. I slowly got up and glared at Gautam and Archana who were now giggling.

'I need one more,' he called out as I made my way to the dais.

Dr. Nitin, one of the doctors from my branch, got up excited and ran on to the dais.

Dr.Amit then connected some electrodes that looked like regular ECG to my forearm. The other end of the wire was connected to the machine on the trolley. He then asked Nitin to come forward and connected similar electrodes to his arm.

Dr.Amit, then moved a white board between Nitin and me so that we couldn't see each other. Then he asked me to rotate or move my hand and palm however I wanted to. I moved my fingers, held the fingers tightly to make a fist and rotated my fist. The audience gasped and then there were murmurs followed by a thunderous applause. I was confused. What was happening?

Dr.Amit's assistants moved the whiteboard away. I noticed that Nitin's arm and fingers were involuntarily moving the way I was moving my hand! I looked at Nitin, who looked back at me shocked.

Dr.Amit thanked us and started speaking as we left the stage.

'Just to recollect what you saw here today. We connected the leads from the lady to our machine which captured the messages coming from her brain and transferred it to the gentleman's hands. So, as she was moving her hands, based on what her brain instructed, the gentleman on the other side was mirroring her actions. His hands were receiving the exact same signal as his brain would have instructed. Of course, this isn't a new phenomenon. It has always been there under electro physiology.'*

I was stunned as I slowly walked back to where Gautam and Archana were sitting. I could see the same amazement in Archana's eyes too.

Being a neurologist, I understood electrical charges and neuroscience. But I had never experienced it firsthand, at least not this dramatically.

He continued speaking for the next thirty minutes as the auditorium listened to an amazing lecture where he told us about the interwoven fields of medicine and electronics. He even showed us a presentation featuring some amazing futuristic gadgets that truly seemed out of the world.

When he wound up his lecture finally, and the floor was open for questions from the audience, we were still trying to digest the magnanimity of the subject we had just heard.

'This Dr. Amit is really popular, isn't he?' I whispered to Archana who pushed her spectacles up on her head and looked at me surprised. Some people had already started asking questions.

(* Based on TED Talk by Greg Gage : How to control someone else's arm with your brain.)

'You haven't been to any of his other lectures?' she asked distractedly as her eyes kept moving back to the dais. I shook my head.

'I'm surprised, Payal, considering how good looking he is,' she said with a sly smile.

'So?' I asked, narrowing my eyes. She shrugged.

'It's not just good looks. He also speaks so well. He has the whole audience rapt. But what I really enjoy about his lectures is to see his passion for his subject. It really shines through,' Archana said, looking away dreamily in the distance. I could clearly see what she meant. Everyone was in awe of him. I looked at Gautam who seemed bored and restless. Typical.

'He's just so good Payal. So good at what he does,' Archana continued and I nodded.

I settled back in my seat, thinking about what I knew of Dr. Amit. I already knew how successful and important he was. He had a PhD in Medical Electronics and he was a successful scientist as well who had written for various science journals. But knowing all that about him hadn't been quite the same as seeing him in action myself.

Then someone asked him a question and we all fell silent.

'Are you working on something related to what you spoke today, Doctor?' he asked.

'Maybe I am,' Dr. Amit said with a mysterious smile. When he didn't elaborate, the man who asked the question persisted.

'Can you tell us what it's about?'

Dr. Amit looked a little amused as he shuffled his papers and shook his head.

'It's a project for the government,' he replied after a beat.

'Is that a secret project?' the same doctor continued.

'Well it wouldn't be much of a secret if I told you, right?' he asked and there were some titters in the audience. The doctor who had asked the question looked a little shamefaced and yet defiant. For some reason Dr. Amit looked around and took a deep breath.

'Since you have brought up the matter...' he said and everyone seemed to hold their breath. I glanced at Archana whose eyes were round and she turned to me, looking slightly awed.

'Secret research work for the government? How cool is that?' she whispered. I had no idea. But her reaction to his words got me excited as well.

Gautam mocked at Archana, 'Secret service like James Bond? Would he say, My name is Dr.Pande, Deshpande' in distinct Sean Connery accent! All three of us giggled.

Dr.Amit was speaking again, but this time there was a quiet kind of force in his voice.

'I've already explained to you about how electronics and medicine are virtually inseparable now. All over the world, there's been a lot of research in this field that has been pushing the boundaries as far as possible. Medicine at present is at a reactionary level. If someone falls sick, only then he goes to a doctor but with this new research, there's a chance of being proactive.

Prevention instead of cure. As we speak, we know there are smartwatches or smart or health bands monitoring our pulse, how many steps we walk and much more. The world of medicine as we know will change and it will happen in our lifetime. Most scientists and researchers are working on this same thing the world over. But we have recently had a breakthrough in terms of development,' he said.

'What kind of breakthrough?' a doctor in the front row asked.

'I'm afraid I can't reveal that,' Dr. Amit said, looking

apologetic. There was silence as everyone digested this. It seemed unfair that he would lead us up to this moment and then back off. But to our surprise, he continued talking.

'If you are really interested and committed, you can stay back and discuss this with me further,' he said, folding his papers and there were protests once more.

'Why can't you tell us now?' someone asked.

'I can't. I'm not allowed to, but I may have an opening for a few volunteers and if they pass certain tests, they will have to sign an NDA and only then, they can know the true nature of this work,' he said. His words lingered in the air for a few seconds until someone spoke again.

'How can we sign up without knowing what it is?'

It had been a while since I'd been a part of such a charged classroom atmosphere and I knew that Dr. Amit was responsible for it. I glanced at the dean who looked mildly worried but didn't say anything. It was like he had left Dr. Amit in charge.

'I cannot reveal the actual nature of our project unless you sign up for it, but maybe I can offer you a little glimpse into it,' he said.

'I'll sign whatever you ask me to, doctor,' a girl behind my bench whispered.

Unfortunately for her, everyone had stopped talking by then and as the room was huge, her words echoed. Someone giggled and then soon a few of the girls behind us were giggling.

Dr. Amit looked in our direction with a sardonic grin on his face and I felt my skin flush when I realized he was staring at me. Had he thought I was the girl who had spoken out?

'Noted. But for now if we can focus on my research I'd be much obliged,' he said mildly. I wanted to die of mortification when I realized that he was talking to me but thankfully he started speaking again.

'All of you have faced situations where patients were brought in too late. When you couldn't save them. You've looked at their family and you've said platitudes about fate and the will of God because you didn't want to blame them for not coming sooner. But what,' he stopped, looking around to ensure that every eye was on him. 'What if you knew that someone was going to have a heart attack? Or a stroke? Or had developed a clot in their brain? What if you could prevent it from turning into a catastrophe? What if you could indeed be a savior in the true sense?'

He let the words linger in the air and in that moment, I knew I was in. I wasn't known to make impulsive decisions ever but this was something that was close to my heart. It was the reason I'd become a doctor in the first place. Not for glory, not for money but to save people. My father had died of a heart attack, alone at home, while my mother was at the supermarket and my brother and I had been playing in the ground. When we came home, our lives had changed forever. I'd vowed that I would become a doctor, not just to save lives, but to save families. To save a way of life.

'Stay back and talk to me if you're interested and we'll see where things go,' he said, nodding to indicate that the lecture was over.

Archana and I looked at each other. Her eyes were shining and she nodded. Many doctors around us started streaming out, some muttering that they didn't have the time for this. I felt a little jolt when I saw Gautam standing up in his seat, turning around to see if I was following suit. What? No way. I shook my head and he frowned.

Dr. Amit spoke again.

'I'd appreciate it if those who want to leave can do so quickly. Those who are staying behind, please move forward and occupy the empty seats,' he said, waving expansively to the seats up in front.

Gautam turned to me. 'Payal, come on!' he whispered. I shook my head and he looked surprised but determined not to leave without me. I realized we were holding up Dr. Amit, so I quickly got up from there and walked out with him. I sensed Dr. Amit's gaze following me as we stood at the threshold of the auditorium.

'I'm staying Gautam,' I said.

Are you serious?' he asked in a low voice. 'Would you actually sign up an NDA to get involved in some government funded research? It sounds very shady to me.'

I felt irritated at his implication. 'Look Gautam, I want to do this. I'm really interested. I understand if you don't want to do this, okay?' I told him.

'I'd like to get started if you don't mind,' Dr. Amit called out, startling me.

'Go if you're not staying,' I said to Gautam. He looked unsettled as he shrugged and left.

'Can you close the door and come back to your seat, Dr...?' Dr. Amit spoke to me. I nodded quickly and shut the door, surprised to see that even the Dean had left. It dawned on me that this was serious stuff we were getting into. But for the first time in a long while I was excited. I realized that he was still looking at me expectantly and then I remembered that he was probably waiting for me to tell him my name.

'Payal. My name is Dr. Payal,' I said, as I hurried to where Archana was sitting. I settled into the seat next to her and looked around a little uncomfortably when I noticed that Dr. Amit was still looking in my direction. But then he shook his head a little, as though to clear it and then stepped away from the dais and moved forward. There were now around fifteen of us.

Dr. Amit started speaking in a low, calming voice and the atmosphere grew more hushed. And so it began.

CHAPTER - 2

'As doctors, your lives are not really your own,' he started when everyone had settled down. 'But we also know that we cannot afford to let our busy lives stop us from staying abreast of the latest advances in technology. We cannot stagnate. We have to learn and move with the times.'

Since the hall was almost empty now, we had formed a closer circle near the front and it seemed like an intimate gathering. I looked around at who else had opted to stay back. Apart from Archana and me, there was Nitin as well, a doctor whom none of us took seriously. I was surprised and wondered what had made him stay back. Maybe he wanted to prove to the world at large that he could be serious if need be because he had a look of utter concentration on his face. Or it could be that he just wanted to stick around because of Archana. If that was the case, he wouldn't last long. Everyone, including Archana, was aware of his crush on her but she chose not to do anything about it. She'd made a face when she saw that he had stayed back.

There were a couple of other girls, doctors I didn't know well enough but going by the look of adoration on their face, I knew why they were here. But it made me feel weird. None of us were teenagers here. So it wasn't the same as mooning over a good looking lecturer. There was no time for it. But then if they were really here just because they admired Dr. Amit, they might figure out soon enough whether they had it in them or not. Jai, one of my friends from MBBS, was a close pal of Gautam's and I felt a little relieved at seeing him. These were people I mostly knew. If we were all getting into something, at least we were in it together.

I wished Gautam too had stayed back. Despite my inner struggle of feelings for him, I didn't want him to miss out on what seemed like a huge opportunity. I brought my thoughts back to the moment when I realized that Dr. Amit had started speaking again.

'One of the many amazing things about living in these times is seeing how functionality has become inversely proportional to size. I'm not talking about your mobiles or TVs or tablet computers where bigger is better. I'm talking about technology that gets more done when it is smaller. Nanotechnology. Nanobots, as they are known the world over, are tiny microscopic robots that have numerous applications. Even for someone like me who knows a thing or two about medical electronics, I can assure you, these nanobots are the next big thing in medicine.'

As Archana said, he was an impassioned speaker. He told us about the research that was being done the world over with Nanobots, and how researchers everywhere were frantic to be at the finish line first. 'Because it would mean glory and fame and a place in history,' he said with a wide smile.

'But it's not like researchers thought up this idea over the past few years. The idea has been around for a long time,' he explained. 'In fact, as early as 1959 Richard Feynman talked about the possibility of 'swallowing the doctor', an idea that he credited to his student Albert Hibbs who suggested that there could be medical uses for nanotechnology.'

'Swallow the doctor?' I repeated in surprise. I thought I'd spoken the words softly but he had heard them. Damn, the man had sharp ears.

'Yes, Dr. Payal,' he turned to me and smiled. 'The idea even back then was that these nanobots, once inside our bodies would proactively work to prevent diseases, attacks and strokes. Thanks to modern technology, Feynman and Hibbs' words are becoming a reality.'

I nodded, and looked down at my notepad because I was aware of his scrutiny.

'So are you working on nanobots in your secret government work?' Nitin asked.

'I can't give exact details but it's something along the lines of monitoring health. To give you a very simple example, you know how a pacemaker works to keep the heart pumping but supposing we embed some intelligence in it, what can it do? It can intelligently identify whether it needs to increase or decrease the blood supply. What if it can sense that the heart is failing? We are doing just this kind of futuristic research that is going to change the world of health monitoring and management. It's proactive monitoring versus reactive treatment.'

We all listened in amazement but with a fair amount of skepticism as well.

'How is this even possible?' Jai asked, looking slightly disbelieving.

'It is possible and we are working to make that happen. Earlier in the lecture, you saw that the brain was able to send signals that we could interpret and send it to other body. How do you think it would be if we had an agent inside our body who kept telling us what's happening inside?' Dr. Amit asked, turning to look at each person with a great deal of intensity.

Jai didn't have the answer to that. He looked around at the rest of us, as though to ascertain what we felt. But Dr. Amit started speaking once more.

'Now, why am I talking to you? We've made a breakthrough and we have started the testing phase. We need talented professionals, especially doctors to monitor and record everything. You will need to undergo a few tests and government agencies will do some background checks then. When you're through with that, you have to sign a Non-

Disclosure Agreement. After that you can visit my lab and see what we're doing,' Dr. Amit replied.

'But why do we need to sign an NDA?' someone asked.

Dr. Amit shook his head. 'It's mandatory. It means, you will not be able to tell the outside world anything about it till it is released to public. It's important work that has been entrusted to me by the government and I cannot take any chances of leaks.'

I realized with a pang of dismay that he was done now. He was going to leave because he was placing some papers in his laptop bag. I don't know why I wanted him to stay a little while longer and keep talking. Listening to him had been so fascinating!

'Oh you're free to go now,' he said absently when someone asked if we could go.

Archana whispered to me that she wanted to stay back and talk to him. I wasn't sure if it was a good idea. He had seemed approachable when he was talking about his topic but now that he was packing up to leave, he looked a bit standoffish.

'Why?' I whispered back as I saw the others leave. Some of the girls looked at him as they walked towards the door, hoping for some sort of acknowledgment from him but he barely looked up. He had picked up a notepad and was flipping over the pages, lost in thought and I shook my head at Archana.

'Let's leave,' I mouthed and although she seemed disappointed, she nodded. She walked ahead of me and when I walked past him, towards the door, he muttered something. I lingered even as the others left and he too seemed to wait for everyone to leave.

'Did you say something?' I asked softly when everyone had left. My heart thundered a bit because I was afraid that he might snap at me.

He shut the notepad and looked at me, a half smile on his face. 'When you were walking past me I noticed you were wearing anklets,' he said.

'So?' I asked, a little baffled.

'Just thought it was an odd coincidence that someone named Payal was wearing payal,' he replied.

I didn't know what to say to that. He had finished packing his laptop bag and I walked ahead of him, hoping to join Archana and the others when he said something again. Since he said it under his breath, I turned around to face him.

'Excuse me?' I asked.

'Nothing,' he said with a secretive smile. I turned around to leave, a little annoyed but eager to get started with this whole nanobot thing as soon as possible. That's when I remembered that he hadn't told us anything about when these tests would be conducted and when we could go to the lab and I turned to him once more.

'Payal aur payal ki jhankar' he said as he left and my query died on my lips.

CHAPTER - 3

Gautam and I had an unspoken ritual everyday where we took a breather from our hectic schedules and tried to meet up for a cup of tea in the hospital cafeteria every evening. Most of the time either he was late or I was, but we knew that we ought to at least try and wait for ten minutes before leaving. For a change, both of us were at the cafeteria at the same time today. It was most unusual.

Although both of us had studied MBBS together, we had taken up different specialties for our MD but had still ended up at the same hospital. I knew he had pulled a lot of strings to make sure that we both stayed near each other, while never actually mentioning it to me or anyone else. It was one of the reasons why I found myself growing more and more attached to him. He was like my guardian angel and while his over protectiveness could get annoying at times, I was happy to have him with me.

After Dr. Amit's seminar, I had left because I needed to check in on some patients. There was the regular OPD work also that had been pushed a little behind schedule and once that was over, I don't know whether it was me or my body that remembered I needed that hit of caffeine. So I found myself in the busy cafeteria where I found Gautam sitting at our usual spot, lost in thought.

I walked over and sat down beside him and nudged his elbow. His eyes widened when he realized that it was me.

'All done?' he asked, pushing a plate of sandwiches towards me. I declined even as I picked up my tea and sipped it.

'Yeah, it was all right,' I said cautiously. Dr. Amit's words of the NDA were still echoing in my head. But Gautam didn't even seem curious about that, to my surprise. I'd been dreading that he would try to dig for information or try to stop me from getting involved.

'You sure you want to get into something with an NDA?' he asked. I shrugged. I was already in.

'Fine,' he said and took a bite of his cheese sandwich.

'Everything okay?' I asked him, as I studied his side profile unobtrusively. He looked somewhat anxious, not a trait I associated with him. He was outgoing and brash and wore his heart on his sleeve. So, this reserved attitude was slightly worrying.

Gautam turned to look at me and my face flushed. It would seem that he had caught me staring at him, which is unusual if you consider how the whole hospital thought of us as a couple. But the truth was, we'd never really discussed it. We'd just gone along with the flow. There had been a lot of girls in my batch who would have given their right arm, or even the arm with which they'd be doing surgeries, to be where I was, sitting next to him. But Gautam had never had eyes for any of them. He'd been with me from the time we'd met and became friends.

I sometimes couldn't understand what he saw in me.

'See anything you like?' he asked with a smile and I felt relief somewhere in the recesses of my heart. This sounded like the Gautam I knew.

'Maybe,' I joked, poking his dimple with my finger. He caught my finger suddenly and I felt my stomach plummet deeply. I'd always pretended that I was absolutely normal about him holding my hand but even that little contact had always left me feeling all sorts of things. I just hadn't made it apparent to anyone, especially Gautam.

'I was just thinking. That scientist fellow seemed to have impressed all the girls,' he said, still holding on to my finger. I extricated it from him and smiled.

'Yeah! You should have seen Archana and how she was behaving,' I muttered.

'What about you?' he asked. I looked up surprised. Was he jealous?

'What about me?' I asked finally.

'Did you also find him attractive?' he asked, looking at his tea cup as though the answers lay there.

'Well, he is a good looking and charismatic man,' I said and his eyes narrowed but he was waiting for me to continue talking.

'But what difference does it make?' I asked finally.

'You're going to be working with him, closely. I...I just...' he couldn't end his sentence but looked at me, his eyes completing what he wanted to say.

I looked down. We'd been supposedly together for so long and yet, we'd never really broached the topic of what we had between us. Gautam was so outgoing and fun loving that he would say 'I love you' to even the lab technicians if they did something correctly. So it had been difficult for me to figure out his actual feelings for me.

'Just what Gautam?' I finally picked up the courage to ask him. I felt disconnected from the rest of the world. I couldn't for the life of me remember where we were even sitting.

He looked up at me and shook his head.

'Nothing,' he said. I felt disappointed. But then he picked up my hand and squeezed it.

'As long as he knows you're mine,' he said. I felt a thrill shooting up my spine at his words. I tried making some witty comeback but I didn't have any words. Without taking his eyes off mine, he reached for his pager because it had buzzed and he got up.

'I have to go now, but we're going to talk about this later,' he said, brushing my cheek lightly with his finger before he left.

I continued sitting there for nearly ten minutes after he left, the tea cold and my mind abuzz with excitement.

Gautam's new alpha male side that seemed to have come up because of Dr. Amit was actually, surprisingly attractive. And I don't think it had anything to do with the brain's neurotransmitters. Of course, Dr. Amit might have his own take on this.

The cafeteria was crowded and I made my way out towards the balcony that looked over the hospital grounds. I breathed in the balmy Delhi air and wondered if it would rain one of these days. The weather had been getting warm and uncomfortable - typical April weather but a good thunderstorm might just be what we needed. A section of the grounds was cut off for the visitor's car park and even as I was thinking of stepping back inside, I noticed Dr. Amit striding towards a parked car.

Since our lecture had taken place earlier in the day I'd assumed he would have left by now. Maybe he had some other things to take care of, I thought as I watched him get inside the car and roll down the windows. He didn't start the car right away. I felt a bit like an intruder watching him but I didn't move from there. Since I could barely make out his features, I was quite positive he couldn't see me either.

I realized that he had started the car and was backing out towards the gates. I wondered how soon it would be till we heard from him again. How soon till we get started?

I stepped back a little when a movement from his car stopped my eye. He was waving goodbye as the car sped out!

---✿✿✿---

CHAPTER - 4

Of the fifteen of us who stayed back that day to listen to Dr. Amit, only four were permitted to move to the next level. Either some of them had performed badly in the test or something else hadn't worked out. Even as I was doing the test, I realized that Archana hadn't been joking when she said it would be very tough to crack. Still, she, Nitin, Jai and I had made it. The four of us were the only doctors from our hospital who were going ahead with Dr. Amit's program.

For days after the test, our regular routine was disrupted by the range of interviews that we had to do with various government outfits including background verifications, family history etc. It was annoying at times because it seemed like such trouble. But Dr. Amit had come to the hospital to meet us, once the four of us had been finalized, and having him around was a completely different experience.

The four of us shared a sense of awe that wasn't easy to dispel. It only spurred us on to excel so that we could be a part of this historic and scientific venture. There was something about Dr. Amit that made him larger than life. For one, he had all those years of experience docked away and he was a good eight to ten years older than us. To be honest, he wasn't as much a doctor as a scientist, and a very intriguing one at that.

I often sensed Gautam's irritation at the amount of time all this was eating into our personal lives. But most of the time, he tried not to say anything. While I appreciated his patience, I wished we could continue the talk that we were having the day Dr. Amit came to speak to us for the first time. It had been the one time Gautam had been really serious with me and I wanted to know where we were headed. Still, Gautam was one of the most transparent people I've known. It was always easy to deduce what he was thinking and how he felt about someone. Unlike Dr. Amit.

Dr. Amit remained a mystery to all of us. He barely spoke to us about anything apart from the subject. Even then, he was serious and forbidding. I often wondered if I'd misheard him that day when he passed a comment about my anklets and my name. It was hard to reconcile this serious man with someone who could make such a frivolous comment. Sometimes the intensity that beamed from his eyes made me nervous. It often seemed like he was carrying the weight of the world on his shoulders and knowing the kind of research he did, he probably was.

I found myself reading up articles about him on the internet and scouring the few interviews that he'd given to science magazines because I wanted to see the man beneath the serious façade. I wanted to see what he was really like. It was a bit like hero worship, more than anything else.

Today he was at the hospital and he called a meeting for the four of us later in the evening so he could prepare us for what was coming up ahead. We had cleared all the hurdles. It was now time for the NDA.

Somehow, Gautam and I had managed to have lunch together today. That in itself was a miracle, considering our clashing schedules. Gautam had been quiet and thoughtful, not unlike the other day and I wondered if finally things would move on when my cell phone vibrated with a message from the head of our department, summoning me.

'I have to go right away,' I said getting up from my chair even as I read it and absently stuffing the rest of my sandwich quickly in my mouth.

'Wait,' he said grabbing my wrist and looking at me seriously. 'We have to talk.' What, now? I'd been waiting for days for him to broach this subject again but the timing is so off. I had to go right away.

'Gautam, can we talk later?' I asked him, as I tried to pull out my wrist from his grip.

'You never seem to have the time Payal,' he said, and I detected only the slightest hint of resentment in his voice.

'Yes, but...'

'I want to marry you,' he said, focusing his eyes on me. Whoa.

He had certainly jumped the gun. Whatever it was, I hadn't expected this, well not so soon.

'Really?' I asked with an artificial amazement.

'Of course,' he said looking absolutely serious.

'But...'

'But what Payal? You know I love you right? I've been in love with you for years and I've waited and waited. It's the right time now,' he said.

I sat down beside him once again, sacrificing another minute or so before going to meet the department head. This was serious.

'We've always had this...this between us,' I started, my voice unsteady. 'And you're the most important person in my life right now. Well, apart from my mother and my brother,' I added with a slight smile. He continued staring at me.

My mind was spinning, trying to come up with the right words. I wanted this. I wanted it with Gautam, but not now. We both needed to do so much more in our lives. 'Talk of marriage seems a bit sudden to me, that's all,' I said finally.

'What's sudden about it? You love me too, right?' he asked, holding my hand again.

I looked down. Gautam meant the World to me and I couldn't imagine a life without him in it. Was this love then? It had to be. I wish I knew for sure. But I was sure of one thing. I couldn't get married so soon.

'Payal, I asked you something,' he said. My phone vibrated once more and I jumped up, startled. I'd forgotten completely about the department head calling me. I had to leave now.

'Look, if we get married now, what's going to happen to our careers? The stipend from the hospital is not enough for a family. So will we end up depending on your parents?' I asked. I know I'd evaded the question he asked but I knew I'd hit the right nerve. Gautam was defensive about his rich family and wanted to make it on his own without any help.

He blew out a breath but before he could speak, I stopped him. 'I have to think about my family too. I need to ensure that my mother is fine and that my brother finishes his education. There's so much I need to do before I can get married. Let's not rush into this. We're both young and we're both not going anywhere. Let's come back to this after some time,' I said. I squeezed his hand and tried to get up but he wouldn't let me.

'You didn't answer my question,' he stated, his eyes all intense, unlike the joking Gautam I knew.

I blew out a breath and nodded. 'I will. Soon.' He stared at me for a few more seconds and then let go of my hand. I almost wished I didn't have to go. After all this time, Gautam had professed his love for me, seriously, and I couldn't even savour the moment.

'Love you Payal!' he said loudly as I turned to leave and I blushed. He was back to his tomfoolery now. I shook my head and smiled and then realized that the person sitting near us would have heard our entire conversation.

I rushed out quickly and then stopped for a second before continuing on forward. I hadn't been able to see the person who had been sitting near us because his back was turned but as I walked out, I'd seen a little of his side profile. I could have sworn it was Dr. Amit.

---❁❁❁---

CHAPTER - 5

I was on my way to Dr.Amit's laboratory finally with Nitin, Jai and Archana and to say that we were excited was an understatement. Apparently their heads of department had also called them and spoken to them and gave them a bit of gyan about dealing with a top secret government project like the one we were getting into. We decided that they were probably jealous they weren't being involved and were just trying to sound cautious and scare us a bit.

After all, the NDA wasn't a big deal. All it had was some serious sounding words to scare us from leaking any info about the project.

Anyhow, after signing the NDA, I texted Gautam and told him that I would have to meet him the following day as I would be going to the lab after my shift. He replied back with a long text that made me roll my eyes when I first read it. I was re-reading it and smiling to myself, thinking how there was something so frivolous and irreverent about Gautam that you couldn't help be charmed. And yet, he could get serious too when it came to me and there was no doubt that I was happy he was in my life.

'Reading a joke?' Dr. Amit asked politely and I straightened up. I didn't realize he had come. He was going to take us to the lab today and we had assembled in the parking lot to wait for him.

'Just a message,' I replied, looking down. Archana nudged me a little and I looked at her. What?

'From your boyfriend, I suppose,' Dr. Amit muttered as he went towards his car and unlocked it. Archana and I looked at each other, puzzled. Archana looked as though she wanted to ask me several questions but I shrugged. Anyway, the four of us got into his car and we drove out of the hospital parking lot.

It was only then, a while later that I realized that Dr. Amit was patiently talking to the others. I tried to focus on what lay ahead. He drove us towards South Delhi and soon we were on the outskirts. The traffic and pollution were considerably less and after some more time, we passed by the Bharadwaj Lake. It was so serene here that it was hard to believe that we were just outside Delhi. We were in the Asola Wild Life Sanctuary. I took a moment to appreciate the beauty and tranquility around me and then looked ahead of me in shock. There was a huge building in front of us surrounded by dense trees. If I wasn't mistaken, there weren't supposed to be any sort of buildings here.

The four of us got out and watched as Dr. Amit drove the car towards the basement parking. He waved to us, indicating that we should go inside. Surprised, we walked towards the rather innocuous looking door and opened it. Inside, there was a room that seemed like a waiting room of sorts as there were chairs and even a couch. It seemed like a typical waiting room of a lowly uneventful office. The four of us felt a bit uncomfortable as it certainly wasn't what we had expected. Thankfully we didn't have to wait for long.

Dr. Amit joined us and continued walking towards another door without a break in his stride. 'Come on!' he said and the four of us surged forward.

Inside, there was a lift and we all got inside, subdued. In the lift, I happened to glance at Dr. Amit and realized that he was staring at me and he looked away swiftly. I looked away too, wondering what the matter was but the lift opened and whatever I was thinking, fled from my mind instantly.

We were here.

This was the laboratory where Dr. Amit was working

on revolutionizing medicine and we were here to help him do it! The lift opened to a smallish room with a desk and the most serious-looking receptionist I had seen in my life. She stopped us and asked us to hand over all our electronic as well as metallic items like jewelry. A little surprised, we looked at Dr. Amit for guidance but he was tapping his foot impatiently on the ground.

'Go on,' he urged us. We switched off our mobile phones and other electronic devices and placed them in the plastic box that the receptionist had kept on the table. Archana looked most reluctant to leave her phone behind but Dr. Amit was shaking his head firmly.

We moved towards the door at the end of the room, hoping it would lead to the laboratory that we were now dying to see.

There were several people in the laboratory already, most of them looking rather important as they worked on computer stations that were arranged around the periphery of the room. There was so much equipment in this room, that my mind was boggled. Apart from the computers, there were a couple of huge machines. There was an electronics circuit board on one of the walls that was lit up and there was a huge screen on another wall. I noticed a couple of doors leading out of the laboratory and noted the names on the doors. Chemistry and Microbiology.

I was impressed, to say the least! To set up such a facility, Dr. Amit must have put a lot of money and his devotion.

Dr. Amit strode into the center of the room and immediately a few of the people looked up from the computers, moved their chairs back and came up to him. Some others also converged towards him and the four of us watched as he consulted with them. One of them handed him a large tablet and he swiped across the screens and looked thoughtful.

He looked up and when he saw that the four of us were still looking unsure, he signaled us. We walked up slowly and I don't know about the others but I was really excited now. He introduced us to the rest of the people there. The names were all a blur to me but at the end of the introduction session, I realized that he had got the most talented individuals working for him in this laboratory. Jai voiced my question aloud.

'How did you get all these people to work for you?' he asked in a whisper when the team melted back to their computer stations and it was just the four of us with Dr. Amit.

'What do you mean?' Dr. Amit looked surprised.

'I mean all these people are super talented. You just told us that the guy there was the top communications expert in the country. And the girl sitting there writing code, you said she was the top ranker in her university. How did you get them all to work for you?'

Dr. Amit smiled sardonically. 'Just like how I got all you guys to work for me,' he said. Then looking a bit serious, he continued, 'I traveled the world to get the best people for this laboratory. Those you see here are the best of their field, whether they are electronics engineers or microbiologists or software engineers. I located people of Indian origin, even those who were living abroad and got them to work for us because this is such a huge project. It's a game changer. Why wouldn't they want to be a part of it?' he asked.

We were all silently contemplating this. Each of us was probably thinking if Dr. Amit had got us here because he considered us to be the best in our fields. Before we could let that thought inflate our ego, Dr. Amit spoke once more.

'I don't know if you've understood by now what exactly we're up to. Our first session when I told you about nanobots and someone asked if we were doing the same, I was evasive and I had to be. But now I can explain everything to you perfectly. Yes, we're working on nanobots too but we call it Microbots here because of the larger size and a little higher functions.'

The four of us quickly looked at each other but he continued talking.

'I know I am talking to a bunch of very good doctors and you all know that a disease is an abnormal condition that affects the body of an organism. It is often construed as a medical condition associated with specific symptoms and signs. It may be caused by factors originally from an external source, such as infectious disease, or it may be caused by internal dysfunctions.'

We listened to him in silence, wondering where this was leading to.

'Let's consider for example, hypertension. It is the most important cause of cerebrovascular disease; it damages the lining of the blood vessels, the endothelium, and exposes the underlying collagen. Now platelets are supposed to repair the blood vessels but it may not happen properly. Continuous hypertension will permanently change the structure of the blood vessels. They can become narrow, stiff, deformed, uneven and changes in blood pressure can affect them in an even worse way.

These Microbots will be able to scan the cells, the blood vessels, and check any deformities to see if everything is as it should be and if not, they will help us take appropriate action,' he addressed us. Wait. What exactly could he mean by this?

'How is it possible?' I spoke my thought out aloud. Dr. Amit turned to me and raised one eyebrow.

'Look around you Dr. Payal. We are making it happen. I need people like you to help us monitor patients who have been administered with the Microbot,' he said.

'You mean you have already started testing it? Is it even ethical?' I asked, surprised.

'Yes, Dr. Payal. It is ethical because the patients are making an informed decision. We are not hiding anything from them. We're talking about terminally ill people here, those in a lot of pain. We have implanted the Microbot in them to ease their pain and improve their quality of life,' he explained. 'Of course, we don't have the approval of any drug controllers because it's still a secret project but the Indian Government has given us the go ahead to start testing with those who have agreed to it.'

'Implanted the Microbot?' Archana asked, her brow bunching up together. I swear all of us felt the same level of confusion. 'Is it like an endoscopy with tubes and wires that is inserted into a patient?'

Dr. Amit merely chuckled. 'Why don't you all come with me?' he said and took us to a corner of the room. On a desk, there was a microscope. He gestured and invited us to peep into the eye piece lens. I was the closest so I bent my head to get a proper look. I looked up swiftly to see Dr. Amit's reaction.

Was this even real?

One by one, everyone peeped into the eye piece. There was a tiny insect like device with tanker roller wheels and an antenna! This was the Microbot?

'This is what we're implanting inside people,' Dr. Amit spoke. It was almost creepy imagining this little thing getting inside your bloodstream.

He then pointed out a huge computer monitor screen mounted on the wall, divided into several tinier screens. Each screen had a name displayed on top. Some data was scrolling on it continuously.

'Each of these screens represent the patients that we are monitoring. Come up close and see,' he said. The four of us peered closely at the screen. Each screen displayed information about the patient and the disease they were suffering from along with other vital data about their health.

'The dot that you see on the screen represents the Microbot that's moving in their bloodstream,' he explained. My eyes widened.

'Amazing,' I murmured, even though I still couldn't understand the enormity of this device. But before I could ask any more questions that would make me look more foolish, someone else beat me to it.

'So what does it do? Does it tell you if someone has got diabetes or high cholesterol?' Nitin asked, his brow furrowing in confusion.

Dr. Amit smiled and shook his head. 'The Microbot cannot analyze and do anything on its own. It's a dumb electronic device that is implanted in the bloodstream to keep a check on various parameters. See, today there are many types of equipment to monitor blood sugar and other variables. The Microbot contains the measuring element of such monitoring devices while the analytical element is installed in the software. Once something is out of the normal range, it sends information to the servers via communication channels and the people receiving this information have to analyze the data and make proper diagnosis.'

'But why do you need people from different areas like software, electronics, or medicine?' Jai asked with a puzzled shrug.

Dr. Amit looked at him patiently and then started speaking. 'See, this whole set up is very unique. Firstly, the Microbot is an electronic device that's microscopic in nature. How do you think we designed it? We needed people who were experts in Electronics to do this for us and believe me, it took us years and years of effort. Once that was done, we had to embed it with intelligence. After all, it had to notice all these parameters and notify the server. So we got in experts from medical electronics, communication engineers and even software engineers to build us analytic engines. After all, how do you think we will be able to sift through all that data which would normally seem meaningless? But thanks to these analytic engines, we are able to make sense of all this data.'

Since the four of us looked far from enlightened, Dr. Amit nodded and asked us to follow him outside the lab to another section which was on another floor so we took the lift and then stepped out minutes later. It seemed like a hospital, but the beds were placed far apart and there were a number of people sleeping on them.

'Come, meet your patients,' he said.

---❀❀❀---

CHAPTER - 6

It took us a little more than three days to get accustomed to the laboratory and our function in it. Dr. Amit was extremely helpful as he helped us connect to the various terminally ill patients there and the gratitude that some of these people felt towards him was heartening. It was like a mini hospice which was completely self-sufficient, having all modern facilities that were otherwise denied to most such setups because of a shortage of funds. Clearly, this hospice was fully funded. The patients here were volunteers for the Microbot program and had given Dr. Amit permission to use it on them. We were all amazed at how much the Microbot had made a difference to their lives.

From what I understood, once the Microbot entered the bloodstream, it traveled around the body, measuring parameters of various organs. Whenever something was out of the normal range, the software would analyze and send out a notification. Based on the feeds the server received, the software would analyze it and provide a scale of comparison.

To help us understand it better, Dr. Amit likened it to an SMS or internet connection. Or like a mobile SIM card for humans. So in effect, we could all walk around normally while there was something that was constantly monitoring us from inside. Pretty much what he meant by 'Swallow the Doctor' in his first lecture to us.

Our job initially was not really well defined and there didn't seem to be any boundaries because we had to keep defining them based on our own expertise. For example, if an artery wall thickened because of calcium and cholesterol accumulating on the walls, the Microbot would only indicate that the artery walls have thickened. However, the software would compare and analyze this data with the previous data, and conclude that since this artery has more deposition than before, it would require medical attention. But neither the software, nor the Microbot know when to raise an alarm, so it was our job to define or train the software to raise the right kind of alarm based on the harm caused or the risk possibility.

Over a period of time, our job was becoming clearer. We had to define the parameters in our field of expertise for the Microbot, so that the whole system could work effectively. I was proud to be a part of such a group that made such a difference to society at large. Or about to make a difference!

Regarding our work with cancer patients, we were actually able to prevent the growth of more cancerous cells. Some of these patients were now relatively healthy and much happier.

These past few days were hectic, nerve-wracking and exhausting but the four of us along with others who were already on the program were also exhilarated. We were on a different kind of high and most of the times, we couldn't quite wait to finish our shift in the hospital before we could come back to the lab. Gautam and I hadn't been able to sit down for our regular afternoon tea in the cafeteria and I felt a little guilty because of the amount of time I was spending away from him.

Gautam was in the Orthopaedic department and he was often busy assisting his mentors with surgeries.

A couple of days after we first visited the laboratory, I hung around outside his department because I was missing him. I'd texted him to meet me there but as I was waiting near one of the pillars, I overheard two people talking. One of them was Gautam and the other was the head of his department, Dr. Vinod who seemed displeased with him for some reason.

I felt uncomfortable and wanted to make my presence felt but Dr. Vinod was berating Gautam and I didn't want him to know that I'd overheard their conversation. So, much to my embarrassment, I stayed behind the pillar, trying to figure out why Gautam was being raked over the coals.

'I cannot forgive such carelessness Gautam! You know this was your last chance and you screwed up again,' Dr. Vinod said. 'What did he mean by last chance?' I thought nervously.

'I know. I really am sorry again,' Gautam said softly. I could hardly reconcile this soft spoken and almost scared person to the jovial guy I knew.

'Sorry? Tell that to the patient! How could you have done something so stupid?' Dr. Vinod fumed. What had Gautam done? I was getting really worried now.

'I...it was...I got confused,' Gautam said.

'And you chose to cut open the wrong hand?' Dr. Vinod asked in a whisper. Oh no! My eyes widened in horror. How could Gautam have made such a big mistake!

'I am not allowing you inside the OT again. You need to prove yourself before you can come inside any OT. You need to prove that you will not be distracted,' Dr. Vinod admonished Gautam.

'But...if I don't complete my quota of surgeries for the log book...'Gautam said, sounding broken, 'I...I won't be able to attend the exam.'

'You should have thought about that before cutting open the wrong hand. This could become a massive scandal for the hospital. We have to think up reasons to tell the relatives why we did this! Can you even imagine what you have done? You've done these surgeries so many times before. How could you do this?' Dr. Vinod fumed and walked away in anger. I didn't know how to face Gautam in the face of such a big disaster. I wanted to support him and be there for him but I was also hesitant. For some reason, I didn't want him to know that I had witnessed his humiliation.

'Hey,' I called out to Gautam who looked up at me surprised. He had been staring out at the road dejected. I pretended that I had just come upon him there.

'What's up?' I asked as I walked up to him. He tried to recover himself but failed.

'I can't talk now,' he said, his voice gruff and he walked away from there. I wanted to run after him and offer him comfort but I felt that he would be embarrassed that I knew what he had done.

I watched him cross the corridor and leave the hospital. His shift wasn't yet over and I knew he would get into more trouble if he left a shift mid-way. Then I got a text from Dr. Amit who asked if I could find out if the four of us were free this weekend. He wanted us to stay back at the laboratory because he was going to try out something new.

'I'll find out,' I texted him back and looked up to see that Gautam was nowhere in sight. What could have gone so wrong? Why had he been so distracted? But I was also curious about what Dr. Amit had in store for us. I found out from the others and informed him that we would be able to stay the weekend at the laboratory.

Later that evening, when we entered the lab as usual depositing our electronic items outside, I noticed that I'd received a text from Gautam. I quickly opened it to read it while the others waited for me impatiently.

'I need to talk to you. I need to see you now,' it said. I was in a dilemma. I looked up at the others who were clearly irritated with the delay I was causing. Feeling annoyed with myself, I told them to carry on and I would join them in five minutes.

I turned around and quickly tapped Gautam's number. He answered on the first ring itself.

'Where are you?' he asked, his voice hoarse as though he'd been crying.

'At the lab,' I told him.

'I want to you to come back. I need you Payal,' he said, his voice breaking.

'What happened? Are you okay?', I asked concerned.

There was a pause and he replied, 'Yes, but wanted to talk to you.' That was a relief.

'I'm sorry. I can't come today, Gautam. Dr. Amit wants us to stay here for the weekend,' I said, hating that I was unable to help him.

'But....'

'Gautam, please understand. I can't come now as I am here in this remote lab with no transport,' I told him. My eyes were on the door that led to the lab. Everyone had already gone inside and I was dying to go and see what was happening there.

'Payal, I'm in deep trouble. I need you. I need to talk to you,' he said, sounding slurred.

'Have you been drinking?' I asked him sharply.

'A little,' he conceded. He knew I hated it when he got drunk.

'Gautam, I'll meet you on Monday. Please don't do anything stupid. I'll come and talk to you. Promise,' I assured him even though I wanted to yell at him for trying to drown his sorrow in alcohol. Now was not the time.

'I love you Payal,' he said. I shut my eyes briefly. Confusion over my feelings for him and my excitement at the work that awaited me warred in my head.

'Same here,' I said finally, and then ended the call, switched off the phone and dropped it in the box. The receptionist looked at me in disapproval as I ran towards the lab and opened the door.

'I can hear Payal ki jhankaar. She's just in time,' I heard Dr. Amit's clear voice calling out, as Archana giggled and Jai rolled his eyes. From Gautam's broken syllables to Dr. Amit's clear cadence, it was a complete extreme.

'Just in time for what?' I asked breathlessly as I joined the others who were standing near a medical observation bed where Dr. Amit was lying down. Shirtless. Seeing him like this, I couldn't relate him with the forbidding and strict man who had lectured us that first day. Or even the doctor we were used to working with all along. Would I ever be able to remove this image from my mind? I glanced at Archana and saw that her eyes were round too. She was having pretty much the same idea, I was sure. Dr. Amit was undeniably hot.

'To see me implant the Microbot in my body,' he said and I blinked. All these people were here surrounding us, but he was looking at me. I took a deep breath and looked away. There were various machines beeping and sending out info somewhere. There was also a large machine with a big injection next to it. It hardly looked like the kind of injections we used in the hospital. There was a red liquid in it which strangely seemed to resemble blood.

I whispered to the senior doctor next to me, 'What's the liquid in the injection?'

'It's his own blood. We took it out over a period of time and made sure that the Microbot was conditioned,' he said. Conditioned?

The injection actually resembled the ones I had seen in Hollywood movies, particularly the lethal ones. The pressure on the injection were being applied by an automated, computer controlled system. The needles - multiple of them - were connected to different parts of the body.

Dr.Amit nodded to Dr. Sundaram, who was the senior most doctor in our setup who took control of the computer and started the injection process.

Once again, I found myself looking at him and realized that his eyes hadn't left mine at all, as the injection slowly pumped the blood into his body.

---❁❁❁---

CHAPTER - 7

We were all still in shock. Why had he injected himself with the Microbot? I think the question was evident on everyone's faces. Dr. Amit straightened his arm, slipped into his shirt and buttoned it up, smiling at us, as he sat up on the bed.

'Why are you all so surprised? I thought by now you all knew what I have been planning all along,' he asked. Had we known? I don't know. It was the first time any of us had seen the Microbot being used actually. Since no one replied to his question, he shrugged.

'Come on everyone,' he said, getting up and beckoning us to follow him to the end of the room where the monitoring screens were located.

'It's not enough to use the Microbot in ill patients. We need to test it on several healthy patients as well. The problem is that the government will not allow it unless the Microbot passes several approval levels and that cannot happen without extensive testing. We've already tested it on guinea pigs and then dogs and monkeys. It took us a couple of years and hundreds of failures to get it right and then we moved the testing to terminally ill patients as volunteers. That was an uphill task and the government played a very important role there. We've been testing it on ill patients for nearly two years now, making sure we get the right combination that would work best inside the human body. It's time to test it on a healthy body now,' he said.

I looked at his face trying to see if there were any changes in him but they wouldn't be immediate, right? And neither would they be visible to us, just like that.

'You can see that I am perfectly fine but that's just now. I wanted you to stay over the weekend so you all could monitor my reaction to the Microbot personally,' he said, gesturing to all of us. 'The reason we need monitoring is because we've seen that the body initially rejects the Microbot as an external invader and that causes fevers and side effects sometimes.'

'So why did you inject it straight away?' Nitin asked, his eyes round.

'We didn't. We took blood samples and we prepared the Microbot to get used to the body's environment. It's after all a tiny metal inside the body. We have to configure it to suit the blood group of the recipient, so that it will behave as if it's a part of the blood composition. So initially a lot of WBC might die fighting. There are chances that my WBC count may drastically go down. Hence I need the best doctors to monitor me.'

Before we could assume he was referring to us, he pointed to the other senior doctor team working on the injecting machine.

'The reason why I wanted you to monitor my reaction was that it would be great if I could get some volunteers who don't mind getting the Microbot inside their systems,' he said, smiling sardonically in the way I'd come to expect from him.

He wanted us to inject the Microbot in our bodies! I was a little late in reacting because the others had started murmuring by then. Archana seemed very excited and so did Nitin.

'Come now. You can see that the Microbot has entered my bloodstream. It will now travel through my body, detecting and measuring parameters and sending information to the system here,' he explained. 'For the first few days, the data would be random as everything is going to be new for the software as well as the Microbot. As a result, there will be a lot of inconsistent data. But then, that is how the baseline data is formed so that any deviation from this will be reported.'

'Now where do you all of you come in? We won't know what should be the ideal data for each and every part of the body. It may be that one parameter may already be high in my body and it might mistakenly be taken as the baseline. For example, I may have high blood sugar when the Microbot entered. Now if that becomes the base, that won't be right. That's where you can help. You will be monitoring the data from every single section of the body and you will define what is normal according to your area of expertise. After that, the data will be compared with values that are globally normal so that we can all make sense of the incoming data and use it for our well-being.'

Everyone in the lab became pretty excited because it certainly felt like we were watching history being made. We all strained to look at the screen and watched as the dot representing the Microbot moved around, presumably inside Dr. Amit's bloodstream.

Soon we all dispersed and focused on our regular work in the lab as well. I thoroughly enjoyed being a part of the work here. As doctors, we dealt with a lot of situations on a daily basis but this was different in many ways. There was research and there was hands on activity as well where we were required to bring in our level of experience into the mix. When we were done for the day, we trooped out, hungry and tired.

Dr. Amit led us to a section of the building that we'd never been to before. It was where some of the people who worked here slept. There was a dining room of sorts and we all sat down to dinner. Archana kept looking at me as though she wanted to say something but she kept quiet. I even raised my eyebrows at her, asking her what the matter was. She looked concerned about something but shrugged instead and mouthed 'Later'.

Over a dinner of methi-alu and chapatis, I noticed that Dr. Amit stayed mostly silent and watched everyone else interact. A couple of times I felt his eyes on me but when I turned to him, he'd be looking in another direction. I wondered if it would be possible to retrieve my phone and make a call to Gautam. I realized that I hadn't thought of him all evening. Feeling guilty, I looked around at the people conversing and wondered how to get an opening into it to ask about the phone.

'Anything you need Dr. Payal?' Dr. Amit spoke softly, leaning forward and I realized that the others continued talking and I was the only one who could hear him. It seemed somewhat intimate.

'Uhm....I just wanted to know if it would be possible to get my phone back? I needed to make a call,' I said, smiling apologetically. He smiled back but his smile didn't quite reach his eyes.

'I'm afraid that's not possible,' he said, leaning back. What?

'But we're going to be here for the whole weekend!' I protested in a whisper, feeling a bit trapped. I wasn't the only one who didn't have access to the outside world but I felt awful. I was now really worried about Gautam. Knowing the mistake he'd done today in surgery, he probably needed someone to talk to. I wished I had gone after him right then. All my emotions were plainly visible to Dr. Amit.

'I thought I told you to read your NDA before signing it. There can be no contact with anyone outside this building while you are working on the Microbot project,' he said in the same soft voice. I looked away, feeling upset. I didn't know what to do.

'What if it's an emergency?' I asked. He looked thoughtful and then leaned forward to speak to me directly.

'Only once. You can use my phone,' he said and pulled out an old phone from his pocket and handed it to me. I looked at it a little surprised before taking it. That was when I noticed that some of the others had felt silent and were looking at us.

'You know how I feel about using technology in the vicinity of my lab,' Dr. Amit addressed the group. Everyone fell silent and I felt my face burn in embarrassment. 'I use only this old phone when I'm here. It's just a phone. No camera, no internet, no Bluetooth, no WiFi. Dr. Payal says there's an emergency and she needs to talk to someone so I'm giving her my phone. You can go back to finishing your dinner.'

Everyone continued looking at me as I clutched the phone and backed the chair to get up from there. I felt all eyes on me as I walked towards one corner of the room and quickly pressed the buttons for Gautam's number. When I turned back to look, I was relieved that no one was looking at me. Most of the people had finished eating and they were getting up.

I looked at the phone in frustration when I realized that the call wasn't getting through. Gautam's number was unreachable. I tried again. Same result. I wished I could call his roommate Roopesh but that wasn't possible because I didn't remember Roopesh's number off hand although it was saved on my phone. Feeling discouraged I walked back to the dining table and handed the phone back to Dr. Amit. I went to Jai and asked him if he remembered anyone's number. He shook his head but he too looked worried.

'Don't worry. Gautam will be fine', he said, trying to comfort me.

He normally avoided getting drunk because he knew how much I hated it but after what happened today, he had turned to alcohol, in my absence. I felt uneasy because I didn't know what he was doing and how he was at the moment but I had to put it out of my mind as we left the room. Dr. Amit was showing everyone where they had to sleep. It was like a dormitory, but with better furniture.

'I hope everything is fine,' he said, as Archana and I walked into the dormitory for women along with some of the others.

'I don't know,' I said, feeling a little cross with him and didn't turn to look at him as I went inside and walked up towards an empty bed. Archana sat down beside me on the bed.

'What did you tell him?' she whispered.

'Nothing, why?' I asked, looking up to the doorway. Dr. Amit wasn't there.

'He kind of looked...a little upset,' Archana said, her eyes on the empty doorway. I shrugged.

'Okay you know something?' she lowered her voice further and I pushed my feet out of my sandals and sat on the bed cross-legged.

'What?' I asked. Archana looked around as though assessing the others who were with us. They were the regulars here and they seemed to know what to do. One of the girls padded up to the door and shut it while another switched off the lights, bathing the room in darkness. Before Archana and I could protest, someone switched on a night light.

In the eerie red orange glow, I looked at Archana who seemed to be debating with herself over something.

'Spill it. You've been dying to tell me something all evening,' I whispered.

'Okay,' she said. 'You're right. You know after Dr. Amit injected the Microbot, I was the one who was regulating his heartbeats and other heart related information, right?'

I nodded. She was the cardio expert in our group.

'I just noticed something weird. His heartbeat would be normal most of the time but...' she looked at me and paused as though wondering to continue or not.

'But?' I asked, curious now.

'His heartrate would shoot up whenever he came near you or spoke to you,' she said in a rush, her eyes wide.

What?

'Why?' I managed to ask.

'I thought maybe you'd know the answer to that,' she said, looking at me in an assessing sort of manner.

I shook my head. 'I don't know,' I spoke slowly. 'What could it mean?'

'It means that you're literally making his heart race,' she said, with a wink.

CHAPTER - 8

Archana's words kept me awake long after everyone else had gone to sleep. What could she possibly mean? I hadn't really paid attention to any of Dr. Amit's readings but now I was painfully aware of his supposed reactions towards me. My sleep was not peaceful. When I woke up the next day with the others, everything felt a little strange.

After a quick breakfast, we were back in the lab. Today since we were here from the morning, I realized that there was so much more work that went into the Microbot program. Yet, Dr. Amit was rather insistent that the four of us be involved in monitoring the health of the patients as well as the few healthy people who had taken the Microbot.

Apparently, despite his dramatic announcement yesterday, he wasn't the only one who had taken it. Some of the others who had been working with him for a long time had taken his lead and asked for it to be injected.

Nitin didn't realize that he was riling up Dr. Amit as he kept asking him about what the Microbot actually did. I could sense that Dr. Amit was close to losing his patience as he explained to him for the umpteenth time that the Microbot didn't possess any intelligence of its own and could not act on its own. It just relayed information that it came across.

'So it won't tell my doctor that I have diabetes?' Nitin asked once more. Dr. Amit sighed and looked skywards as though for patience.

'Dr. Nitin, the Microbot is a tiny, microscopic device. It's just like an electronic chip that is introduced into our bloodstream. It can only traverse the human body and report only observation data. The software analyzes any anomalies and by that, I mean any parameters that have strayed from the normal. It cannot send an SMS to your doctor saying anything about your health,' he said. Poor Nitin still didn't look too convinced and he glanced at Archana as if expecting her to help him out. Archana rolled her eyes and shook her head. She'd been pretty annoyed that he'd been accepted in the Microbot program.

Just then, Jai asked, 'Dr.Amit, how do we know for sure that this is a well-designed and properly executed project like the ones we hear are being done in more developed countries?'

Dr.Amit's faced turned red. He seemed to be struggling to regain his composure, as he asked, 'Do you doubt our competence, Dr. Jai?' he asked and I could sense the underlying anger in his words as he stressed on the word 'competence'.

All of us stared at Jai, trying to signal to him to shut up without being too obvious but he ignored us and continued speaking. 'Yes, we know you have all these talented people here for this job. But it's not like everyone is a scientist here of the highest caliber. I mean, do they know every single aspect of electronics, medicine, software, firmware, robotics and all that is needed for this project? Isn't that too much to expect from this relatively small team that you have?'

Dr.Amit smiled and waved at Dr.Sundaram, who was walking past us towards his desk and called out to him. 'Did you hear what he just said, doc? They want proof that we know everything even though they're here, where all the action is taking place!'

I felt like squirming. Dr. Amit's attitude was bordering on dangerously-close-to-exploding now and I wanted to yell at Jai for having got himself in the crossfire like this. But I stood by, waiting to see what would happen.

Dr.Sundaram laughed and spoke, even as he walked towards his workstation without a break in his stride. 'Amit, you're the pro. Why don't you show them what you know and what you don't. I'm sure the kids will be impressed.'

I frowned. Kids? Us?

Amit turned towards Jai and while there was still a smile on his face, no one else was amused. 'Why don't you choose any of the encyclopedias and books from there?' he said, pointing towards the rows of bookshelves adjacent to where Dr. Sundaram was sitting.

'And?' Jai looked stymied.

'And I'm saying you can ask me anything you find in any of those books,' Dr. Amit said. My eyes grew round. 'Any subject,' he reiterated, quickly glancing over at all of us. I looked away quickly even as I felt his gaze on me for the barest of second, noting that the others in the lab too had become interested now. Was this going to be an embarrassing moment for Dr. Amit now? Or would he actually impress us with his knowledge?

Most of the others had left their workstations but some of the seniors like Dr. Sundaram continued with their work, looking already lost to the world. Jai looked hesitant but he walked towards one of the bookshelves and pulled out a fat encyclopedia from it. He flipped the pages and stopped, looking up at Dr. Amit, as though mentally asking him if he was sure.

'Go ahead,' Dr. Amit raised his hands expansively, a little theatrically. Oh my god, I winced. Jai was holding an encyclopedia in his hand. How could Dr. Amit possibly know everything in the encyclopedia?

Jai flipped some more pages and then stopped. He looked up and then said, 'Erinome'.

Dr. Amit smiled widely. 'Really? That one's easy. It's one of the 39 known moons of Jupiter.' I looked up surprised.

Okay, for someone like him, it might have been pretty easy. As though reading my thoughts, he turned to me suddenly.

'Why don't you come and help your friend, Dr. Payal?' he addressed me. Startled, I recovered my wits and nodded. I walked up towards Jai and pulled out a couple of more big books feeling a little weird about how this was progressing.

It soon turned into a free for all match. We kept bombarding him with complicated terms from physics, microbiology, organic chemistry and even technology. He got the answers right, all the time! It was crazy! How could one man have learnt all the encyclopedias?

Jai too was relentless. As though he'd been personally challenged he asked question after question, each one, tougher than the previous one. I gave up when he correctly answered that Nystagmus was the term used to describe fast and uncontrollable movements of the eye. I shut the book and shook my head, speechless. Jai, too, looked stunned. I could see that a fine line of sweat was trickling down his temple as he shut his book too. Dr. Amit had not only answered all the questions correctly, he'd known them in detail! Like he was some sort of human encyclopedia.

Archana and Nitin looked shocked as well and the others in the lab who had gathered close to us, smiled, as though glad that their Dr. Amit had proved himself.

Oh he had proved himself, and how!

In fact they started clapping and we all joined in. Dr. Amit gracefully bowed, but I caught him winking at Dr. Sundaram who only smiled as if he knew Dr.Amit would get it right.

'Are you convinced now?' he asked Jai who was dumbfounded. He could only nod silently. But before anyone could say anything else, Nitin volunteered to have the Microbot injected in himself. There was a new resolve in his eyes and we all looked at him amazed.

'Are you sure?' Dr. Amit asked, looking surprised himself. Nitin nodded.

'I trust you Dr. Amit and since you too have got it injected, I know it can't possibly be harmful. Maybe once I have it in my body, I'll understand what it does properly,' Nitin said. In a strange sort of way, he made sense.

Archana looked impressed with his reasoning and we all watched as Dr. Amit prepared Nitin for the procedure. Only Jai and I looked a bit wary.

'Will I have to wait as long as you did?' Nitin asked Dr. Amit who seemed momentarily confused.

'What?'

'I meant, you said that the body had to prepare for the Microbot and for that we have to do a lot of tests. How long will it be till I get the Microbot in my system?' Nitin asked, as though he couldn't wait for it to happen right now.

'Oh, that! Right. As you can see, we are constantly developing the Microbot. Since I had opted for this a while back, I had to be injected with a slightly older version. But the new version we have here is the nearly perfected prototype. It will assimilate into your body in no time. There might be a few side effects but they will be much less than what you would have had, if you'd been injected with an earlier version,' he explained patiently.

'So will you inject me with it now?' Nitin asked, a little nervously. Dr. Amit nodded.

'First let's take some of your blood,' he said as he led Nitin towards the bed. The rest of us were soon assigned to monitor Nitin as Dr. Amit prepared him for the Microbot. We were, of course, expected to monitor Dr. Amit and some others as well.

After Nitin was injected, he spent almost an hour near the screen that showed his health statistics. The first thing he said was, 'Shit. I have high cholesterol.' We all laughed at that even though it was no laughing matter. Nitin, with his chubby build and his fondness for rich food, having high cholesterol was not a surprise to any of us. Nitin's wealthy family had easily paid for his medical education but it was a testament to his hard work that he had found himself in the Microbot program.

After Nitin, it was Archana who said she was ready. I looked at her surprised. We had been sitting together all this while and she had never let on that she wanted to try the Microbot too! Her eyes were shining with excitement as she stepped forward. For the next few hours, we got busy, taking her blood out and slowly getting the Microbot to adjust to the 'hostile' environment. This was later released back in to her veins, along with the Microbot, of course.

Dr. Amit looked at me pointedly as we watched Archana get injected. I didn't say anything. We spent most of the day going over our findings and I was so immersed in it, I realized that I hadn't thought about Gautam at all. Sometime around lunch, I remembered that I hadn't been able to contact him yesterday. I looked at Dr. Amit who was discussing something with his software people and knew that he wouldn't be happy if I asked to use his phone now. So I hung back and then realized that Archana kept giving me odd looks.

I went up to her and sat down beside her as she looked at the screens that displayed the data of those who had the Microbot in them, including her. While there was a huge amount of information to be analyzed, Archana was responsible only for the cardiology part of it.

'What is it?' I asked her. She shook her head and I looked away impatiently. Dr. Amit had finished talking and he came up to us.

'Is there a problem?' he asked. Archana shook her head vigorously but tapped some keys on the keyboard and looked busy. Dr. Amit shrugged and walked away. After he left, she showed the screen to me.

'What?' I asked, looking at what seemed to be the normal spikes in Dr. Amit's heart rate.

'This,' she said, and tapped a few buttons. I realized she had taken a screenshot when he had come near us to show the situation and yes, she was right. Dr. Amit's heart readings were all over the place.

I looked down, not sure of what to make out of it. All I knew was that it made me a little uncomfortable. Archana however seemed to think it was cute.

'I wish I was the one who made his heart race,' she whispered when we were heading out at the end of that day back to our dorms. Dinner had been a quiet and subdued affair for some reason. Or maybe people were talking as normal and I was lost in my own thoughts that I didn't notice.

'Shut up!' I whispered back to her and then remembered that I needed to talk to Gautam.

'I'll just be back,' I told her and went back outside, hoping to catch hold of Dr. Amit before he disappeared to his own room. Luckily he was there talking to Nitin. I was surprised at how amenable he seemed with Nitin now. Earlier on it had seemed like he couldn't stand talking to him. Jai was on the sidelines, looking at the two of them critically.

When Dr. Amit saw me approaching he excused himself from the two of them and walked up towards me.

'Any problem, Dr. Payal?' he asked.

'I needed your phone,' I said, looking down unable to meet his piercing gaze.

'Right. You need to check up on your boyfriend, I suppose,' he said, pulling out his phone and handing it to me. I wasn't sure if it was sarcasm I detected in his tone.

I took the phone from him and went towards a corner of the room, realizing that only the two of us remained in the dining hall now. Everyone else had gone to sleep. I dialed Gautam's number hoping to talk to him this time at least.

His phone rang for a few minutes before finally he answered. My heart leaped when I heard his voice but then I realized it didn't sound like him at all.

'Gautam, is that you?' I asked, wincing at how stupid that question sounded.

'Who's this?' he asked.

'Payal here. I'm calling from Dr. Amit's phone,' I said, turning away towards the wall so I wouldn't have to look at Dr. Amit who seemed to be lingering in the room. I suppose he didn't want to leave his phone unattended even for a little while, my privacy be damned.

'Right. Dr. Amit's phone,' Gautam said, his voice slurring a little.

'What do you mean?' I asked him sharply.

'I suppose saving the World is more important to you than I,' he said, his voice bitter. 'I suppose I should be grateful that you found the time to call me finally.'

'I called you yesterday too but your phone was unreachable,' I protested. He didn't hear me as he went on.

'My life is ruined,' he said. I frowned. What did he mean?

'I needed you yesterday Payal. Where were you? When are you coming back? I can't do this on my own,' he said.

'Can't do what?' I asked, feeling a little angry, 'And what do you mean that your life is ruined?'

'I can't explain it over the phone. I made a big mistake yesterday during a surgery and Dr. Vinod has banned me from the OT. Then today….' He broke down.

'Listen, Gautam! Hold on! What did you do today?' I asked, painfully aware that Dr. Amit's eyes were on me and his ears were tuned to the conversation.

'You have to come back. You should come back. Just tell that big shot Amit that you don't want to do his stupid research. I need you. I'm more important than his research,' Gautam ranted. I felt my patience snap at his words.

'Gautam, don't act like a small kid. We've been through so much worse before. And you were so brave every single time. Pull your chin up. I'll be there soon. And please try and understand! I can't just leave everything here and come back!'

'You can if you want to. It's not like he's signed you into slavery. Just say you don't want to do it because your fiancé won't let you,' Gautam said.

'Let me?' I whispered back angrily. I was on the verge of saying something very bitter to him but I didn't want to talk to him when my primary emotion was anger. 'It's already late evening. One more day. I'll meet you on Monday, Gautam,' I said and ended the call. I took a few deep breaths to bring my anger under control.

But it wasn't easy. I just couldn't forget Gautam's words that he was more important than the stupid research. I jumped when I realized that Dr. Amit was standing right behind me and I turned around to face him.

'Everything okay?' he asked softly, putting his hand out for the phone. I looked at him squarely for a few seconds although it seemed longer. I don't know what it was that prompted me to do it.

'Everything is okay. It will be even better tomorrow when I take the Microbot,' I replied. I carried the look on his face back to my dorm, even as I tried to drown out Gautam's bitter voice.

---✿✿✿---

CHAPTER - 9

I didn't feel any different. It was like a regular injection, though a bit longer. The others were looking at me expectantly after I'd allowed Dr.Sundaram and Dr. Amit to inject the Microbot into my arm the next day.

'Let's get back to work,' I said crisply and sat down at my computer where I was monitoring the brain readings of those who had injected the Microbot in their bodies. I was looking forward to finishing my work here today so that we could go back to the hospital this evening. Even though I was angry with Gautam, I wanted to try and meet him tonight once I went back. Maybe things would become normal once I sat down and spoke to him.

Dr. Amit was absent from the main laboratory for a large period of time. I couldn't help but notice his absence. I looked around, wondering where he could have gone when he normally liked to work with us and enter all our observations in his laptop. Oddly, when he returned, the first thing I felt was relief. Was Archana's observation about the effect I supposedly had on his heart rate, affecting my behavior too? No, it couldn't be, I reasoned immediately.

I smiled at him and he looked a little surprised. Given our on and off behavior with each other, I suppose he was used to me being distant with him. He smiled back and we continued as before.

As the day wore on, I realized that Nitin of all people, had been right. Having volunteered to inject the Microbot in myself, I felt exhilarated now. I fully understood what it would mean to have this technology accessible to everyone.

I was able to see and read every single parameter inside my body. We all were setting the base parameters. In effect we had all swallowed the doctors! Well, all of us, except Jai, but he would come around soon too, I hoped.

The way the Microbot worked was remarkable. If someone was going to have a stroke, the Microbot could most likely save their lives by passing on the message to the analysts because even the few minutes before a stroke occurred were precious. All day, my respect for Dr. Amit and his hard work grew. I realized how difficult it must have been to cross all those hurdles and I wished I'd been there from the beginning of his amazing journey.

When we were discussing some details, he came over and listened to us and then spoke a little about what was up ahead. Jai turned away from his system and stepped up closer to listen to us. I glanced at him and got the feeling that he had another question to ask.

'Don't you think monitoring patients is like invasion of privacy?'

Bingo. I swerved to see what Dr. Amit would say to something that had been at the back of my head too.

Dr.Amit cocked his head and then spoke, 'Ethical and legal are two different concepts now. Security cover is no longer considered a threat but need. For example, if you walk down a well-known street you may be covered and followed by multiple cameras. That's not called invasion of privacy. It's just security.'

'You think you can spy on anyone with your camera smartphone but do you know that your GPS enabled device is actually letting someone else from a remote location spy on your every move? Also, with big data analytics every message and email is being screened by Government agencies! Why? To prevent terrorism. And for that, we're okay with it, in a way. What is legal, what is ethical and what is necessary - the lines have blurred and it is all very complex now.'

He paused in his speech, looking a little distant for some reason and then snapping out of it, he spoke again briskly.

'In our case, though, we take an informed consent from the person whom we are monitoring. He or she signs up for the program being fully aware of the fact that they will be monitored for health. Although, when we roll this out to the general public, there might have to be some rules to be followed. But first we need to test the Microbot extensively on healthy people to prove that there are no repercussions and side effects. Once that's done, we can aim to get the government approval and after that...' he trailed away.

'After that?' Archana asked, looking up from her screen. Dr. Amit shrugged elegantly.

'Who knows, maybe even the Nobel,' he said with a wink as he walked away. Wow!

The three of us turned to Jai as if on cue. 'Did you hear that? The Nobel!' I whispered.

'So?' he raised both eyebrows in an exaggerated manner. 'He gets the Nobel. What do I get?'

'Come on! We'll be in the team that got him the Nobel!' I said, feeling excited.

He shook his head adamantly. 'Forget the Nobel okay? That's a long shot. About injecting the Microbot, you said it doesn't feel any different than normal so why should I get it?' he argued with me.

'What about the long term benefits? Won't it be helpful if you get it and find out once and for all, about the status of your health?' I asked him. He continued shaking his head. The three of us looked at each other and I shrugged. There was only so much one could do to convince someone.

As the day wore on, I realized that during the past two

days here in the laboratory, my life had changed somehow. Yes, like the others, I too had signed on a consent form and let Dr. Amit inject me with the Microbot. But that just wasn't the reason for my change. In a way, my weekend trip away from the hospital had put things in perspective for me with Gautam too.

A part of me felt the tiniest twinge of guilt. Gautam's behavior with me had changed so suddenly that I didn't know what to think. He'd never sounded so angry in all the time I'd known him. I knew that he counted on me to be there when he needed me and I felt like I had betrayed him by coming here. But as soon as that thought came, it evaporated. I was just doing my job!

I caught Dr. Amit looking at me and I looked down, feeling a bit shy. What was the deal with him and the number of times he kept checking me out? I recalled Archana's words the other night about how his heartbeats accelerated when I was in his proximity and the simple fact amazed me. Science did not lie. If his heart raced, it had to do with me and what he felt for me. I lifted my eyes and looked back at him and he smiled before going back to his laptop.

I found myself walking past his workstation more often that day and our wordless interaction had increased many times over. Maybe it was because he seemed so much more approachable that I found myself talking to him that evening as we finished our work for the day.

'So you just live here? Work at the lab? Come and inspire people like us with your speeches?' I teased him.

'What else is there to do?' he asked, as he watched the others leave.

'What about a personal life? No family, no friends?' I asked and then realized I must have sounded so impudent. 'I'm sorry, I didn't mean to be intrusive.'

He shook his head. 'I don't have a family any more, Dr.

Payal,' he said. 'They died when I was in engineering college.' I winced.

Oops!

'I'm sorry to hear that,' I said, feeling a little guilty. He nodded and continued.

'There was a car accident and...they didn't survive it,' he said, his face looking drawn as he recalled what was probably the worst time of his life.

'Oh god, I'm so sorry,' I whispered. How awful.

'I've devoted my life to work ever since then. There's no one else to live for, right? And if I am successful, I just think of the number of lives I can save, the number of families that can stay whole,' he said softly. My respect for him grew in leaps and bounds.

'You are amazing,' I said, blushing a little because I couldn't believe I was saying these things to him.

He didn't say anything but he looked up and smiled in a way that momentarily made me realize many things at once. Like the fact that even though he was so handsome and popular, he was a lonely person who didn't seem to have a single friend.

'Thank you, Dr. Payal,' he said. Everyone had left now and it was just the two of us. I got up too because I had to leave.

'What about friends?' I asked him, unwilling to let the conversation get over for some reason.

'My work consumes me totally. I don't have time for friends and they too don't have time for me. I don't know how it happened but once I got involved in the Microbot project, I realized I had distanced myself from everyone. Now, it's only my work and me,' he said, shaking his head sadly.

'That's too bad,' I said as I walked away from there, waving a goodbye to him.

'Dr. Payal,' he called out and I stopped and turned, surprised.

'I do have time these days for a friend, as long as it's you,' he said and my eyes widened. I felt something lift in my heart.

I nodded, not sure if I could say the right words. Then willing myself to speak, I said, 'Then you should call me Payal from now on,' I said. He shook his head resolutely even though he continued smiling at me.

'No. That's not what I'm going to call you,' he said. I was surprised. What then?

'I think you know already,' he said, and looked in the direction of my silver anklets. I walked out from there, wondering if the smile on my face made me look foolish or radiant. Whatever it was, I knew that things were not going to be the same around here from now on.

CHAPTER - 10

By the time we reached the hospital, it was late evening and I wasn't in the mood for a confrontation with Gautam. I wanted to sleep - my limbs were tired and aching from the work we had done over the weekend. It may not have seemed like much but mental exhaustion was something else altogether. But before I could sleep, I had to drop in quickly to check the charts of my patients to see if everything was in order.

The four of us had initially been a bit taken aback when we'd been told to pack for the weekend. Being doctors first, we were worried about our patients. But Dr. Amit had assured us that it would be taken care of. With all the stuff that was happening with Gautam and injecting the Microbot and getting to know Dr. Amit a little better, I had put my patients out of my mind for the weekend. But now that we were back, I was anxious and wanted to check in on them.

Thankfully, no one had required any emergency attendance and I felt relieved as I walked back to my quarters with Archana. The feeling of contentment that I'd felt just some hours ago had vanished. There was a sense of dread inside me for some reason that had to do with facing Gautam actually. But just as we turned towards our building, I spotted Jai running towards us and I was shocked to see the look on his face.

'What happened Jai?' I asked him as he stopped before us panting.

'Gautam has been expelled from the hospital,' he said, sounding breathless.

'Expelled? What do you mean?' I felt the blood drain from my face.

'I mean Dr. Vinod kicked him out of the hospital,' Jai said, looking at me as though I was responsible.

'But why?' I asked, feeling shocked.

Jai shook his head. 'It seems he made some mistake on Friday and Dr. Vinod told him not to do any more surgeries until he had proved himself. But Gautam didn't listen. On Saturday he went into the OT when he was drunk,' Jai whispered as though he couldn't believe it himself.

'Drunk?' I repeated. I remembered how he had sounded on Friday evening itself when I'd got a call from him. I had told him I couldn't talk to him and had gone on inside to the lab.

Jai nodded. Archana shook her head as though she too couldn't believe it.

'Yes, and it seems Dr. Vinod didn't want him in the OT and Gautam actually got into a scuffle with him after which Dr. Vinod kicked him out. He's not in the quarters any more but everyone is talking about it,' Jai said.

Oh no! This was what Gautam had meant when he said that his life was ruined. I took a deep breath and lifted my phone to call him. But Jai shook his head.

'His phone is not reachable. I've tried. I don't know where he's gone Payal,' he said, looking distressed.

'I'll keep trying,' I said, wondering what I could do to make this right. How could things have gone so wrong in one weekend? I felt the full force of guilt crash into me when I realized that if I'd been here on Friday evening, none of this would have happened. He wouldn't have gone on a drinking spree and definitely would not have the audacity to challenge Dr. Vinod who was his mentor.

Jai left while Archana and I made our way back to the dimly lit compound where our quarters were. Both of us were quiet. I kept trying his number every two minutes but it was unreachable. By the time we reached our place, I was frustrated enough to want to fling my phone at the wall.

I thought it was obvious that I was not in the mood to talk but Archana just went on and on about how irresponsible it had been of Gautam to go into the OT when he was drunk. Finally, I snapped at her, 'I don't want to talk about this,' I said. She looked at me squarely and then shrugged.

'What do you want to talk about then?' she asked.

'Nothing,' I replied because my mind was already clamoring with different thoughts.

'Fine,' she said and turned to go to her room. Then she turned around and spoke once more. 'But I hope you'll put this out of your mind when you go to the lab tomorrow. We have a lot of work there. Dr. Amit won't be pleased if you're too distracted.'

I watched her go, not sure how to reply to her. My boyfriend was missing and she wanted to talk about work! I had to find him first and I had no idea how to do that. I didn't want to call up his parents and alarm them if he hadn't gone there.

I went to bed, holding my phone in my hand, redialing his number in the hope that it would connect. But after nearly half an hour of trying I gave up. I put the phone down on the bedside table and shut my eyes wondering how it had all gone so wrong.

Gautam and I go back so long that I don't quite remember how or when we met. We'd been together in MBBS and we even started doing our residency in the same Government hospital before moving here. In fact, there were a few incidents during our residency in that government hospital that had cemented our friendship firmly.

My mind drifted back to those days where my primary emotion was one of fear of not being able to do enough. I had channeled all my energy into becoming a doctor so that I could change the lives of my mother and brother, and I didn't have time for anything else. Gautam could always get a laugh out of me though, even when I was moody or upset. But one day he looked disturbed and it was my turn to ask him what had gone wrong.

Apparently, one of his senior Doctors had mistreated a patient who had a fractured elbow. Gautam had been aghast at what the patient had been subject to, just because he was poor and couldn't afford to go to a private hospital. He was a laborer at a construction site and he had slipped and fallen down from the scaffolding one day, right on his elbow, shattering it. The senior doctor had been rude and made offensive remarks and had generally treated the poor man as dirt.

Gautam's words had opened my eyes that day and I became more observant about what was happening around me. Everywhere, it was the same case. Poor patients who came to the Government hospital with hopes in their eyes were either being turned away or being treated very badly. Doctors who had taken the Hippocratic Oath had merely muttered the words without taking it to heart like Gautam or I had.

Once when a doctor sent away a patient who had gangrene in his foot, I decided enough was enough. With Gautam's help, we enlisted more young doctors who were disgusted by the practices of their seniors in the hospital and together we started a movement of sorts. Any patient who was turned away was being redirected to us and we tried our best to help them.

The movement didn't go unnoticed by the hospital authorities and Gautam and I were summoned to the management for spearheading it. But before we could be ostracized for being 'trouble-makers', a few friends of ours had managed to get articles written about the two of us in the local newspapers. Then there were blogs and social media where the two of us suddenly became heroes. The tables were turned on the hospital because their malpractice had now come under the scanner of the Indian Medical Association. The medical superintendent was fired and the new woman who was the replacement actually listened to our suggestions and ideas and promised to implement them in the hospital.

Gautam and I had spent so much time together on this campaign that when he asked me out on dinner, I didn't even think much about it. It was a natural progression from being just friends to being more than that.

Gautam and I both remembered those days, but differently. He used to say that it was when he really fell in love with me. I would tell him that he opened my eyes to the suffering around me and stopped me from being self-centered. Even though I couldn't really define whether what I felt for him was love, I knew that Gautam was really important to me.

I forgot our fight on the phone yesterday. I forgot the harsh words we'd exchanged. All I wanted was to talk to him, just hug him once more and see for myself if he was fine.

---❁❁❁---

CHAPTER - 11

The moment I opened my eyes in the morning, I reached out for my phone. There was a new message! I quickly tapped it open and then read it in surprise. It wasn't from Gautam but it was from Dr. Amit. At first the crushing sense of disappointment I felt that Gautam hadn't got in touch was so huge that I couldn't bring myself to read Dr. Amit's words. I kept the phone aside and showered and came back, feeling only slightly better. I picked up the phone once again and read the message.

'Good morning. Hope you're fine! Any side effects?' the message read. I shut my eyes briefly to recall if I did feel any side effects. According to Dr. Amit, the initial versions of the Microbot had caused fevers in some people and some others had developed a few rashes. But those side effects were in ill patients. We were some of the first few healthy people who had taken it although we had taken the much revised version.

'Just a bit of a headache and I don't know if it's because of that,' I tapped out. It was true. There was a slight pain at the back of my skull and it throbbed as I pressed down on it.

'Oh. It might be a side effect. Ask Archana if she too has it,' he replied back. I wasn't in the mood to talk to Archana and didn't really choose to think about why he couldn't ask her himself. But our conversation last evening came back to me and I remembered how he'd said we would be friends which is why he was being more open to me.

I didn't reply to him but as I got ready to leave for the hospital, I realized that the pain wasn't there. Or if it was there I'd got used to it. Anyway I couldn't make out the difference. Archana looked at me a little warily.

'Have you heard from Gautam?' she asked carefully as though assessing my mood. I shook my head. The weird part was that although I was despondent about it, I didn't really feel it. I didn't feel the despair I felt last night. Somehow it seemed to have been lifted.

Before we reached the hospital, I tried his number one more time. It was still unreachable. Sighing, I put my phone on silent and went to work.

On the way I remembered to ask Archana if she'd felt any side effects. She looked thoughtful. 'Just a light headache,' she said and I looked at her, surprised. So the headache must have been a side effect. 'It was quite prominent when I woke up. But it's almost gone now,' she added. I should remember to tell this to Dr. Amit, I thought but then we were caught up checking in on our patients and it slipped my mind.

I was completely busy most of the day, making up for missing the weekend. When the four of us met once more at the parking lot where Jai would drive us down to the lab, all four of us were exhausted.

'I didn't know this would be so tiring,' Nitin muttered as Jai drove through the busy Delhi traffic. I remembered then to ask Nitin if he too had any side effects. Nitin bunched up his forehead. 'Nothing out of the ordinary. I'm not sure,' he said.

'What do you mean? You either have a side effect or you don't,' Archana challenged him. 'Like I had this pain at the back of my head in the morning but it's almost gone now. Did you also have something like that?' Both of us were a little surprised when Nitin said he hadn't. Of course it was entirely possible that the Microbot reacted differently to different people.

Jai was quiet on the way and I asked him if he'd heard from Gautam. He shook his head as he made the turn that would take us to Asola. I felt the worry worm itself back. Where could he have gone? Why wasn't he reaching out to us? But once we reached the lab, I felt Gautam recede from my mind. Dr. Amit had a new battery of tests that he wanted to be conducted on everyone who had taken the Microbot and we got involved in it completely.

'So the headache is gone?' Dr. Amit asked softly as I made some notes. I looked up surprised. I hadn't heard him come at all. I think I forgot his question as I stared at him, realizing just how good looking he was. The female doctors who had been enamored during his first lecture had good enough reason and although I too had noticed his good looks, but a little more objectively then, it was hard not to fall under his spell.

'Anything wrong?' he asked as I continued staring at him.

'No, nothing is wrong. I'm fine now,' I said, unable to meet his clear gaze.

I felt distinctly pleased when he pulled up a chair and sat down near me during a break. In fact, the pleasure I felt at his presence seemed to magnify by the minute and it eclipsed everything else I'd been feeling all day. The exhaustion, the worry, the concern, they were all replaced by the pleasure of sharing his company. I subdued the pang of guilt that loomed up when Gautam's name popped into my head and tried to focus on what he was saying.

'Did you know that until recently, I couldn't stand doctors?' he said in a low voice so only I could hear him. I looked at him startled. What did he mean?

'But...aren't you a doctor yourself?' I asked. He looked at me as though I was daft.

'I'm an engineer but my focus is on Medical Electronics. I'm not a doctor like you or any of the others here. I'm called 'Dr' Amit because of my PhD,' he said. I nodded, a little embarrassed but also impressed, remembering some of the things he'd told us in his first lecture.

'But why didn't you like doctors?' I asked, remembering how he had started the conversation. He looked down a moment as though composing himself.

'I told you about how my parents died, right?' he asked.

'Car accident,' I repeated slowly.

'It wasn't just a car accident, Payal,' he elaborated. I leaned forward, interested in what he was telling. I didn't realize that the two of us made a cozy picture sitting close together, heads bent, talking until I looked up and saw Archana lifting one eyebrow questioningly. I ignored her and tried to focus on what he was saying.

'What do you mean?' I asked.

'Both of them didn't die immediately. My father was on life support for nearly ten days after the accident. My mother had a badly fractured hip and she was bed ridden and in a lot of pain. I was just a student myself and the costs of having both parents in the hospital escalated so much that I had to mortgage our house. But even then, I couldn't save my father,' he said, looking into the distance. I worried my lower lip anxiously, feeling terrible for him. He continued talking.

'I went crazy trying to get to talk to doctors, asking them what they were doing and how they could help my parents. When my father didn't come out of the coma after ten days, they called me and explained that even if I pumped more money into my father's treatment, it was useless. They advised me to take him off the life support and focus on saving my mother.'

He went silent for a bit after that and my heart ached at the thought of the young man who had to make such a difficult decision all on his own. He took a deep breath as though fortifying himself and then continued.

'All they kept saying was they didn't know why he wasn't responding to their treatment. All the doctors I asked had the same answer and that frustrated me. If doctors themselves couldn't surmise what was happening inside the human body, what was the point of it all? Then something one doctor told me just stayed in my head. He said that they were just monitoring reactions and they couldn't actually get inside the body to find out what was happening. And he would keep saying about how the 'body is not telling us' anything. Those were the words that stuck with me, even after I gave them the nod to remove the life support,' he said, looking down at his hands.

'And your mother?' I whispered.

'I stopped trusting doctors from that day because I felt that there was no point to their education if they could not answer a basic question about what was happening inside the human body.'

I listened to him in silence. 'What changed your mind?' I asked.

'Necessity. My mother died within twenty days of my father's death. She had got an infection from her surgery and she didn't survive it. I was devastated. I thought she would be fine. I thought one day maybe we could salvage our lives somehow and move on but she didn't give me the chance,' he said.

When he looked up, I saw the tears in his eyes and my heart melted. He blinked quickly and then looked away as though trying to regain control of himself. I don't know what made me do it, but I leaned over and placed my hand on his. He looked at me, surprised.

I smiled and squeezed his hand and he interlinked his fingers with mine. I have no idea what was happening to me but I only wanted to comfort him. I wished the others weren't here. But he squeezed my fingers lightly and let go and I looked away, not sure of what I was doing any more.

'The Microbot project is my life, Payal. I couldn't save my parents but I studied, worked hard and worked relentlessly so that this ground breaking technology will save many other lives. I took the words of those doctors and made it a prayer that I have lived by, all these years. But then, I got so involved in my research that I didn't have time for anything else. Now I look at my contemporaries and see them all married and having families and I feel like I have left all that behind. Or rather, I'm left behind as everyone else has moved on.'

'So? You're still young. You can still find someone I'm sure,' I said, smiling at him.

He stared at me so intently that I had to look away.

'Not just someone Payal,' he said, before he got up and walked away.

---❁❁❁---

CHAPTER - 12

Archana got hold of me just as we were finishing up that evening. It was pretty late and to say that we were exhausted would be an understatement. With all the tests that we were doing, Dr. Amit said that we would be ready to try and get government approval for it in a month. When Jai looked skeptical that it would be ready so soon, Dr. Amit reminded him that he'd been working on developing the Microbot for years, and testing it for an even longer time. 'I've been working on this for more than a decade now. It's finally the end of the road,' he'd said, his eyes lighting up with excitement.

The way in which Archana grabbed my arm surprised me. 'What's the matter?' I asked as we all switched on our phones outside the building. Archana looked around at Nitin and Jai who were talking as they walked towards the car.

'There's something I need to tell you about the cardiology reports,' she said. My face fell. What could she mean? Did one of us have heart trouble?

'It's not what you think,' she amended quickly.

'Then?' I asked, lowering my voice to match hers.

'Remember I said that Dr. Amit's heart readings would go haywire whenever he came near you?' she asked, as we both slowed down.

I nodded.

'Well, I've been noticing the same thing happening with your readings as well,' she said. I whipped up my head to look at her in surprise. I didn't know what to make of it so I kept quiet but Archana being Archana wouldn't let go easily.

'I saw the two of you talking earlier,' she insisted. I shrugged.

'So?'

'And I've seen the way he looks at you. Or the way you look at him when you think no one is observing you,' she whispered.

'What do you want me to say?' I asked her, feeling a bit annoyed.

'Why would I want you to say anything?' she asked, looking surprised. 'I just thought that if you and Dr. Amit have feelings for each other, then you should get them out in the open and face them. The more I see the two of you together, the more I feel that you look perfect with him.'

I looked down, unable to process why my heart was leaping so much inside my chest. Literally and medically speaking, I should have been able to pinpoint a reason for my heart's behavior. But I couldn't.

'I think you're falling in love with him,' Archana whispered dramatically as she opened the door of the car and sat down. I stood outside the car for so long that only when Jai honked the horn, I looked up startled.

No way! How was that possible? I was in love with Gautam, wasn't I?

I got inside the car and tried Gautam's number even though my heart was beating madly at Archana's suggestion. Was Dr. Amit the Mr. Right I'd been looking for without even realizing about it? I thought Gautam and I had something, but it had never been like this. Never this intense. It had simply never felt as right as this did.

Gautam's phone was still not reachable. I looked at Jai in the rear-view mirror as he looked at me and shrugged. There was something in his eyes, a look of censure that I couldn't quite figure out. Was he blaming me for Gautam's disappearance? That was...that was completely unfair.

I didn't say anything as I leaned back into the seat and shut my eyes. Immediately, Dr. Amit's face swam before my eyes and I sighed. Maybe Archana was right. Maybe I was falling for him. And given his reactions to me, as well as the cryptic things that he said to me sometimes, I was positive that he too had feelings for me.

We reached our hospital quarters in silence. I got out with Archana who seemed strangely subdued and I wondered if it was because she too harbored some feelings for Dr. Amit. After all, which girl in her right mind wouldn't? For me, good looks were never enough. Intelligence and compassion occupied a higher ranking in my head and Dr. Amit seemed to have plenty of both.

In my room as I got ready to sleep, I got a text message and I knew it was from Dr. Amit. It was a simple good night message. I typed back a reply and hit 'Send' and went to sleep with a smile on my face, somehow forgetting my misgivings with Gautam and the way he'd disappeared.

The following morning, I decided I would call up his parents and ask them if he'd gone to them. Feeling a bit uneasy, I called them and to my disappointment, they hadn't heard from him in more than a week. They immediately got worried and Gautam's father said that he would file a missing person's report. I thought it was a good idea and I tried to ignore the sick feeling in my stomach. Gautam had to be all right. He had to be.

But once we got busy with work, I had to put him out of my mind. For some reason, it was not easy to put Dr. Amit out of my mind. My hand kept wandering over to the phone to check if he'd sent any messages but he hadn't. I realized I was excited at the prospect of visiting the lab this evening. I was looking forward to it. When I saw Jai during lunch though, I felt a shaft of guilt at remembering Gautam. I filled him in on the latest and saw his eyes narrow. He looked like he wanted to say something to me but then thought better of it and shut his mouth.

'What is it Jai?' I asked him, feeling a bit nervous.

'I...I don't know if I should tell you this,' he said, looking around at the cafeteria where we were sitting.

'What?' I asked, leaning forward, feeling worried.

'On Friday, Gautam had a talk with me before he messed up that operation,' Jai said. My eyes became round.

'About what?' I asked, fiddling with my dupatta.

'You,' he said, looking uncomfortable. I looked down at my lap.

'What about me?' I asked.

'He said he wanted to marry you and you wouldn't give him a concrete answer because you weren't ready,' Jai started. I nodded.

When I realized that Jai was looking at me with a funny expression, I had the sudden realization that he thought I was responsible for Gautam's mistake in the OT, albeit inadvertently.

'Jai, it's unfair to blame me for his mistake! I just said that we're not ready yet. How could we get married until our feet are firm on the ground and we have some earnings in the bank? That's not a no! How could that lead to him cutting the wrong hand in the OT?' I asked, anger evident in my tone.

I got up from there and walked away in a huff.

I hoped Gautam's parents would be able to track him down soon. People say that distance makes the heart grow fonder but in my case, although I was worried about him and prayed he was safe, this distance had just made it really clear what I didn't want in my life.

---❁❁❁---

CHAPTER - 13

We were simply swamped the next few days, both in the hospital and the lab. There was so much work to be done that there were times, we just stayed back at the lab, sleeping in the dorms because it was too tiring to travel back. Of course, it meant that we would have to get up early to leave for the hospital but we were at least spared one commute.

As for Gautam, I'd wanted to call his parents and ask if he'd been found but there was simply no time. I would notice Jai looking at me speculatively sometimes and it would irk me. I think I was trying to mask my guilt with annoyance. It was one of the reasons why I didn't ask Jai if he'd heard anything from Gautam or his parents.

Things between Dr. Amit and I progressed swiftly now and it seemed like I had no control over it. We always managed to get a place to ourselves during lunch or dinner during the times when we stayed back at the lab and we'd talk. I had thought that he was a reserved kind of man whose do-not-approach vibe was rather intimidating but once that outer shell had cracked, I realized there was so much about him that I admired and liked.

I could never get used to how much he seemed to know. Really, he seemed to know almost anything to do with medicine or electronics. It was like he'd absorbed the entire subject! A few times when there were some theoretical aspects of our work that we found confusing, he would excuse himself for a little while, saying he needed to brush up his knowledge. Then he would come back in an hour or so, and actually teach us with enough competence as though he had written several books on the subject himself!

Some days, I wouldn't realize that the rest of the group had finished dinner and already retired as we continued talking. The fire in his eyes as he spoke about his plans, his passion for creating something that would help humanity as a whole, truly reached out to me.

As the date for the government approval neared, we were all frantic with worry, trying to make sure the presentation that Dr. Amit had to give was perfect.

The presentation had to include all the trials that we had done with ill people as well as healthy persons and he would have to demonstrate how the Microbot worked. These people from the government had the power to give the project the go-ahead, making it publicly available, but on the other hand they could also axe it. Dr. Amit was confident they would see the good that the Microbot can do and would definitely want us to take it forward.

One day in the lab we were just wrapping up our work for the day when Jai came up to me and I realized that maybe he had news about Gautam. It was now close to 10 days since he'd left the hospital and 'disappeared'.

'Any news about Gautam?' I asked, curbing that sudden spike of guilt at his name. Jai looked at me surprised.

'I thought you already knew,' he said.

'What?' I asked, feeling a thump inside. 'Have they found him?'

'Of course. Long back. I thought you would have spoken to him also. And he wasn't lost or anything,' Jai said. I felt bewildered. It seemed like I'd been in some kind of time capsule where I had no idea what had been happening.

'What do you mean long back and where was he all this while? Why isn't he back in the hospital? Why hasn't he called me?' I asked him.

'Look, I thought you would have spoken to him by now. But he's fine. The day Dr. Vinod sent him away from the hospital, he got drunk once more and he managed to lose his wallet and his phone got stolen. He crashed at a friend's place and got himself sorted and by then his parents were frantic with worry. He got in touch with them and he's fine now. Well, as fine as he can be,' Jai said, looking bitter.

I was relieved to hear that Gautam was fine but couldn't understand why he hadn't contacted me.

'What do you mean?' I asked, almost afraid of the answer Jai might have.

'He's going to try to speak to Dr. Vinod once more although that stuck up fellow is not willing to give him another chance. If he doesn't then, I don't know where he can go to finish his residency,' Jai said.

'I'll call him when we get back today,' I said, sounding as though I was promising myself. Jai looked at me with a funny expression on his face and nodded.

'You do that,' he said, although I sensed he was skeptical for some reason.

I glanced at Dr. Amit who was nearby, and I had a feeling he had heard our conversation. I felt a bit uncomfortable. These past few days, we'd grown so close that Gautam had slipped from my mind completely. Maybe he was wondering what I would do now that Gautam was back. I wanted to reassure him that there was nothing left between Gautam and me but I held back. I wasn't yet sure of the equation I had with him yet, enough to make assumptions about our 'relationship'.

'Was there anything else you were going to tell me?' I asked Jai, realizing that he had approached me first. Jai looked a little uncomfortable as though he was extremely conscious of where we were.

'Don't do this to Gautam, Payal,' he said, softly. 'He needs you. Don't abandon him now.'

I looked at Jai sharply.

'You can't force feelings upon someone, Jai,' I said finally, fully aware that Dr. Amit too might hear us.

'But you guys were in love with each other,' Jai said, looking at me confused.

I didn't know what to say to that. I just shook my head and my heart thumped loudly when I realized that Dr. Amit was looking at me.

'You won't understand that, Jai. It's more complicated than you think,' I shrugged and moved away from there.

As we were headed out though, I realized that Dr. Amit and some of the software guys were still in the lab. Actually, I'd never seen them leave. It was a bit creepy to realize that they lived here almost all the time even though I knew that they too went to sleep in the dorm. I lingered, wanting to explain the whole Gautam situation to Dr. Amit but he didn't seem to have time. When it seemed like the others were almost ready to leave, I turned around to say good-bye to him but he wasn't there.

Feeling disappointed for some reason, I walked away with the others but each step I took away from the lab made it feel like my feet were made of lead. I don't know why but I didn't want to go back today. Although I should have been relieved that Gautam was fine, I couldn't think about him at all. In fact his face was just a hazy picture in my head. All I wanted to do was to ensure that Dr. Amit knew that I didn't have any feelings for Gautam anymore. My mind kept telling me to stay back. I did not want to go. I was deluged under such a huge tidal wave of emotions, all directing me towards Amit that I couldn't bring myself to move.

Archana and Nitin were surprised when I stayed back inside the lift. Jai looked at me, his eyes narrowed.

'What's going on?' Archana asked as Nitin placed his hand near the door to prevent the door from closing. I just shook my head.

'I...I can't come back today to the hospital,' I said in a low voice. My heart was beating madly and I felt like a 16 year old girl who had a crush on a boy. All these emotions were so new! I'd never felt anything like this before with Gautam and to be honest, I didn't think I was capable of them.

Gautam kept telling me his feelings but I could never bring myself to express what I felt, because I hadn't felt anything like this in my life. My feelings for Amit took on a new level, and it seemed I was discovering a new aspect to myself. I too was capable of having these emotions, this desperation of being emotionally close to someone, and that someone was Amit.

'But why?' Nitin asked. I looked at Archana, hoping that she would understand. My eyes pleaded with hers silently and amazingly she seemed to get my drift.

'Let's go guys. She'll come tomorrow,' Archana said, tugging at Nitin's arm so that the lift doors would close. Nitin stepped away and the lift doors started sliding together slowly. As the doors clicked shut and the lift moved upwards, I knew that Jai had looked at me with disapproval. I didn't care.

When I walked back to the lab, my eyes were desperately seeking out Dr. Amit. He still hadn't returned to the lab. One of the software chaps swiveled around in his chair and looked at me, a little amused.

'Didn't you just leave?' he asked. I barely registered his words.

'Where's Dr. Amit?' I asked him and he looked around at his colleagues for an answer. None of them knew and he shrugged.

It was weird, how I felt like I knew so much about him and yet, didn't know so many things. Like where he was now, for instance.

'Sometimes he likes to go and stand on the balcony and

look out at the lake,' someone suggested. I whipped my head around. It was one of the senior doctors. We all worked in pockets here. Even though we were a part of this big team, we barely knew the others except those in our immediate teams. Dr. Amit was the force that held us together, I realized, as I walked outside the lab.

I had seen the balcony he was referring to only once and had wanted to check it out but couldn't because we'd never really had the time. I wondered what he was doing there at this time. It was on another floor and I didn't bother with the lift as I ran up the stairs and stopped at the corridor. I didn't know what I was doing any more but I let my feet propel me forward. The balcony was at the end of the corridor and was shut off by a door.

I walked towards it, my heart thumping loudly. When I opened the door, I saw that he was standing towards one side, looking out. From his side profile, I could see that he looked pensive. I cleared my throat and he looked at me calmly, as though he was expecting me.

Neither of us spoke for a few moments. He was probably wondering what I was doing when I had apparently left with the others but he didn't ask me that question. Instead he was looking at me speculatively, as though waiting for me to speak.

'There go your friends,' he said softly and I moved up closer to look down from the balcony. It was a wide balcony from where we could see the Bharadwaj lake glitter in the distance. Right now, you could hardly see anything because dusk had fallen. There was the sound of birds as they flew to their nests, rustling sounds as the wild life sanctuary we were surrounded by settled down for the night.

I could see the car with Nitin, Jai and Archana take the turn towards the highway and leave and even then, I didn't feel bereft. I felt completely at home.

'You watch us leave every single day?' I asked in response to his words. He smiled a half smile and nodded.

'And wait for the next evening when you will come,' he spoke. I held my breath because I didn't know what to say. His words had released a clamoring inside me and I stepped forward, to be closer to him.

He held his hand out and I took it and he pulled me closer. This moment, everything about it was just perfect. The serene atmosphere, the slight chill in the air, quiet forest sounds drifting up to us, and if you strained your ears, you could even hear the ripples on the lake. But I was most attuned to this man in front of me.

'Then you would have known that today I didn't leave with them,' I said. He smiled.

'I was waiting for you here,' he replied and lifted his finger to trace a line on the side of my face. 'But of course, I heard you much before you opened the door.'

'You mean my payal ki jhankar?' I managed to ask even though I could barely think because of his proximity and that one finger that kept contact with my face.

In that moment, if I'd been plucked out of his arms and if someone asked me my name, I probably wouldn't have remembered it. Trying to find some courage to take the next step, I tried to explain what I was feeling but it overwhelmed me. I'd never felt this way for anyone. It had never been so keen, so acute, almost to the point of being painful.

'I...I couldn't leave today,' I said finally. 'I didn't want to.'

'I know,' he said simply before lowering his head to kiss me.

CHAPTER - 14

I had always thought that my future was pretty clear cut when it concerned my ambitions and my profession. I had always known what I wanted to do. But I'd never been in love before. Well, certainly not like this. It was all consuming, and every waking moment, all I wanted was to be with Amit. I didn't leave the lab for a couple of days after that because the very thought of going away, putting so much distance between us made me feel anxious and unhappy.

Archana was happy for me and Nitin seemed puzzled by this sudden change in my prerogatives. It was Jai though, who looked very displeased. I ignored him most of the time and any how there was no time for any idle chit chat after that. We were swamped because the government officials would be visiting the lab the following week and everything had to be perfect for the presentation.

Amit too was busy most of the time but he always managed to make time for me every evening and we'd spend at least half an hour on the balcony that I'd come to think of as 'ours' now. A few people from different teams were to be selected who would help Amit with the presentation and I wondered if I would be chosen.

'Of course you'll be chosen,' Nitin said but without any rancor. 'I mean, you're the doc's girlfriend and everything.'

'As if that's a criteria!' I protested on the way back to the hospital one night. As the car wound out of the lane, I twisted my neck to see if I could spot Amit at the balcony but it was too dark to make out anything. I knew though, that he was there. I knew he wasn't pleased that I was going back but I had to return now and then, right?

'I wish you'd never leave,' he'd muttered to me gruffly as he pulled me into his embrace when I went to say goodbye to him. It felt that way to me too but I didn't say anything.

'I still have to finish my residency at the hospital,' I reminded him.

'Once the government gives its nod to my Microbot, then, maybe you could just ditch that and come work with me,' he said. I looked to see if he was teasing but he wasn't.

'I can't ditch my residency,' I replied softly, vaguely aware that if Gautam had suggested something like this I would have given him a scathing reply. Since any thought of Gautam always brought along guilt, I quickly suppressed it.

'Yeah, I know. I was joking,' Amit amended before letting go of me.

As the car moved through the darkened highway, I felt the first stirrings of unease. I couldn't quite pinpoint it. I was supposed to have called Gautam nearly four days ago when Jai had told me that he was trying to get back into the hospital. It was like Amit had eclipsed everything. He had become such a larger than life presence for me.

I knew that if I asked Jai anything now about Gautam, he would make some disapproving remark and that would just annoy me so I kept quiet. Nitin however kept talking about the government approval that was due.

'You know, I'll be glad when this gets over. Once the government says yes, then we can just move back to our lives,' he said. I looked at him in shock.

'What do you mean?' I asked.

'Arrey! How long will you do this volunteering business for Dr. Amit? We have exams coming up at the end of this year and unless we crack those, we're not going to get any decent positions,' Nitin said.

'Leave it, Nitin,' Jai replied, his voice caustic. 'She doesn't have to worry about exams and other stuff like us ordinary people. She doesn't have to worry about getting a job because she already has one with her beloved Dr. Amit.'

I was stung by his words but I didn't reply. Archana shot me a commiserating glance and I smiled back at her in the darkness, weakly.

I focused on reaching my room and calling up Gautam so I could ask him what he was doing. With that single minded determination, I stayed silent and waited until I could reach home. My phone flashed with a message and I picked it up. It was from Amit. I miss you, it said and I smiled, tapping back my reply immediately.

Back in our quarters, Archana went to take a shower and I waited in my room, mustering the courage to talk to Gautam. It came crashing down on me that what I'd done with him was extremely unfair. I'd told him that we would talk about getting married and I'd even been ready. I just hadn't expected to fall in love with Amit in the meantime.

Finally, I dialed his number, my heart pounding as the phone rang. He answered warily.

'How are you Gautam?' I asked softly, glad to be able to hear his voice.

There was silence. I cleared my throat uneasily.

'Where are you?' he asked suddenly.

'I'm in the hospital quarters,' I replied.

'I don't want to talk to you Payal,' Gautam said.

'I'm sorry for everything Gautam,' I said, wincing because suddenly it was plain as day to me, that despite everything that had happened with Amit, I still didn't want to lose Gautam's friendship.

'I know what you've been up to and I don't want to talk to you,' he repeated. His words however, triggered a different reaction in me.

'What do you mean? If you are angry, shout at me, scold me. But don't ignore me like the way you are doing now. You did not even tell me once you were back!' I asked him sharply.

'I know what's been cooking between you and that doctor. I know why you've distanced yourself from me. I don't want your pity, okay?'

'Pity?' I repeated, surprised. 'I just...'

'Thanks for everything Payal,' he bit out the words and ended the call. I looked at the phone trying to connect Gautam's normally happy face with this bitter and angry voice. He was like a complete stranger. I felt bereft of his friendship and I sank on the bed, wondering how everything could have gone so wrong.

There was a heaviness in my heart that refused to go. Just a month back, Gautam had been the person I was closest to, here in Delhi. He was not just my friend but he was also my family.

I went to sleep troubled but over the next few days I tried to put Gautam away from my mind. From the somewhat venomous glances I was getting from Jai, I figured out that Gautam had been unable to get back into the hospital. I was worried about him but it seemed like there was no one I could share my worries with. I realized that maybe Jai had been telling Gautam everything that was happening with me and Amit.

CHAPTER - 15

Back in the lab, things were indeed getting extremely hectic. It was now crowded with all the 'experts' who were tweaking the presentation to make it perfect for Saturday when the government officials would come. Nobody was surprised when I was chosen to help Amit for the presentation.

On Saturday, everyone seemed excited about the impending visit. One nod from them and everyone's lives would change, starting with Amit's. Maybe even mine, I wondered. I'd seen first-hand what a wonderful device the Microbot was, how it had helped all those sick people and among the team members here who had taken it, one of them found out about a clot in his brain. Actually, since neurology was my department, I had been the one to discover it. Thankfully, we had found out before anything else could happen and he had taken the treatment for it. It had spurred all of us that day to see such a positive and practical use of the Microbot, and I even spotted Jai looking over at us, as though he was tempted to join the group. But he resisted for some reason.

Anyway, the presentation was to take place at the lab and no extraneous people were allowed. Only those who had been assigned the roles of showcasing each area that was monitored could be inside the lab. The nervous system was my department while Archana was assigned to heart and blood circulation. Similarly many others helped monitor different areas of health. The senior doctors who were with us were super experts and only some of us were newbies, even though we had done our MD.

It was to be a closed door meeting and I was anxious for Amit. I hoped everything would progress as it should. When the government officials arrived, everyone seemed tense. These were definitely biggies. Jai looked excited when he spotted someone among the group who had emerged outside the lift.

'That's the Health Minister!' he whispered as they were led inside the lab. I took a deep breath and followed Amit and the others inside. The lab had been rearranged for the presentation. Chairs had been placed in a semi-circle and a projector had been placed in the front. The delegation that came for review sat down and Amit spoke to each one of them, smiling, shaking hands and telling them about the project. Finally, he went up and started the projector and started speaking.

At some point in the presentation that took nearly two hours, where Amit explained each and every facet of the Microbot, I hazarded a look at the faces of the audience. I was nervous when Amit had asked me along with some of the others to come up and tell them about our experience with the Microbot but now that we were helping Amit in the background, I could breathe easier. Every member of the delegation looked rapt as Amit explained how the Microbot could be used to change so many lives for the better. When he finally wound up, many of them asked questions, just like we'd asked when we first came on board.

Amit answered their questions patiently and told them of the extensive testing that he had already carried out and the results that they had yielded. Time and again, I shot glances at the Health Minister because he had been the one who had brought the Microbot project under government funding. He looked thoughtful although the word 'astute' also figured in my mind when I looked at him. He was listening to the reactions of his posse as well as surmising what to do. Just give it the green light, I urged him mentally, as I looked over at Amit. My heart seemed to be overflowing with love for him.

All the stuff with Gautam in the past few days and how he had cut himself from me had left a gaping hole in my heart. I realized how lonely I was and there was no one to turn to, except now that I had Amit, things had started looking better for me.

The Health Minister motioned to Amit and told him that they would like to discuss this further among themselves. We were all asked to leave the lab. Even Amit. All of us trooped outside, feeling almost victorious because of the wide smiles that the VIPs seemed to have on their faces. They all loved the Microbot and the idea of an impending medical revolution.

Amit was quiet as we waited outside in the hall, wondering what was being discussed.

'These people have my future in their hands,' he muttered to me as I sat down next to him. I reached out for his hand and took it. He clasped my hand tightly and lifted it to kiss my knuckles. I was anxious for him too. So much depended on the government approval.

Nearly half an hour later, one of the aides came outside and asked only Amit to come back into the lab.

'Good luck,' I whispered as he walked inside and shut the door behind him.

---✿✿✿---

CHAPTER - 16

Once again, we were waiting but this time without Amit. I looked at the others and realized that Nitin and Jai had no idea how things had progressed inside the lab. I went over to them and sat down and told them about the presentation. Nitin listened eagerly as Archana too supplied her version of events. Jai listened to me in silence.

'What happens next?' Archana asked. I shrugged.

'Let's see,' I replied. I looked out towards the lab and realized that the door had opened and the government delegation were streaming out. The meeting was over? But the door was closed once again and we all looked at each other surprised.

'The Health Minister is still in there,' Jai noted.

Now it was pure agony, waiting to know why he had stayed back. What had he told Amit? Why hadn't he left with the others? After half an hour, he emerged outside and his aide who had been waiting near the lift, hurriedly pressed the button so that the minister wouldn't have to wait.

We looked at each other, wondering what had happened. Should we go inside? The other team of software people and doctors went back inside, almost eager to get back to their work. The four of us too went back inside cautiously. But, Amit wasn't there.

Where had he disappeared? I looked around at the chairs where the VIPs had sat, at how impassioned Amit had been when he had explained how the Microbot would help people. And now, the lab was like a vacant space without him. I didn't want to get back to any work before I knew what happened.

There was a feeling in the pit of my stomach that maybe things hadn't worked out. But I shushed it immediately.

That was impossible. The Microbot after all its version revisions (some 23 of them) was now perfect to be launched for the Indian public. Amit was sure it would be accepted everywhere. Feeling restless, I went up to see if he was at our balcony but he wasn't. Its emptiness radiated some sort of gloom towards me. I felt even more desperate to see him now.

I had never really ventured towards the floor that he occupied as his own living quarters. He had once told me that he had a house in Delhi but he hardly lived there and he had made the lab his home. Feeling a bit nervous, I went back to the lift and pressed the button for his floor. Had he gone to his room upstairs?

I stepped out of the lift, feeling as though I was stepping out of my own body. It seemed like it wasn't really me, this person here and in a way it was so true. I had changed so much in the past few months.

I walked outside nervously, wondering why he would want to shut himself by coming here. A quick glance at all the rooms showed that they were all open except one. I went up to the closed door and knocked on it. There was no response. I just knew he was in there so I didn't give up and knocked harder. A few seconds later, the door opened.

Amit barely looked at me as he opened the door and went back inside.

'Amit! What happened?' I asked as I stepped inside the room. He was sitting on a bed, his head in his hands. He took a deep breath and then looked up. I felt myself recoil from the blank look in his eyes.

'They rejected it Payal,' he said, putting his head back in his hands.

'What?' I was shocked and I moved forward and sat down beside him. He didn't budge.

'Amit, what happened?' I asked, trying to make him respond. He shook his head, and spoke but his voice was muffled.

'Amit, look at me!' I pleaded with him and forced him to look up.

'They said they couldn't give the go-ahead to make the project public,' he said. But why?

'What happened? I thought they were really impressed with it,' I said. He sighed out loudly.

'They were. But when they decided to have a meeting about it and sent us out, they realized that they couldn't bring it into the market right away.'

'Which means that they didn't reject it outright?' I asked, looking for some sort of silver lining.

He shook his head fiercely. 'No, it's as good as being rejected. Apparently, they were against the idea of a 'revolutionary' product. They wanted something 'evolutionary'.'

'What does that mean?' I asked, frowning. He looked up, straight ahead and spoke but he seemed like a stranger to me.

'According to them, a revolution is good when there are problems because it can straighten out many things. When things are stable, a revolution just upsets the apple cart. In our case, if we brought the Microbot to the public, it would mean that many people would get displaced from their jobs. Right now there are massive structures in place to manage health and if we released the Microbot, it would affect a lot of people, even local doctors,' he said with a snort.

'And you don't think that will happen?' I asked.

'No! It won't. Think about it. Instead of people losing

jobs, it will create more jobs for people. Think of the number of qualified people we will need to monitor and administer proactive treatment! And they were ruing about the bandwidth that they would need to connect so many people when the truth is that since we will be using mobile service providers to connect and communicate to the Microbot, it will all work out hunky dory for both the service providers and the government who will definitely make more money.'

I digested this slowly. What Amit said did make sense but it would be pointless not to take note of what the government was also saying. They were right in their own way.

But before I could say anything else, he went on.

'They said that they loved the idea of my product. They thought it was simply amazing,' he said, sounding bitter.

'Then?' I asked surprised.

'That's the whole point. They want us to 'evolve' the Microbot into the market slowly. They want to start from the top of the pyramid by giving it to VIPs and top government officials,' he said.

'But that means...they haven't rejected it right?' I asked again, a little eagerly.

'Yes, but what they want me to do is to give it to those who are at the helm of affairs. This is not how I envisioned this product. In fact, the common people who are at the bottom of the pyramid will probably get it last, may be a couple of decades later. What's the point?' he said, getting up and walking towards a window. I looked at his back, trying to make sense of his words.

'Amit, try and look at the positive side of this. It's not been rejected completely!' I tried to make him understand. He shook his head.

'He gave me the example of Internet in the US. The US military had the Internet since the 60s during the cold war.

But they released it to the public only in the mid-90s. Now if they had made their development public that time itself, can you think where we would be right now? But, all said and done, this is not what I had in mind Payal,' he continued, staring outside, his hands in his pockets.

'But...'

'They told me that I should continue with the research and refine the product because some of the VIPs want to take it. We will need to monitor them and...' He broke off, and banged his fist on the window in exasperation. I winced.

'Amit, this is still a start. It's not all bad,' I reasoned with him.

'This is not how it had played out in my head Payal!' he said loudly. 'I had given them a life changing product. Something that was surely going to get me the Nobel. Now, I can't do a thing about it. No one will know that I am the creator of this product. I have to stay in the background while some businessmen and politicians use it for their own means!' he said.

Put that way, it indeed sounded like a terrible compromise.

'Amit, just calm down for a bit. Don't get so angry,' I said, getting up to go and stand beside him. He turned to me then and took my hands in his.

'This is it Payal. I'm defeated. All my years of hard work, everything has gone down the drain. Now there's no Nobel in sight. No one will recognize me and the common man on the street will definitely not benefit from my hard work. There's nothing I can do about it,' he said, looking down.

I could sense his despair, it was that strong. Bracing myself, I shook my head.

'No, you can still continue your research and one day they will see sense and give you the revolution you wanted,' I said.

He shut his eyes briefly and then opened them and smiled bitterly. 'Can you guess why the Health Minister stayed back to talk to me?' he asked. I shook my head.

'He said there was still a way for this to work in my favor,' Amit said.

'What do you mean?' I asked, confused. After all, I'd been telling him the same thing but Amit was making it sound like something else altogether.

'Come, sit down. I'll explain,' he said.

---✿✿✿---

CHAPTER - 17

'So when I went inside and these people shredded my dreams in minutes, the Health Minister stayed back. I was pretty much broken when I heard their ideas about how they would get the Microbot for people at various important levels in the country. That's when the Health Minister told them that he wanted to speak to me alone,' Amit said, turning away from the window.

I looked at Amit, wishing I could do something to ease his pain. He continued talking.

'Everyone had left and the Health Minister asked me to sit down next to him. When I did, he told me that I was being stupid by getting worked up over nothing. He said that this was the first step for me.'

'First step where?' I asked, confused.

'First step up,' Amit replied.

'Meaning?'

'He told me that giving the Microbot to high level leaders is important because if ever their lives were at stake because of health reasons, it could affect the entire country and hence the economy. And this was the perfect opening for me, to get close with big politicians and businessmen. This was the best chance for me to leverage my knowledge and take advantage of all these decision makers who were now depending on me,' Amit said.

'Payal, I'm giving them a world-class revolutionary product and in return this is what I get? Connections?' he asked, looking disgusted.

The light from the sinking sun streamed in from the window behind and lit him up around the edges, giving him a halo all around his body. I could barely focus on his words because I was just realizing what he meant to me.

'Don't you see Payal? All my life I've slaved over this Microbot. I've lost so many years of my life because I wanted to make something that would change everyone's lives. I was this close to my dream and now they've shattered it,' he said bitterly. He moved away from the window and walked towards his desk. The light too had evaporated and the room was getting darker.

'I'm a scientist, Payal. Not a politician or a businessman. What good will these so called connections do to me?' he said, sinking his head into his hands. I didn't know the right thing to say because whatever I told him, he just kept getting more upset.

'Amit,' I said finally, taking a deep breath. 'You have to get past this.'

He looked up at me, his eyes boring into mine, desperation looming in them.

'What is there for me to do now? What is the point of continuing the research?' he said.

I shook my head vehemently. 'You can't give up now Amit. Not now,' I told him, getting up from the bed. I sat down before him on my knees. He looked at me, surprised.

'So what if it didn't go down your way? You've got their attention and who knows what this may lead to?' I asked.

'I got their attention four years ago which is when the Health Minister stepped in and offered to fund the research. After slogging for all those years, government approval was the last step for success. And now, it's been snatched away from me,' he said.

What could I tell him to make him change his mind? How could I make him look beyond this revolution vs evolution concept that the government officials had spun? Of course, in hindsight what they said did make sense but Amit was not being objective. He was too close to the situation to see anything clearly.

'Amit, you have to look at the larger picture,' I said finally, placing a hand upon his knee.

'What do you mean by larger picture?' he asked angrily.

'Because you've worked too hard to give up now. Because that is not how you eat an elephant,' I said with a smile, suddenly remembering something my mother used to tell me whenever I was faced with a seemingly insurmountable task.

Amit looked startled. 'What?' he asked.

I shrugged. 'How would you go about eating an elephant? You can't gulp it down right?' I asked. There was a shadow of a smile on his face.

'Well, I suppose the elephant would have something to say about that,' he joked. I nodded briefly but pushed on.

'You have to eat it piece by piece,' I completed the sentence. The trick worked and he grinned.

'But my dear Payal. Didn't you know that I am a vegetarian?' he quipped, getting up from there, and pulling me along with him.

'This is a metaphorical elephant, Amit. So think of this as the first phase. Everything will follow in its own time. Think about it practically. It's just not possible to implement this whole program in one shot. Until today, until you explained what they said to you back there, I hadn't really figured out how big this project was,' I said, leaning into him.

He sighed. 'It's just that...I had such hope. So many dreams,' he said.

'And that's a good thing. You must have hope. You must dream. Or would you have thought it would be possible to actually create something like the Microbot? You had a dream and now it's time to wake up from that dream and realize it. Why can't you think of this as the first phase? I really think it's like an approval by the government to roll it out,' I said trying to convince him.

He listened to me in silence, as though debating with himself internally. Some of the things that the government officials said had sparked a few thoughts in my head and I spoke out aloud.

'Amit, do you really think we have the infrastructure to monitor and manage 1.2 billion Indians? And what about manufacturing the Microbot? Or...or... monitoring everything and the logistical power to do that?' I said, picking up his hand. He looked at me thoughtfully but I realized that there was a lot more I needed to tell him. Practical things that he had probably not thought of in the heat of the moment.

'Even with the government's support, do you think that scale is possible overnight? What will happen to the existing hospital infrastructure? Where will you get the doctors you need to proactively work on patient's needs? Think. I think this is the best foot forward for you. You are rolling your project out but for a select few as a sample. Once you have the perfected model to roll out to the public, you can always go back to them with the model.'

He smiled grimly. But I wasn't done yet. 'And what the Health Minister told you about making connections? It's up to you whether you want to use them or not. Who knows? Maybe they might come in handy one day,' I said.

Finally, he nodded. 'Thanks for coming up to look for me, Payal. I was so depressed just now, because I couldn't see past this as a failure,' he said.

Feeling relieved, I nodded. I couldn't bear to see him so upset. But now that he seemed better, I felt good too. I shut my eyes and without realizing what I was saying, I said, 'I love you Amit.'

'Payal,' he said softly and I nodded, pushing myself closer into his embrace. It felt right to be here, with him. My mind was tired from all that had happened today. I felt at peace for the first time that day, and yet, it was tinged with some uneasiness. As though I was missing something obvious. But I brushed it aside. This was what I wanted to do and this was where I was meant to be.

'I don't know what I would have done without you,' he said, stroking my hair.

'I want you to be happy,' I said, smiling into his shoulder.

'I'm still angry about how things turned out today. I'm still dissatisfied about what is lined up for me. But at least one thing went right,' he said. I stepped back to look into his face.

'What?' I asked, a little shyly. All this was still so new to me. On one hand I'd just professed my love for him and on the other, I was still coming to terms with it.

'You,' he said, leaning in to kiss my forehead.

CHAPTER - 18

The day of the government inspection had been a momentous occasion in more ways than one. Although we hadn't got the direct approval that we had wanted, I had managed to convince Amit that things weren't so bad. But that day as he came back downstairs with me to talk to the rest of the team and outline the plan for the future, I realized that something had changed. He had changed somehow. He was bitter and despite my love and assurance, he hadn't shaken it off entirely. A part of him still resented this hold on his dreams that the government had put. All I could hope was that in time, he would understand that it was for the best.

The group had been waiting in the laboratory unsure of their next step when Amit and I walked back inside. He was holding my hand and he squeezed it lightly before letting go, as though deriving some strength from me. He addressed the group and then told them what had happened. To my surprise, he didn't paint the whole episode as if it had been a failure, as he had done upstairs with me.

He told them that the government would unroll the Microbot in stages and not right away as we had thought and when he explained everything in his usual calm and mild manner, no one was disappointed or upset.

'So it's work as usual for everyone,' he called out, clapping his hands and moving on to his workstation. I walked away towards Archana and the others.

'Everything okay?' she whispered as I sat down beside her. I turned to look at Amit and he too looked at me just then. I smiled and he smiled back and my heart was filled with joy.

'It's fine,' I whispered back to Archana. 'He was a bit worried about how things had turned out at first.'

'Oh,' she said. 'It didn't look that way. I mean he didn't seem upset at all.'

'Well, I convinced him to look at the larger picture,' I said, smiling. Archana didn't look like she believed me.

'What?' I asked her when she didn't say anything.

'Well, when you guys walked back inside, he seemed confident about everything and you were the one who was unsure. That's why I asked you if everything was all right,' she said.

'It's not like that Archana. When I went upstairs, he was completely in despair. He just wasn't listening to reason. He had wanted full government approval right away. He kept lamenting about how his dream wasn't coming true,' I said earnestly.

'Then?' Archana asked surprised.

'I told him that this is a start and how he should focus on that. It took some time but he came around,' I said.

'Hmm.'

'I told him I loved him,' I said, looking down, blushing a little. Archana gasped lightly and punched my shoulder.

'No wonder he looked so happy!' she said. I looked up at her and smiled. 'Are you happy?'

I nodded. 'Very. It's like my life was leading up to this moment,' I said.

Archana was looking at me enviously.

'You're so lucky!' she nudged me.

'Oh please. You have been the object of someone's attention right from the time we started working here together,' I teased her. She made a face.

'Him? Uh, no thanks!' she said, quickly glancing at Nitin who was busy at his computer. I felt sorry for the poor chap actually. He tried so hard to make Archana like him.

'Poor guy,' I murmured and looked up to see Jai glaring at me. What was his problem? And then just like Pavlov's experiments with the dog, looking at Jai reminded me of Gautam. And guilt once again piled on my chest like a ton of bricks.

I tried telling myself that Gautam was my past. Amit was my present and future. But try telling that to the heart.

CHAPTER - 19

It took me some time to realize that the Health Minister had been right in his own way.

After that eventful day, Amit was no longer just a researcher/scientist doing his own thing in a laboratory. The government guys who had been at the presentation had been bowled over by the Microbot and had wanted it for themselves. They had also told other officials about this remarkable device and soon they were all queuing up to get the Microbot into them. Our lab had become like a magnet for them, drawing all the eager ministers and power brokers who were constantly looking for ways to enhance their health. Manufacturing, testing, making sure that the Microbot was compatible with the identified individuals, the list of tasks was endless.

Our workload had grown and Nitin and Jai were often seen to be complaining that this 'volunteer' work had indeed gone on for quite some time now. Archana and I missed the days before the presentation. It wasn't like those days had been laid back but compared to the activity now, they had definitely been easier for us to handle.

My guilt towards how I had treated Gautam loomed large in my heart. We hadn't even begun and we'd ended. Although we'd been together for some time now, it wasn't until that day in the cafeteria that I learnt of the seriousness of his feelings. Thinking about that felt strange now. Because I remember being excited and happy about where we were headed. I had no idea that my feelings would change so dramatically, leaving him in the lurch like this.

In retrospect, I felt ashamed of my behavior towards him and wished there was a chance for me to make amends. But with the busy schedule that the lab seemed to have been plunged into, there was no time for anything else.

Almost every other day we would have a new government official, calling up for an appointment once the Health Ministry had identified them as eligible for the Microbot to be injected in their bodies. We would then have to run the whole battery of tests for them before injecting it, and then our real work started because we would have to monitor them actively.

One day Amit overheard Nitin and Jai complaining about the 'volunteering' aspect of the work.

'It's not like we can even use this work experience in our resume because the project is still classified,' Jai fumed.

'Then you should be compensated for it,' Amit said from behind.

Jai turned around, feeling a little chastened. He tried to justify himself but Amit wouldn't let him. He told them that he would pay all of us for each patient that we were monitoring and when we heard the amount he was going to pay us, we were all pleasantly surprised. It actually bordered on shock, to be honest. We knew that just some of the really senior doctors at the hospital took home that kind of money.

When I asked Amit how he could afford to pay us so much, later that day at our balcony, he shrugged. 'You don't think I'm injecting the Microbot into all these ministers for free, do you?' he asked.

'But even then...' I faltered.

'All those connections that the Health Minister mentioned the other day. They're actually working out to be pretty useful,' he added, with a smile.

'Oh,' I was surprised. I didn't know that he had taken up on the offer from the minister.

'Don't worry, we'll be fine,' he assured me. I nodded, not sure of how I felt about this.

'I think the others will be getting back to the hospital. It's time I left too,' I said, backing out. He clamped his hand on my wrist.

'Stay today Payal. Please,' he said, looking at me with such intensity in his eyes.

'I want to, Amit,' I said softly. 'But...'

'But what's stopping you?' he asked, framing my face with his hands.

Honestly, I didn't know. Everything was just happening so quickly!

'What's the problem?' he asked when I didn't speak. But before I could say anything, his phone buzzed and he looked at it. His eyes grew round with shock. What had happened?

'This is amazing,' he whispered still looking at his phone screen.

'What?' I asked, feeling concerned.

'You are not going to believe this!' he said.

'What?' I was getting worried now. He certainly looked excited but what could be the news?

'Guess who wants the Microbot?' he asked me.

'Stop playing games Amit! Who?' I asked, trying to pull his phone from his hands. He stepped away playfully.

'The Prime Minister!'

CHAPTER - 20

I couldn't quite believe how fast two months had sped by. The government inspection had taken place in early June and now it was August already. A lot had happened in our lives in the interim. After the Prime Minister had become one of our monitored 'patients', our credibility inside the elite circle had shot up tremendously. I still remembered that day when the lab was vacated of all extraneous personnel, even me.

We were in the hospital that day, on one of our rare free days from the lab and we were finally able to breathe easily. Of course, we had all been put out that we wouldn't get to meet the Prime Minister after all our hard work for the past few months. Jai made quite a few disparaging remarks about Amit, saying things like when it was time to claim credit, Amit wanted it all. It was unfair, I argued. We had come upon the scene last. Amit had been working on it for nearly a decade. It was his baby and he was entitled to all the credit.

'Whatever,' Jai had scoffed as he dunked a biscuit in his tea, lifted it, and bit off the edge. The four of us, because we were now working so much together had inevitably grown close.

Archana and Nitin chattered on about what they were going to do after the exams and once their residency was over. Only Jai and I were silent.

'What are your plans?' I asked Jai.

'Not as exciting as yours, surely,' he remarked. His words set me off.

'Why are you always this way with me?' I snapped in anger. 'Always making snide comments and sleazy suggestions!'

Jai was a bit taken aback but he recovered quickly. 'I just call it like I see it,' he said, defending himself.

'And what do you see?' I asked angrily. Nitin and Archana looked at the two of us in concern but I couldn't stop myself.

Jai squared his shoulders. 'Do you even remember Gautam? Have you spared a single thought to what he's doing these days? Where he is? How he's faring?'

I flushed guiltily. 'Of course. I think about him a lot,' I said. 'I even tried speaking to him once but he didn't want to talk to me.'

Jai looked like he didn't believe me. 'Really!'

I insisted. 'He just made some mean comments about Amit and me and said he didn't want to talk to me. He didn't even give me a chance to explain anything to him!'

I narrowed my eyes as something clicked into place in my head.

'You! You fed him stories about Amit and me!' I accused him.

A look of guilt flashed over Jai's face.

'What stories? It was the truth!' Jai retorted, recovering his composure.

'Easy you two. You're attracting all sorts of attention,' Nitin whispered. I didn't care.

'If you hadn't told him anything, I might have been able to talk to him. To help him,' I said.

'Help him? How? By getting him a job in your boyfriend's lab?' Jai asked sarcastically.

'You don't seem to have any problem with the money you're making there,' I countered hotly.

'Okay, let's stop fighting,' Jai said, as though he wanted to make peace. To hell with it. I was spoiling for a fight. Actually it wasn't Jai I wanted to fight with. There was a lot of stuff that I'd bottled inside and it was all coming out.

'Aren't you his friend too? What are you doing to help him?' I asked Jai.

'For starters, I got him a job,' Jai replied. I looked up, startled.

'What kind of job? And why isn't he trying to finish his residency?' I asked.

'He's not interested in finishing his residency any more. I got him a job at a clinic,' Jai bit out. A clinic?

'You mean he's not going to be a....'

'...an orthopaedic surgeon? No. He's not,' Jai said, getting up from there.

'But why doesn't he want to finish his residency?' I asked, my throat blocked with emotion. Gautam had been so eager and enthusiastic and he'd had all these dreams. How could all that have disappeared?

Jai looked at me squarely. 'Why do you even care?' he asked, tiredly.

'Of course I care. He's my friend,' I said, the words sounding false to my ears. Jai just scowled and rolled his eyes, walking away.

I watched him leave, feeling shattered inside. It was surely some sort of domino effect starting with my joining the Microbot program that had caused Gautam to fall out of our radar.

'Which clinic?' I called out, feeling like a masochist. Jai turned around.

'There's a clinic near City Square Mall,' he said as he left.

Nitin and Archana seemed uncomfortable with what had just happened. But Archana leaned forward and squeezed my arm. 'Don't worry. It will be all right,' she assured me.

What will be all right? I wanted to ask her.

'Forget all this!' she said as she got up from her chair. 'Amit is with the Prime Minister of India this very moment, when the four of us are simply chattering like monkeys.'

CHAPTER - 21

If Amit was phenomenally busy, there was a good reason for it. I accepted it as the normal progression of things in our life. Not only did he have to meet with important ministers as he was the face behind the Microbot, he was also personally responsible for setting up the communication systems with the help of the government.

I tried to think of it like setting up mobile towers or setting up tie-ups with existing mobile networks throughout the country so that no matter where the person with the Microbot went, their information would still be received by those who were monitoring them. It seemed as though Amit had now understood the government's reluctance in making the Microbot public because it would be nearly impossible to pull it off at such a large scale in one go. I knew that he was still upset about the fact that his glory had been snatched away but he was careful not to show it.

Since the Prime Minister too had taken on the Microbot, there was so much to be monitored that it was nearly impossible for us to do it on our own. Since every aspect was important, Amit had to hire fresh MBBS graduates who were given the task of monitoring the readings. Of course, they didn't know exactly what they were doing and Amit had set them up at another building not far from the lab where the communication systems had been established as well. I was amazed at how fast these buildings came up and how smoothly things worked out when the government was working hand in hand with you.

These young people came in wide eyed and eager and were given the job of monitoring the new 'patients' but they had not been told about the Microbot. They didn't know that they were part of a path-breaking technology and neither did they know about the level of government involvement. They were just asked to measure parameters of different readings and they did it with enthusiasm. It seemed like the whole thing had evolved into a system, and had become an industry of sorts. More like an extension that went beyond Medical Transcription.

Typically, MBBS and paramedical students were given training for Medical Transcription and they were involved in capturing and typing voice instructions from doctors abroad. But this wasn't just like data entry. It needed more skills because they had to understand each parameter. I realized that an entirely different industry had been born and it gave hope and employment opportunities to so many people across the country. This is what Amit had meant when he said that no one would lose their jobs. In fact there would be more jobs.

I tried not to neglect the hospital and my patients because I knew that I had to finish my residency come what may. It was just that when I was with Amit, I was fine. I didn't think much about the future and where we were going. I was happy to be in the moment and even if he was busy, I didn't mind it so much. But when he was away traveling, or when I was back in the hospital quarters on my own, it seemed like my mind started working overtime. It went into all sorts of directions. There was confusion about Amit and my future together. There was unhappiness at being apart from him. There was jealousy also, of the number of women who were most likely being wowed by him wherever he went. There was guilt. Yes, that familiar guilt wedged itself into my mind every now and then, reminding me of how I had treated Gautam.

That wasn't my fault, I told myself repeatedly but my conscience wasn't listening. It snapped up and kept prodding me, making me wish I could contact him in some way. I wanted to see him, talk some sense into him and try to persuade him to finish his residency. But it was like there was never any time off.

All these feelings overwhelmed me and I tried to shut them off so I could sleep in peace but my insecurity over my relationship with Amit propelled them in my head every now and then.

Archana's blind loyalty to Amit irritated me sometimes. She would just pay no attention to my doubts and I would have to shut up and let my thoughts remain in my head. When the topic was not Amit, we were like the best of friends. After all, we spent so much time together.

On Independence Day, most of the people in the lab were working. We tried to work in shifts but since each department had a defined role, it was difficult to assign the patients you were monitoring to someone else. The students in the other building just collected the data, sorted it and passed it on to us. All this had to be done at the same time or the very existence of the Microbot was pointless if we couldn't be proactive in our approach to identifying diseases and symptoms.

So on August 15th, Archana and I were among the few people in the lab and since Amit was also there, it didn't seem like such a bummer for me. After all, we doctors were used to working on holidays as well. Since we had a streamlined system now, data from all the active Microbots went to the other building where the new batch of trainees sifted through it, raised any red flags if parameters were out of the normal ranges and passed on all the information to us. Since the trainees didn't know what they were monitoring and Amit wanted it to remain that way, each person who had the Microbot in their body was given a specific code number and all the information received for that number was filed separately.

There were a few such numbers that we managed here in the lab directly. Some numbers that we couldn't afford to wait till the information was passed on to us. Like those belonging to the Health Minister and his posse. Or the Prime Minister.

Every day, the group of senior doctors along with us monitored the Prime Minister's readings and we felt a sense of awe that we were so directly connected to the most important person in India.

'All those spikes in his brain activity, he must be thinking so many parallel things in his mind. Amazing!' I murmured to Archana, looking at my computer screen that showed his neurological activity. I glanced at my watch. It was time for the Prime Minister's address to the nation from the Red Fort.

'Obviously, he isn't the most powerful man in India for nothing!' she whispered back as she checked the readings of his heart. It amazed me, how we had learned to work in sync with the Microbot. 'Look at his heart rate. It's on overdrive.'

I leaned sideways and looked at her computer screen and frowned.

'Archana. Look at that,' I pointed at one of the blinking readings that had just come in.

'What?' she said, and then her eyes grew wide and she turned to look at me. From the readings we'd just seen, the blood flow to his heart had been acutely impaired.

'He's going to have a heart attack!' I whispered, pushing my chair back and getting up. We had to find Amit!

CHAPTER - 22

Where was Amit when we needed him? No one knew where he'd disappeared to! I was frantic with worry and I informed one of the senior doctors who began to look even more worried than me. Thankfully Amit came in just then and it wasn't the time to ask him about his constant disappearances even when he was supposed to be in the lab.

We quickly updated him about the situation and he sprang into action almost immediately. He called the Health Minister and informed him that the Microbot had detected a heart problem for the Prime Minister that would lead to an inevitable heart attack if not treated right away.

Amit ended the call quickly and looked around, calling out names. He assembled a team of people who would head out to the Red Fort immediately and take care of the PM. Archana, Jai and I were a part of the team too and without even a minute to waste, we left. The roads were empty because it was Independence Day and yet it seemed like we wouldn't reach there soon enough. Even when we were on the move, we were connected to the main computer through Amit's laptop with a remote connection on 4G. This was such an awesome combination of medical science, communication and software technology on display and yet, no one in the outside world knew about it!

Amit was on the phone with the Health Minister throughout the journey who kept updating us. According to the minister, the PM looked fine and he didn't want to raise any alarm. It was almost like he didn't believe us and he was humoring us. Amit looked frustrated.

'I hope that the doctors there will handle the situation if something happens,' he muttered as he ended the call. We were still a few minutes away from the Red Fort.

'Will they let us in just like that?' I wondered out aloud.

'The Health Minister will take care of that,' Amit responded. We were all tense, our nerves strung tight. It was hard to believe that we were the only ones who knew about this impending disaster. Everything was so surreal. It felt like we were bomb defusing experts in a movie who were being rushed in to save the situation.

After we reached the Red Fort, everything was a blur. Amit and a couple of the senior doctors got into a scuffle with the Prime Minister's security because they weren't letting us through.

I could see the Prime Minister getting up from his seat to walk towards the dais, from where he would address the nation.

My heart was pumping hard, and I was unable to process that this was me, Payal, who was here in the middle of all this action. Amit called up the Health Minister, even as the security detail starting shoving us back and finally he got through.

'It's going to happen any minute!' he barked into the phone when the Health Minister answered the call.

'No, they're not letting us in!' Amit replied to a question that the Health Minister presumably asked. From my position on the sidelines, I could see the Prime Minister walk up towards the dais. He had a smile on his face but I was worried now.

It would be simply catastrophic if he had a heart attack with nation's glare!

His step faltered for just a second but he straightened himself and reached the mike.

Maybe it was that one second of indecision that finally pushed things in our favor.

The Health Minister had seen it too and he realized that we were right. Immediately, the security guy nearest to Amit got a phone call and he answered it with his Bluetooth headset. I assumed the Health Minister had told them to back off because then, all of a sudden, the security stopped hassling us and led us towards the Prime Minister.

We quickly marched towards the ramparts with Amit and we were joined by the Health Minister. Without any further delay, the Prime Minister's security detail led him away along with us to the nearest hospital. I saw the look of utter confusion on the faces of people and some of the ministers too, looked shocked. They all seemed to be wondering why the Prime Minister had suddenly disappeared just before his speech.

The doctors with us had already administered aspirin and other medication that were known to stop the adverse effects of a heart attack, before the Prime Minister had even left the premises. The adrenalin rush was as strong as ever as we ran outside and got back into our vehicle to follow the vehicle that was taking away the PM.

I admired the way Amit handled the situation despite the initial scuffle he had got into. Anyone in his place would have also lost their patience. But after that it had been simply amazing the way he had calmed down everyone else and spoken to the Prime Minister with quiet authority.

Once the Prime Minister was in the hospital and was being taken care of, the whole team could finally breathe easily. We were still in the hospital waiting area which had been declared a no-entry zone by the Prime Minister's security people, while outside there was a barrage of media that had managed to find out that he was here.

We were wondering how we could get out without attracting attention when the Health Minister walked up to us. Amit who was speaking to one of the senior doctors stood up and went to him. Since I was lingering nearby, just looking for an excuse to be near Amit, I could clearly hear what was being said.

'That was amazing work Amit,' the Health Minister said, shaking Amit's hands heartily.

'I hope he's fine sir,' Amit replied modestly.

'Oh you gave him those medication in the nick of time and getting him here was the best thing to do. The doctors here are marveling at how fortuitous it was. I couldn't tell them that fate had nothing to do with it but the work of a very talented scientist!' He patted Amit's shoulder warmly and continued talking.

'Just think of what you have managed to achieve. You saved the Prime Minister and you saved the country in one go,' he said.

'The Microbot saved him sir,' Amit said.

'But you made the Microbot. You see how this one incident will change your life,' the Health Minister spoke.

'What do you mean?' Amit asked.

'This whole thing with the Prime Minister may have just opened the floodgates of important people who want to get the Microbot in them,' he explained.

I groaned inwardly on hearing this. We were completely strapped for time as it was. This meant that Amit would just get busier. The Health Minister confirmed my suspicions.

'Because of your product and your quick thinking team, today you saved the life of the most important man in the country Amit. Things are just going to get bigger and better from here onwards,' he said.

Amit only smiled and turned from there, leading the Health Minister away. Jai walked up to me and Archana followed as well. They looked at me enquiringly but I shrugged. I didn't think it would be right to discuss what I'd overheard just now.

'Let's sit down. We can leave when Amit comes back,' I suggested instead. The TV in the waiting area had been muted but the news channel that was on, kept showing scenes of excited reporters from the Red Fort, who were most likely recapping the events of the day. Since no one had access to the footage of the Prime Minister being taken away by us, no one knew that we were even involved.

Only then I understood why Amit had been so frustrated at first because despite being the creator of such a path breaking product, no one knew who he was. Today it had been Archana and I who had discovered the impending heart attack and yet, looking at the way things were proceeding, it didn't look like anyone in our team even remembered that important fact.

Amit came back beaming and we left through the back entrance to avoid the media. In the van, we were all talking about how things had turned out and Amit briefly told us what the Health Minister had told him. About how this was going to make us even more busy.

Amit who was sitting in the front turned sideways and caught my eye. His gaze was warm and full of love. I felt something click into place as I smiled back at him, radiantly.

He was happy, so I was happy.

---❁❁❁---

CHAPTER - 23

Things changed rapidly after that. Now, it was no longer ministers and other powerful people that Amit was working with. He was asked to give a presentation to the Armed Forces which included the Army, the Navy and the Air Force. All of us were a bit taken aback. Apparently, the Armed Forces who were in present in full swing during Independence Day had seen how the Prime Minister had been saved by the Microbot and they wanted to know more about it. From what I knew the Air Force had already bought into the concept but the Army still needed to be convinced.

We were now constantly in a flurry of activity because of the additional Microbot users that we had to monitor and we also had to help Amit prepare for the presentation. Nitin and Jai with their Endocrinology background, Archana with her cardiology and I, with my neurology expertise had become really essential to Amit although we were still juniors when you considered the numerous senior experts he had on board. It was just that now there were so many different levels of people who were involved that the four of us considered ourselves a part of the old wave and we felt more knowledgeable and superior.

Every day we saw proof of how the Microbot was helping so many people and our respect for Amit's vision grew. But along with that, a nagging feeling had sprung up recently. I felt that the man I knew, the impassioned person who had wanted to change medical history was slipping away from my fingers. That was the man I'd fallen in love with and the lesser I saw of him, as he was so busy flying around, setting up communication centers, the more I wondered if he had changed.

On the eve before the second presentation, Amit and I lingered for a while on our balcony. It was a balmy evening and also a rare occasion when we had some time off together. I knew the following day was going to be hectic but I was glad that we had these few stolen moments with each other now.

Even so, Amit seemed pensive and his mind was far away. I recognized the familiar feelings that gripped my body whenever he was near, and I'd accepted them as a part of being in love with him. Despite the fact that both of us were in love with each other, I couldn't quite figure out how my reactions to him were still so fresh and unchanged. It must be true love, I thought happily, placing my head on his shoulder as we looked out.

'What is going on in that head of yours?' I finally asked when I realized that he'd hardly reacted to my presence.

'Nothing. Just wondering how things will go tomorrow,' he said.

'You've got this in the bag, Dr. Amit. Don't worry,' I said, sliding my arm around his waist. He turned to me and in that instant, I felt a jolt, like he was someone I didn't know at all.

'That's what we thought the last time and see what happened,' he said wryly. The feeling disappeared and I smiled at him.

'But now you're a pro at this. And the Health Minister himself said that the Prime Minister was very impressed. Surely that has to count for something,' I added.

'Let's see,' he said cryptically. 'I have to leave tomorrow after the presentation.'

'Again?' I asked, pouting. He'd already been away most of this week.

'I'm busy Payal. You know that,' he said, rubbing his thumb across the top of my cheek. I leaned into him, wishing he didn't have to leave because when he wasn't around, the doubts came creeping in. Doubts that surprised me because they made me realize that despite our love for each other, I was insecure about our relationship.

'I want to know where we're going,' I mumbled.

'What do you mean?' he asked, surprised.

'Where are we going with this. You. I. We can't just continue like this. We have to make plans for the future,' I said earnestly. The thought had been eating me up from within for a while now. We never seemed to have time for that all important talk! I knew what I wanted and even though I knew that with my work and everything, marriage was going to be an uphill task, I still wanted it. It felt like the only way I could tie down Amit finally.

'Do we have to do this now?' he asked, and there was a sense of déjá vu. I remembered asking Gautam the same words. Shushing that thought quickly, I turned to Amit.

'Yes. We can't keep postponing it. I want you to meet my family,' I said. His eyes widened and he smiled.

'Are you sure?' he asked.

'Hundred percent,' I assured him, wishing he would finally acknowledge what we had between us was going to the next level.

'Okay. Let's have this talk when I get back,' he said.

'Why not now?' I asked, feeling out of sorts. This time he was going to be away for nearly four days.

'Because it's not the right time,' he said.

'There never is the right time. You're just too busy!' I burst out.

'But...'

'And what is it that you do exactly?' I asked, feeling irrationally upset. I knew I was behaving like a clingy girlfriend, the kind I hated but I couldn't help myself.

'You know what I do,' he said, his voice firm. I felt like he had distanced himself from me already.

'But what do you do when you go away? Who do you meet? ', the words escaped before I could stop myself.

Amit looked at me quietly and that riled me more than anything he would say.

'Remember how you were the one who convinced me that the Health Minister was right? You were the one who told me to take that road. And that is exactly what I am doing,' he asserted.

'But what does that include?' I asked, feeling helpless.

'We're tying up with different mobile carriers across the country to deliver our service for the people who have the Microbot in them. The government has to come up with a way to make sure that there is mobile access for the Microbot to detect any problems. And we have to set up mobile towers where there aren't any. That's what is keeping me busy. And you know, this project is still under wraps, so it's not something that we can hire some marketing and sales guys to do! You have to remember Payal, that I'm doing this for both of us,' he said.

I sighed loudly. 'Okay. I just...I just don't like it, that's all,' I said.

'I still have to do it. It's my job,' he said, stepping away from the balcony. 'It's getting chilly. Come on down.' I watched him walk away, unable to stop the elusive feeling that the distance between us was growing and it wasn't just physically.

---❁❁❁---

CHAPTER - 24

Some girls just cannot resist the idea of a man in uniform. Apparently Archana and I both were like these 'some girls'. The following day, we watched with breathless anticipation as the three most important men from the Armed Forces, the Chief of Army Staff, the Chief of Naval Staff and the Chief of Indian Air force arrived at our lab with a contingent each, of their lieutenants. The Air Force and Army Chief seemed to go back a long way going by their conversation, as they met up at the lab.

The Army Chief thumped the Air Force Chief's back loudly. He turned to one of his people and narrated how twenty years ago, the Army had been commanded to move from Tango to Walothang and the Air Force helped out by ferrying the heavy loads on vintage M18 helicopters.

'I still remember, one of his pilots came and complained that the pongos were loading more than 2.5 tons into the chopper,' he reminisced.

'Pongos?' I whispered to Archana who shook her head, clearly baffled. My whisper must have carried over to the Army Chief who suddenly caught my eye and smiled.

'It's what the Air Force calls us Army men, my dear girl,' he said expansively. I nodded, feeling a little shy at being singled out suddenly. I glanced at Amit who was standing by, looking polite but I knew that he was impatient to make his presentation. The Army Chief however was impervious as he continued narrating his story.

'You know what my friend said then?' he turned to one of his men. The man smiled and nodded, clearly having heard the story plenty of times before.

The Army Chief continued, unfazed, even as the Air Force Chief smiled fondly.

'He told his pilots not to crib and do 'utthak baitak' and then they will be able to take the load,' the Army Chief grinned. 'He stood by us like a rock. Now you know why we call him Rock?'

'Sir, can you please take your seat here?' Amit interrupted hesitantly, unable to rein in his impatience. The Army Chief raised an eyebrow and then proceeded to sit down stiffly. He was surrounded by dashing officers who sat in a semi-circle of chairs, and altogether, they made an impressive sight. Amit however didn't look daunted by them at all. I realized the difference between the first presentation and this one. That time he'd been unsure and nervous because the Government had something he needed. Now he was comfortable, assured and confident because the tables were turned. They needed what he had.

Among the sea of different uniforms, I watched avidly as Amit spoke to them and explained the concept of the Microbot. He walked past each workstation, explaining the different roles that all of us played in monitoring the people who had the Microbot inside them.

'So if I have the Microbot in me, and I'm out traveling somewhere, how will you know if something happens to me?' the Air Force Chief asked Amit. The Army General was observing them shrewdly.

'Sir, we have a main control center that is connected to all the Microbots,' he said. I looked at Amit, a little surprised. When the Microbot was just being used for us, we hadn't had any control center but now that it was being implemented to so many people, Amit had set up one obviously because it was required. Now I knew the reason why he kept traveling because obviously setting up this control center must be a tremendous task, especially considering that he could not share the information with anyone outside the circle. Why just outside, he hadn't discussed it even with us!

'Directly?' the Air Force Chief looked slightly dubious.

'No, that's not how it works. Each Microbot is connected to a mobile tower which in turn is connected to the control center. The messages that the Microbot sends are transmitted to this control center where they are decrypted and then monitored by doctors,' Amit explained.

The air seemed to zing with electricity as Amit told them how we had saved the Prime Minister.

'So when my colleagues received the information from the Prime Minister's Microbot,' Amit began and I looked at Archana with a slight smile. She shrugged lightly. 'They realized that it indicated reduced blood flow to his heart, and that usually signified the beginning of a heart attack. They contacted me and I immediately knew what had to be done and I arranged for a team to rush there and take care of the situation.'

'Why didn't you call the Health Minister and tell him about the Prime Minister's condition instead of rushing there yourself?' the Army Chief asked, eyes narrowed shrewdly.

'I did call him. He didn't believe me,' Amit replied smoothly.

'If you couldn't convince him, I don't see how you can convince us,' the General scoffed.

'Well, you did see the results of our hard work when we saved the Prime Minister,' Amit countered.

'I still think that you wanted to make a grand entrance and that you endangered the Prime Minister's life by trying to do it all yourself,' the General said. I looked at Archana in surprise.

'You're free to have your opinion Sir, but if you talk to the Health Minister, you will know that none of this was staged for our maximum benefit as you are implying. You can talk to my team members and they will tell you about the fight we got into with the Prime Minister's security because they wouldn't let us go near him. And where's the question of a grand entrance when no one even knew of what we had accomplished?' Amit asked quietly.

The General's face remained impassive but the Air Force Chief and the Navy Chief of Staff had more questions for Amit at the end of the presentation.

'While this Microbot sounds interesting and useful, how will it work when we are in the middle of the sea?' the Navy Chief asked.

'Or when our pilots are at high altitudes?' the Air Force chief asked.

'At the moment, the Microbot will be able to communicate to us only in the presence of these mobile towers. Once it goes out of that range, we will not be able to receive communication from it,' Amit said.

'Then I don't think it will be so useful for our officers,' the Navy Chief said, looking almost regretful. 'When we really need it, we are almost always out at sea. It doesn't make sense to get my men to implant something in their bodies which won't even help, them.' May be, once it is satellite ready, we'll look at it again.

Oh no, I thought. The Army Chief hadn't looked convinced in the first place and now the Navy was also backing out. Amit's face looked slightly strained.

'I think we will go for it, provided the product is approved by the Institute of Aviation Medicine,' the Air Force chief said after sometime. He turned to his colleagues and the Army and Navy Chief. 'If we have this Microbot implanted then we will be able to know the health condition of any pilot before he goes on a flight. ' The Army Chief still looked doubtful but Amit's face lit up.

'Exactly! Thank you, Chief. We'll get it run through the Institute. Of course, the Health Ministry should approve, I believe,' Amit said, looking thrilled that the Air Force Chief had finally understood what he was saying.

'We'll try this out in phases of course,' the Air Force chief said, shaking Amit's hand.

'Absolutely Sir. I think the Microbot will serve a very useful purpose here,' Amit said brightly. 'If you are able to monitor a pilot's condition closely before sending him on any important flight, then think of the lives you will save in any untoward circumstances!'

The Army General snorted.

'My boys are already fit and fine. We don't need your little electronic blips in their bloodstreams,' the General said disdainfully. I wondered why he was so antagonistic towards Amit. Maybe he just didn't trust people easily. Well, his loss, I thought to myself, annoyed at his attitude.

Amit narrowed his eyes a little at the way he'd denounced the Microbot but there wasn't anything he could do. The General seemed to have made up his mind. All the different lieutenants were milling around talking to us and Archana had already sighed over an Air Force lieutenant who was talking to one of the doctors.

'They're all so handsome,' she whispered. I didn't respond because my eyes were fixed on Amit. He seemed like a different person today. Maybe it had to do with his confidence in the Microbot. Even though he hardly seemed like the man who had joked about my anklets or the pained man who had struggled with his parents' death, I realized that watching him go up step by step was strangely fulfilling. And yet at the same time. I wanted him all to myself. I shook my head to clear the insidious thoughts that nevertheless entered sooner or later.

When the presentation was over and the uniformed visitors had left, we could all breathe easily. When we were settling back into work, I realized he was hovering near me. I looked up at him and felt that familiar jolt of attraction that canceled out all the negativity I'd been feeling lately. I smiled at him.

'May I sit?' he asked and I rolled my chair to the side so he could sit down on a chair that he'd pulled up.

The thrum of feelings that I experienced whenever he was near had seemed to have reached a crescendo. I fiddled with the keyboard uneasily.

'So how was the presentation?' he asked softly. I turned sideways to look at him.

'Great as usual,' I said. But Amit didn't look convinced.

'Why do I get the feeling there's a 'but' in there?' he asked. I sighed.

'It's just that you and I, I thought we're a team. I was just taken aback to learn that there's some control center now,' I admitted.

'But that's not a secret. How did you think we managed to connect so many people to the Microbot without one?' he asked, looking stymied.

'Okay,' I said, feeling a little foolish. 'But where's it?'

'Oh it's in a good location. We can go visit it sometime,' he averred and then before I could ask anything, he said, 'I'm leaving early tomorrow morning. But when I come back, we will talk about that...stuff you wanted to discuss,' he promised, lifting my hand to kiss my knuckles.

'Okay,' I said feeling infinitely happier than I'd been just a few minutes ago. Of course, things never turn out the way we plan them to, but I had no idea of knowing that.

---✿✿✿---

CHAPTER - 25

Much later, I wondered if it was fate or mere coincidence. In mid-September, when Amit had left the city once again on his numerous work related visits, right after the presentation to the Armed Forces, I was feeling quite sick. I couldn't get up from bed to work at the hospital and I was positive I wouldn't be able to go to the lab either. Anyhow without Amit, the prospect of working at the lab seemed dreary.

For doctors, even falling ill was a luxury. Sometime around 11 am after taking a nap, I realized I was feeling better but I still wanted to take the day off. I took a shower and felt fresh and clean and wondered how I was going to spend the rest of the day. Amit had texted me in the morning, his usual message asking what I was doing but I hadn't felt like responding.

Since Archana had said she would tell the hospital I was not well, I felt free, like a young person, alone in the city. There was so much to do, to see and I wished there was someone with me. I decided to take a chance on my own and went to the Metro nearby. For someone who had lived in Delhi for so many years, I had hardly explored the city as much as I'd wanted to. Studies and then work had left me with very little time. Even when I did, Gautam was always there, so I never had to look for places on my own.

I got off at Rajouri Garden and looked around amazed at the number of malls this place had. Sometimes, memory is a strange thing. It rears its head at the strangest of times. I suddenly remembered that Gautam had brought me here to one of the malls once, on one of our rare dates outside the hospital. He had insisted that for one day, we should forget we were doctors. We could behave like any other normal couple, he had said. Naturally we'd ended up fighting over something silly, I couldn't remember now, but he'd been so happy then. Even our fight hadn't dimmed his mood. He proclaimed that 'normal' couples fought too.

The reminder of Gautam urged me forward and I stepped inside one of the malls, without even thinking of where I was going. I had to get away from the onslaught of guilt that was sure to follow if I thought of Gautam. The only way I'd learnt to deal with these thoughts was to block them as soon as I had them but today, there was nothing to distract me.

I stepped inside Lifestyle and browsed through the clothes, wondering if I should update my wardrobe. After spending at least half an hour there, I almost wished Archana had been there with me. At least she may have had some ideas on what worked for me and what didn't. I usually didn't have a clue and so usually stuck with Indian ethnic because that was a look that had worked for me for so many years. I tried on a few Western outfits and checked myself in the long mirror outside.

'Those anklets don't work with those capris,' a woman who was heading into one of the changing rooms murmured. I shot her a look. I didn't need her advice. Still, I went back into the room and decided I'd buy the aqua green top and the black capri pants. I felt the urge to do something different and new and after buying the clothes, I went back and changed into them. On an impulse, I bent down and removed my anklets. I dropped them inside my handbag and stuffing my old clothes in another bag, I stepped outside.

Honestly, I'd wanted to get rid of the anklets for a long time but Amit was so fond of them and the tinkling noise they made that I hadn't had the heart to do it. I headed towards the food court feeling tons lighter already.

But just as I was settling down to eat a quiet meal of exorbitantly priced Pav Bhaji, I faltered. Gautam was sitting on the table towards my right. I had spotted him but he hadn't. Instinct told me to get up from there and run. But I couldn't seem to move. He too was alone and he was eating. Almost as if he sensed me staring at him, he looked to his left, and blinked.

Seeing him brought a rush of emotions inside me, emotions that I'd thought had been buried when I fell in love with Amit. What was wrong with me? How was it possible to feel this way? After what seemed like endless minutes, he pushed his chair back and lifted his plate and came towards me. I felt panicked. He was going to join me at the table here.

When he sat down, I stared at his face, realizing that it had been months since I'd seen him. And the force with which I'd missed him came rushing down over me at that moment.

'How are you?' he asked finally.

'I'm fine,' I replied. How strange this was! This was the person I'd been the closest to for so many years and now we were talking like strangers.

'How have you been Gautam?' I managed to ask finally.

'Can't you see?' he asked bitterly.

'You look fine,' I lied. Actually, Gautam looked pretty terrible. He had bags under his eyes and he hadn't shaved for several days.

'Nice joke, Payal,' he said. 'You look fabulous though.'

I looked down at my clothes, realizing he'd never seen me in clothes like this before.

'Thanks,' I murmured.

'I never thought I'd see you here. I don't know if you're real or a dream,' he said, picking up his spoon and eating the bright orange biryani.

'I took a day off,' I said quietly.

'Wow. And your Dr. Amit let you?' Gautam asked. I felt the familiar hackles rise but I paid no heed to them.

'He's not in town,' I replied as I broke off a bit of my pav.

Gautam's eyebrows rose. 'Ah. Makes sense now.'

'Why do you always behave like this?' I snapped.

'Because you're blinded by him,' he snapped back at me. Blinded?

'I'm in love with him,' I said slowly and Gautam winced, as though from pain.

'There was a time when I was confident I would hear you say those words for me,' he said quietly.

I looked down at my plate.

'Things change, Gautam,' I said, wishing I'd never come here.

'Whatever you say. I just...I just...' he looked away as though even looking at me was too painful for him.

'You just what?' I asked him, unable to stop myself.

'I just wish I knew why you did this to me,' he said, looking back at me, his eyes blazing. I swallowed nervously.

'These things happen; I couldn't help falling in love with him.' I explained lamely.

'No they don't. We were going to discuss marriage plans for god's sake!' he said fiercely. I looked around warily. 'The next thing I know you've cozied up to this famous guy and dumped me totally when I needed you most.'

'It wasn't like that,' I said, realizing that I had no explanation for my actions.

'Then what was it like, Payal? Tell me. I want to know,' he said, his eyes serious and intense.

'Why didn't you finish your residency in the hospital?' I asked him, hoping to change the topic.

'And bump into you every day? No thanks,' he sneered.

'But you were going to become an Orthopaedic Surgeon!' I protested, trying not to think of how much his words hurt me.

'Dr. Vinod said I didn't have it in me,' he bit out angrily.

'So? You could have tried another hospital,' I persisted. He shook his head.

'Leave it Payal. I lost interest in it,' he said.

'So...where do you work now?'

'At a clinic nearby,' he said. That was when it clicked to me that Jai had told me that Gautam was working near City Square Mall. I hadn't even noticed which mall I'd gone into when I came here.

We were silent for a while and then he pushed his plate and scraped his chair back.

'I can't do this. I can't sit here in front of you and behave like we used to be good friends,' he said. 'Not when I'm still in love with you.'

I think the shock was evident on my face. 'But...'

'But what Payal? You think feelings can just go away? They can't. The day that Dr. Amit stepped into our hospital was the last day I had any happiness in my life,' he said, walking away.

I wanted to stop him but I knew I wouldn't have any words to tell him. At least not any he'd want to hear.

My day was now completely ruined. I just wanted to get back to the hospital now. I got up from there, collecting my bags and walked away from the food court when my mobile phone rang. A little exasperated, I shifted the bags from one hand to the other and then dug in my bag for my phone. It was Amit.

'Hey,' I said, as I answered.

'What's up? How are you?' he asked.

'The same,' I answered, stepping on to an escalator that was moving down.

'Where are you right now?' he asked.

I don't know why, but I lied. 'In the hospital,' I told him, looking around at the people milling around me.

'I thought you were at a mall,' he said faintly. I was shocked. How could he possibly have known?

'Why would you think I'm at a mall?' I asked finally.

'Just...nothing...just the background noise levels made me think you were in a mall,' he said.

'I...I was in the cafeteria,' I lied once more, wincing. Why was I doing this?

'Ah! Okay,' he said, sounding convinced.

I reached the end of the escalator and looked around, wishing I could banish the thoughts that were crowding my head. Especially because I'd lied to Amit. Twice. Was it the guilt of having met Gautam?

'Listen, I'm getting back tonight and I want to talk to you. It's important,' he said.

'Okay,' I replied and then after we said our goodbyes I ended the call.

I went back to the hospital, trying to shush the internal monologue in my head that kept going on and on about why I'd lied to Amit. Was I worried that he'd be jealous if he found out I'd spoken to Gautam? No. Amit was perfectly aware of my history with Gautam but he also knew that I was in love with him now.

Amit's asking if I was in a mall shook me a little. Meeting Gautam and then lying to Amit - what was I doing?

---✿✿✿---

CHAPTER - 26

'You're coming to the lab this evening, right?' It was Amit once again on phone. He asked without any preliminaries.

'I...' I wasn't sure. Nitin and Jai hadn't said anything about going today. It was one of those rare days when we didn't have to go to the lab.

'I'll tell Nitin to drive you up here. I want to see you today,' he said when I didn't say anything.

'Okay,' I said, not entirely sure why he wanted to meet me suddenly. I think my complaints that he barely spent time with me must have finally hit home.

Feeling a little happy about that, I dressed up again and went out. Nitin was waiting for me in the car park and I walked up to him.

'Thanks for driving me to the lab,' I told Nitin. He shrugged.

'No big deal,' he said.

We got inside the car and on the way Nitin got talking.

'Jai told me you met Gautam today?' he asked casually. I did mention that to Jai after meeting Gautam. I wasn't comfortable with Jai discussing it with his roommate though! I didn't want to be the subject of gossip!

'Y-yes. I met him at City Square Mall today,' I said uneasily.

'How's he?'

'Okay. Not so good actually,' I admitted.

'Why?'

'He's just...he's going through a bad time,' I improvised.

'For what it's worth, I think you made the right choice Payal,' Nitin said, turning to look at me briefly. His words should have reassured me but instead, it felt a little weird coming from him.

'Why do you say that?' I asked, unable to stop myself.

'Look at what Dr. Amit is doing! He's so successful and he's going to make a big name for himself one day. And look at Gautam. One little thing went wrong and he just went haywire. Obviously Dr. Amit is the right person for you,' Nitin said confidently.

I didn't reply because he sounded right. I just couldn't reconcile this with why I'd lied to Amit today about where I'd been. Nitin turned the car silently.

'Where are we going?' I asked Nitin, surprised because he was not driving in the direction of the lab.

'Oh, I forgot to tell you. Change of plans. Dr. Amit called and told me to bring you to Janakpuri instead.'

'What? Why? Who's in Janakpuri?' I asked, surprised. Nitin shrugged.

'He asked, and I said I would do it. We should be there soon,' Nitin said, taking a turn on the road. What was this new development? Why were we going to one of Delhi's most affluent localities? I thought Amit had wanted to talk to me.

Nitin spoke to Amit on the phone a couple of times and then followed directions to a tree lined avenue which was flanked by huge bungalows on both sides. I looked around, impressed. Finally, Nitin stopped the car in front of a huge bungalow. I stepped out uncertainly. Nitin checked the address on the gate and nodded.

'Yep, this is the one,' he said. He was still in the car.

'Aren't you coming?' I asked, surprised. I felt a dip of irrational fear in my stomach.

He shook his head. 'Boss wants to see you. Not me,' he said with a wink. I cringed a little at the way he addressed Amit as 'boss' suddenly.

'But how will I get back?' I asked.

'He'll drop you back, right?' Nitin asked, backing the car and driving away, leaving me there.

What a day, I thought, as I pushed the gate open and went up to the door and rang the doorbell. It was opened after a few minutes by Amit who beamed at me.

'You're in perfect time,' he said, stepping back to let me enter.

I walked inside, wondering why he looked so much at home in this palatial bungalow but he led me to a dimly lit hall that was decorated tastefully. He insisted I sit down on one of the plush sofas and smiling at him, I did.

'What do you think of this place?' he asked, waving his hands expansively.

'It's amazing,' I shrugged. 'Whose house it?'

Amit smiled in response and sat down beside me and took my hands in his.

'This house is mine, Payal, but I would like nothing better than to share it with you,' he said.

My eyes grew round. What did he mean? Seeing the confusion on my face, he quickly explained.

'I had bought it a month back. I was getting it refurbished and I wanted it to be a surprise for you.'

I looked around again, trying to take in what he was saying. I couldn't believe that he owned such a big house. This bungalow must have cost crores.

'What was that you said, about sharing this house with me?' I asked him slowly.

He stood up and pulled me along with him.

'I know you've been upset with me because I don't spend too much time with you. But I was busy doing all this for us. I love you Payal. I've loved you since the moment I saw you in that classroom,' he said, his eyes intense. My heart sped up and I realized my breathing had become shallow.

'I want to meet your mother and brother as soon as it's possible,' he said.

'Why?' I asked him.

'Isn't it obvious? I want to ask your mother for your hand in marriage,' he said.

'You're going to ask her, and not me?' I managed to ask.

'Of course not. Why do you think I brought you here instead of the lab?' he asked, lifting my hand and kissing it gently.

'Will you marry me, Payal?'

I felt blood rushing in my ears.

'Payal?' he asked expectantly. I nodded.

'Yes,' I said, and flung myself into his arms. He held me tightly, his face buried in my neck.

All the uneasiness of the day disappeared when Amit slipped a gorgeous diamond ring on my finger. I didn't know it was possible to be this happy! The moment I realized that this was going to be my home, it took on a completely different meaning. This was going to be our place! Amit's and mine and it was certainly a dream home. Amit had taken care of everything. I had no idea that he'd actually listened to the things I'd spoken but he'd apparently tuned in to all my likes and dislikes and he'd planned the entire house around that. I discovered that every little thing had mattered as I walked around the house with him. The fact that he'd remembered things like my favorite colors was a bit overwhelming and romantic. It was all so beautiful. And must have cost a bomb. There were five bedrooms and we didn't even look into each of them in detail.

He slowly asked, 'I hope your mom and your brother will come here to live with us once we get married?'

I looked up pleasantly surprised. Nothing in the whole world could make me happier.

He continued talking, 'I really want to be a part of a family once again, Payal,' he said. He looked calm but I could also sense the child like happiness he radiated. My heart clenched in response, as I felt just how vulnerable he was.

Amit showed around the house to me and I exclaimed in wonder. He told me about how he had been planning this surprise for a while now. I realized that because he was probably busy with all this, it was why I'd been feeling distanced from him lately. I immediately banished the negative thoughts that had been creeping into my head in his absence.

Even though Amit had been away, he had still been thinking of me. It warmed my heart and I fell more in love with him.

CHAPTER - 27

I had decided to move in with Amit. He said he would take care of everything at the hospital. I knew Archana would be shocked when I told her the news but she was actually quite thrilled for me. I had expected her to chide me about going away to live with Amit but she just waved it off.

'You both are in love. You want to be with each other. It makes perfect sense,' she said as she helped me pack. The only person who looked put out was Jai but he didn't say anything to me. I just sensed his disapproval as they saw me off a week later, as I drove away with Amit.

'I'll see you in the hospital,' I waved out to them and then turned to Amit, who looked at me happily.

'You look like you have everything you ever wanted!' I teased him.

'Almost,' he said, reaching out to grasp my hand firmly. As the roads sped away behind us, I realized I was leaving behind my old life and its ways. I still had to talk to my mother about Amit but he had promised me that we would visit her together very soon.

Once I was settled in with Amit, I thought less and less about Gautam. That was fine by me because I hated the guilt that swamped me whenever I thought of him. Anyhow, there was hardly any time. Amit had arranged for a number of people to come from his home town, as house help and they took up a lot of time as we tried to manage my new home together. Some of these people had known Amit right from the time he was a child and so there was a sense of comfort and warmth when they were around.

Both Amit and I were really busy. I had the hospital as well as the lab and he was still flying around the country on various important deals.

Some of these deals even took place at our home. On some days I'd come back from the hospital and see huge and important looking cars in our driveway. I was constantly amazed at how fast Amit had moved up the ladder. All these VIPs were visiting our home because they needed Amit.

A couple of times, he had even introduced me to some of them as his fiancée before taking them away to his study where they talked for hours. I usually saw them again on their way out as they shook hands with him. Obviously things were going well. One time I got back from the hospital a little earlier than usual and he introduced me to some NRI who was a geologist. They were in the middle of a chat in the living room, instead of Amit's study and I overheard the visitor mention something about 'mutual benefit' and that kind of stuck in my head as I went inside, to freshen up. When I came out after sometime, the man had left.

I asked Amit what work a geologist had with him. Ministers and VIPs, I understood. But a geologist? Amit looked amused at my curiosity. We sat down together in the living room and he tried to explain. According to him, the government had discovered a source of alternate energy but to make it work, they needed technological and expert support. This man, the NRI, had come to Amit after being referred to him by a friend of Amit's who lived in the US.

'So? How can you help?' I asked. Amit gestured with his hands and shrugged. When I still didn't get it, he sighed.

'Come on. I'm sure you would have understood. He wants me to put in a word for him with the right minister, since they all know me so well now,' Amit said.

Oh. 'And what was that about mutual benefit?' I asked, feeling curious.

'Oh that. He was probably referring to a finder's fee,' he said.

'What's that?' I asked, a frown on my face. He leaned in close and rubbed my forehead with his thumb.

'Stop frowning. You'll get lines on your forehead. A finder's fee is a perfectly legal percentage or commission that I will get for introducing him to the right minister,' he said.

'But that...that makes you like a broker, right?' I asked, realizing that I wasn't so comfortable about how this was all turning out.

I think he sensed my unease and his eyebrows shot up.

'Seriously? You have that look on your face now? You were the one who convinced me to pursue these 'connections' that the Health Minister told me about, right? I did, and this is where I am. Where we are,' he said, waving his hands expansively around. Oh well. I rested my head on his shoulders and shut my eyes. He knew what he was doing. I trusted him.

---✿✿✿---

CHAPTER - 28

The Microbot had been successfully implanted in several Air Force pilots and at the lab, Archana was often found sighing over some of them when they came. I found it amusing and she did not.

'You've got it all set. Not so for us though,' she said when I told her that she was taking this obsession with Air Force pilots a little too seriously.

I was a bit taken aback. 'Relax. You're busy like crazy now. But I'm sure you will find someone eventually,' I told her.

She shook her head dejected. 'I don't know. I can't see any of these handsome chaps falling madly in love with me. I just don't have it in me,' she said.

'What nonsense. You're one of the prettiest doctors in our hospital. Ask Nitin, he'll tell you for sure,' I reassured her teasingly and she rolled her eyes but brightened considerably. 'And also the brainiest. Do you think you'd have got into this Microbot program otherwise?'

'Yeah. I wish Dr. Amit had a twin who would fall in love with me though,' she said and I burst out laughing.

'Not possible. He's one of a kind,' I said, a little proudly.

'Don't I know it,' she said as she got back to her work.

The monitoring process had become much more streamlined now that we had the medical graduates working with us. Things worked smoothly and almost effortlessly. We'd had a couple of exciting incidents where the Microbot had pointed out that one of the political party leaders was possibly developing an angina and he was not in Delhi at the moment. But we still managed to alert him and he had himself checked into the nearest hospital where a possible fatality had been averted. Needless to say the minister had become Amit's number one fan and had even visited us at home to talk to Amit.

My thoughts were brought back to Archana when she said something about one of the pilots.

'Oh God. This one is even more dashing,' she whispered as he registered himself at the desk.

I grinned.

'I just wished there was something that could make him fall in love with me,' she said vehemently and I patted her back.

'As if that's possible!' I said, watching the pilot as he got ready to be implanted.

'Yeah. I know. I just wished it was possible,' Archana said.

After the initial set up, we showed him the way the Microbot worked inside his body and honestly speaking, he seemed a bit taken up with Archana too as he hovered near us, expressing his amazement that the Microbot even though it was inside him, could tell us what was going on.

'This is really great,' he said for the umpteenth time.

'Umm...you might have a few side effects initially as your body gets accustomed to the Microbot,' Archana told him with a smile.

He waved it off. 'I know. I've been told about this already. I hope it gets over soon because I have to be on duty in a couple of days,' he said.

'Well, you're perfectly healthy so you should be soon,' I said, looking over the findings and smiling at him.

'What do you do when you're not on duty?' Archana asked flirtatiously. I left both of them together, Archana and Mohan (that was his name) as they talked about some of the nice places in Delhi that they hadn't yet seen.

I glanced at Mohan's brain scans as the Microbot started feeding us information and noticed the spikes in his brain activity.

After a while Mohan left but there were definitely stars in Archana's eyes. I listened to her in amusement and realized that Jai and Nitin were feeling left out. In fact, Nitin looked quite dejected at seeing Archana's face light up as she talked about Mohan. I felt sorry for him and nudged Archana to stop going on about Mohan in front of the guys.

She looked disgruntled at first and then nodded reluctantly. But instead of shutting up, she started referring to Mohan by the last two digits of his patient ID number.

At first I didn't understand. Who is no.78, I wondered when she kept mentioning that she wanted to get ready for her date with no.78. Then I realized that she was referring to Mohan's patient ID number which was technically MD11078. I shook my head at her, in exasperation.

Later that night, when I was back in the bungalow, I realized I should have gone away with Archana to the hospital quarters for the night. Amit was away and being alone in this huge house made me quite nervous. The servants also disappeared into their quarters after eight and it became quite lonely. But Archana had really fixed a date with Mohan and I didn't want to be a third wheel when finally her personal life seemed to be picking up.

I wandered around the huge house, wondering what we would do with all these rooms. So far we used only a couple of them. Feeling a bit antsy I thought that maybe I should check out some of them and see what potential they had for the future. The rooms were nothing special but were huge and I thought maybe I could renovate them for my mom and brother when they would come to live with us.

Feeling more bored than ever, I walked towards Amit's study, because I was missing him and I wanted to be in a place where his presence was palpable. I turned the doorknob and pushed open the door.

---❁❁❁---

CHAPTER - 29

I stepped inside and my hands lingered on the walls trying to find the light switch. When I finally found it, and switched it on, I looked around, a little disappointed. Being here reminded me of Amit more than ever and feeling like a lovesick puppy, I walked towards his desk. The room was furnished elegantly with wooden bookshelves that were neatly arranged with books, mostly scientific ones. Despite his constant presence in the study, there was a distinct unused feeling to the room, especially the books. They looked too neat, as though they hadn't been touched after they'd been arranged on the shelves.

I rounded his desk and sat down at his chair and leaned back comfortably. I must have sat there for a while, thinking about the past and the future and how everything in life was uncertain. When I came to Delhi, all I had in mind was that I had to become a doctor and a good one at that. The very best actually.

I had stars in my eyes and today, those stars were still there but there was something different about them. I hadn't expected to find myself in one of the most expensive localities in Delhi, in such a huge bungalow, engaged to a brilliant man like Amit. There was nothing wrong with this picture. It was just that I hadn't chosen to take this path. The path had chosen me.

Feeling philosophical, I texted Archana, asking her how her date went. There was silence at first and then she texted back, all exclamation marks and smiley faces that it had gone perfectly. I smiled at her enthusiasm and then kept my phone on the desk, absently opening one of the drawers. I froze.

There were pictures of me. Several of them. What astounded me was that these pictures were taken when I was still with Gautam. Before I'd even started work at the lab. In several of them, Gautam was with me and I bit my lower lip when I saw the look in his eyes. It had taken a photo for me to realize that the look in his eyes meant that he really loved me.

With slightly trembling hands, I pushed the photos back where I'd found it, wondering if I should ask Amit about them. Why had he taken these photos? Why did he still keep them? I was reminded of his words that he had fallen in love with me as soon as he'd seen me. What had seemed romantic then had just acquired a stalker-ish edge to it now but I didn't want to think about it.

I shut the drawer and left the room, deciding to ask Amit when he came back the following day. But the next morning, he hadn't arrived even as I got ready to leave for the hospital. I waited as long as I could before leaving a message for him on the dining table that we needed to talk. I had called his cell phone but it was switched off, meaning he was still on the flight.

All day Archana raved about Mohan and how brave and handsome he was. I couldn't help feeling a stab of envy at the newness of her feelings and how she seemed to be positively glowing. I tried to recall a moment in my own love story with Amit and whether I'd felt like this at any point of time. But all I could think was that my feelings for Amit had just fallen upon me like a ton of bricks. There had been none of this delicious uncertainty of whether Mohan would call Archana again or not.

'So when are you meeting him next?' I asked, pushing away those traitorous thoughts.

'He's joining his duty in a couple of days but he's promised me that when he gets back to Delhi, he will call me up,' Archana said with a dreamy smile.

'So he's gone to...'

'He's at the Hindon Air Force Station so he's not that far away,' she said as we walked together.

'Who's not that far away?' Nitin asked, as he appeared beside us from nowhere. I looked at him surprised. Being in love with Amit had put blinkers on my eyes and I'd stopped really noticing my friends. Nitin had lost weight considerably in the past few months. He looked leaner and there was something quite different about him.

'Oh just someone I've started seeing,' Archana dismissed with a smile.

'But who?' he persisted. I wished Nitin would stop asking. He was just going to be hurt when he found out. If only Archana had seen him as someone who could be more than a friend to her, he would have been infinitely happier. But feelings couldn't be forced upon anyone. I knew that from personal experience.

'No.78 if you insist,' Archana said and walked away, waving at us.

'She's had 77 boyfriends before this guy?' Nitin turned to me, his face paling. I laughed although I felt sad for him.

'No, that's not what she means,' I said, trying to be kind as we walked towards the desk. We were both signing out for the day.

'Then?' he asked, and I sighed unhappily. Nitin didn't stand a chance against the dashing Mohan.

'You shouldn't have waited for so long,' I told him and his face colored.

'I...' he started to say something and then stopped as though unsure of his own words.

'It's okay, Nitin. These things happen,' I told him as I patted him awkwardly on the shoulder.

When I reached home, I was still thinking about Nitin and Archana and then I remembered that I had to talk to Amit about my photos. But when I went inside, he was getting ready.

'Where are you going?' I asked him as I shrugged out of my doctor's coat.

'We have an important dinner today. I need you to get ready soon!' he said, straightening his sleeves.

'Where?' I asked, mentally groaning because I was not in the mood for socializing.

'It's at the house of an old friend of mine. Tariq wants both of us to come. He's inviting some special guests today as well,' Amit said, looking at me through the reflection in the mirror.

'I'm tired,' I said plainly as I deposited my bag on the floor. He turned around with a smile and kissed the back of my neck.

'You'll feel better if you come,' he said.

'Really? I'll feel better in a house full of strangers and VIPs?' I snapped at him.

'Payal,' he said, a slight warning tone in his voice. 'It will do us both good to come out and meet people. We have to think of this as the next step in our lives. This is how it's going to be.'

I sighed, nodded and went for a shower. I had hoped to hash things out with Amit about the photos and spend some quiet time at home with him, maybe watching TV. But now I had to get dressed to the teeth and make sparkling conversation as well.

We reached Tariq's house in half an hour and as we got out of the car, I asked Amit, 'You said you didn't have any friends. So who are all these people suddenly coming out of nowhere?'

He shrugged. 'They're not friends as such. Just people I've known for a long while. They've just woken up to my special qualities of persuasion with politicians,' he said with a wink. Although it was done to reassure me, I felt out of sorts when I realized this was to be a business dinner.

I was right. Inside the house, we were seated in the living room along with a few other people who were all important for various reasons. I felt discomfited making small talk with all these so-called big people so I picked up a magazine, even though Amit was right beside me.

I sensed someone had come to sit next to Amit and was talking to him with a great deal of urgency in his tone. 'I just heard he will be here Amit,' he said. I lifted my head to look at this man and he smiled at me. Amit quickly introduced us. This man was Roshan. Another of his 'friends' apparently.

Even though I flipped the pages of the magazine, I was able to hear his conversation with Amit. Apparently Roshan wanted to start a tech university and needed approval from a certain minister who was sure to be attending the dinner. How did I land up here, I wondered, amongst all these movers and shakers?

My eyes fell on one of the pages and I realized that I'd seen the man in the article somewhere. The headline screamed out words like 'scam' and 'high level involvement' and then I realized with a dip in my stomach that this was the same man who had visited Amit at home. The man who had wanted to pitch his expertise to the government, offering them technical support for their alternate energy source. The geologist.

CHAPTER - 30

I felt the blood drain from my face as I read the damning words in the article. What if Amit also got pulled into this mire for having done the introductions, I wondered. But before I could alert Amit to it, we were asked to join the others for dinner.

It was an elaborate affair and I realized that the Minister for Human Resources Development, the one Roshan had wanted an introduction to, had finally managed to come. I couldn't even enjoy what I was eating because of the nervousness brewing inside my stomach. I had to discuss so many things with Amit but he looked completely at ease as he talked to everyone. He was hardly aware of me beside him because he was completely engrossed in explaining something.

I realized that Amit had become one of those important people that only other important people knew about. Even though he was behind the scenes, he had orchestrated so many deals with these people that everyone turned to him, hoping he would be able to work his magic. The Minister for Human Resources was not someone I had met at the lab and I had certainly met my share of politicians. He had not yet visited the lab and I sensed Amit was trying to get him to come. Although he couldn't discuss the Microbot openly, I figured that both Amit and the Minister knew what he was talking about.

When dinner was over, most people lingered in the drawing room making small talk. That was when Amit chose to introduce his friend Roshan to the minister. I watched them from afar as Amit told the Minister about Roshan. Feeling bored, I tuned out and watched the moonlight streaming on the lawn. It was a lovely night. When I turned around, I realized that the three of them were walking towards a room. Great, I thought, annoyed. Amit was taking them to a private place to talk while I lingered here among people I didn't know.

I should have just stayed at home, I fumed. I was nothing more than Amit's sidekick...hardly his fiancée. I had a good mind to just leave but knew that Amit wouldn't be pleased so I stuck around. When Amit, Roshan and the Minister emerged, I sensed that all was not well.

The minister was in a hurry to leave and Roshan clearly looked disappointed. Amit grabbed my elbow and timed our exit to match with that of the minister. I realized he was still trying to talk to him.

'I told you Amit. I'm not interested,' the Minister whispered harshly. I felt Amit stiffen beside me even as Roshan joined us. This was getting more awkward than I thought. Thankfully, no one at the party was even aware that something ugly was playing out here on the driveway.

The Minister was waiting for his car to be brought in front and I realized that while he could have waited inside, he had wanted to avoid talking to Amit. His aides were hovering near him but Amit and Roshan were still trying to make their point.

'We'll take care of everything, Sir. Just give us a chance,' Roshan said and the Minister turned to him and then Amit. It was like I wasn't even there.

'I came here today for dinner at a friend's house. I had no idea you were going to try and coerce me into doing something I do not want to do,' he said.

'No one is coercing you,' Amit said quietly.

'Well, it definitely feels like you're taking advantage of our acquaintance,' he said gruffly. 'I am not for sale.' Saying so, the minister sat in his car and left, leaving Amit, Roshan and I, standing on the drive. Amit was emanating quiet anger and that made me uncomfortable as we sat in the car to go back home. I'd never seen him look so livid before.

There was no way I could raise any of the topics I'd wanted to talk to him earlier I thought as he drove back home in silence. I felt like I was caught between two worlds. One - my work in the hospital that was comforting and familiar, and two - this world of Amit's hobnobbing with important people for obscure reasons.

I didn't know where I fit anymore.

CHAPTER - 31

As for other things, Archana and Mohan were now going strong. I felt a little sad for Nitin when I saw how upset he seemed with these developments.

'Be happy for her. Be happy that she's happy,' I told him once. He looked at me as though I was an alien from outer space. Why was that such a strange concept for men, I wondered. Mohan was spending more time in Delhi now because he was one of the pilots who usually ferried around ministers in their helicopters and naturally Archana and he were spending a lot of time together.

'Your no.78 is turning out to be quite a permanent fixture here,' I commented to Archana one day at the lab. He kept popping up at the lab, supposedly to ask questions about the Microbot in his body but we all knew that he was only here to be with Archana.

She blushed a little. 'Yeah. I think he's the one,' she whispered to me. I smiled. I was genuinely happy for her. This was what she'd wanted for a long time. Someone she felt about strongly and who would reciprocate her feelings. But I chanced a look at Nitin as he went about his work on his computer, and I shook my head in resignation.

And although I was glad that things were working out for Archana so well, deep inside it was a reflection of my worry over how little Amit and I were communicating these days.

One day, a rare occasion when both Amit and I were at the house at the same time, we were watching TV in silence. I wondered if it would be the right time to speak to him about the various things that we needed to discuss. He looked strained and tired. The endless travels and stress must be taking a toll on him. How I wished things between us were like the earlier days when we could talk to each other so easily. Clearing my throat, I spoke.

'Is everything all right, Amit?' I asked.

He turned to look at me. 'Yes why do you ask?'

'I was just...wondering...you seemed a little worried,' I said.

'Just the usual. Coordination with so many agencies and these useless people add to the stress of not completing their commitment on time. Nothing out of the ordinary,' he shrugged with a wry smile. I had a good mind to check out his Microbot reports the next time we were in the lab just to make sure everything was all right with him, health-wise.

'Amit there's something I wanted to talk to you about,' I told him, feeling a little better after having made that decision.

'What?' he asked. I opened my mouth to talk when my phone started buzzing insistently. A little annoyed, I looked at the screen to see who it was. Archana. I looked at Amit apologetically but he was already back to staring at the TV so I answered it.

'Hey, what is it?' I asked her.

'Payal! Switch on the TV right now!' she said, her voice wavering. I realized she was crying.

'What happened? The TV's on,' I said.

'I can't talk! See news right now' she hiccupped and ended the call.

I looked at Amit who wasn't even curious about my conversation with Archana. I picked up the remote from the coffee table and switched channels wondering what she had wanted me to see on TV. And then, I stopped as a scene of horrific destruction came on one of the News Channels.

There had been a helicopter crash where all the passengers including the pilot had died. It had taken place just outside Delhi and the news channels were telecasting a live feed from the scene where the fire was being brought under control.

Had Archana wanted me to see this? But why, I wondered.

Then my phone buzzed again. It was a message from her. I tapped it open and felt my throat dry up instantly.

'Mohan was the pilot of that helicopter,' read the message. No! I looked again at the TV screen where the ticker tape announced that there were no survivors.

Mohan was dead? I looked at Amit who also looked shocked. In fact his face had turned white.

'Amit! Archana's boyfriend Mohan was the pilot of that helicopter,' I forced the words out. He looked at me uncomprehendingly and then shook his head.

'Oh, that's such a tragedy,' he said, his voice quivering. 'But look who that helicopter was carrying.'

I didn't think Archana would be able to recover from this at all. Mohan had been such a young and vibrant man. How this could have happened to him, I thought as I forced myself to look at the TV. Shock slammed into me.

The helicopter had been carrying the Minister of Human Resource Development.

---❁❁❁---

CHAPTER - 32

Amit drove me to the hospital quarters so I could be with Archana. I couldn't talk at all. Sometimes these tragedies just happened out of the blue and struck you down. It was just that we never thought it would happen to us. Amit told me to stay the night with her because she clearly needed support.

I smiled at him thankfully and then frowned when I realized he was driving away.

'You're not coming?' I asked, wondering how he could go without talking to Archana. He shook his head.

'I don't think she would appreciate my presence. You're her friend and I'm her boss. You go on,' he said and I nodded, although I wasn't convinced with his explanation.

I went up in a hurry and saw that the bedroom door was open and a few girls were there trying to talk to her. Archana was silently staring at the TV. I sent everyone on their way and switched off the TV. She looked at me only then, tears streaming down her face. I hugged her and tried to console her but she didn't say a word.

I knew it was pointless trying to talk to her so I just sat with her while she cried. There was a knock on the door and then Jai stepped inside.

'I just heard,' he said quietly as he sat down beside us.

'Where's Nitin?' I asked. He shrugged.

'He went out somewhere quite some time back,' Jai replied.

Archana who was sobbing, finally cleared her throat and spoke, 'Thanks for coming here both of you. But I just want to be alone.'

Jai and I looked at each other then and knew instinctively that it wouldn't be a good idea to leave her alone.

I shook my head and took Archana to her room and tucked her in bed. Jai quickly brought an injection to help her relax. She was still sobbing and my heart broke for her. She had been so happy for these past few days and all of it had been snatched away by the hand of fate.

When she drifted off to sleep, I came back outside where Jai had switched on the TV and was watching the coverage. I told him about having met the Minister so recently. But he was frowning at the TV for some reason.

'What?' I asked.

He shook his head. 'I've been catching the news on all the channels and none of them have given the pilot's name. So how did Archana know?'

Oh!

We both tried to come up with possible ways she could have known it was him. 'Maybe he called her before getting on the helicopter,' I suggested.

'Possible,' Jai murmured.

'Whatever, I'll ask her tomorrow when she's feeling better,' I said, turning to look at the room.

'You think she'll be better by tomorrow?' Jai asked skeptically.

'No. She won't. Where's Nitin? I thought he would have wanted to be there for her at a time like this,' I said.

'He came back from the hospital and then said he had to go somewhere. He didn't tell me where,' Jai said.

We watched the news for a little more while, feeling more

depressed and then finally Jai left. I curled up on the sofa to spend the night, wondering what Amit was doing. The next day Archana appeared better but she refused to take leave from the hospital. I kept telling her that she needed some time off.

'If I stay away from work, I will just think too much Payal,' she said quietly and left. I sighed. She was right. Plunging back into work was the best thing to do.

I barely saw Amit that day. I came home, got dressed and went to the hospital and he wasn't around. Later that evening, at the lab, we were working like it was a normal day but I'd glance up at Archana every now and then and she looked a bit lost. Nitin seemed uncomfortable in her presence, and he barely spoke to her which was strange, I thought.

It was amazing just what could change in a single day. Until yesterday, everything was fine in our world and now, nothing would be the same again. I saw that Archana was struggling to behave normally and I wished she hadn't come.

'You should have stayed at home,' I told her again. She didn't answer. Her eyes looked glazed and tired. I knew it wasn't probably the right time but we couldn't evade the topic forever.

'Archana, when you messaged me last night, saying that the pilot was Mohan, the TV channels were not showing his name at that point. So how did you know?' I asked.

She looked up at me, her eyes widening like a deer caught in spotlights. She got up from there, almost fumbling and excused herself to go to the rest room. I looked at Jai and shrugged. He looked thoughtful and then after a few minutes, he approached me.

'I looked up the logs of who was working here yesterday evening on the lab computer,' he said.

'None of us were. It was our day off,' I reminded him. He shook his head.

'Archana was here,' he said.

'What?'

He nodded. Both of us watched as Archana stepped back into the lab, looking pale and upset.

---✿✿✿---

CHAPTER - 33

It was obvious that Archana was avoiding both of us when she returned to the lab. She feigned sickness when we tried to speak to her but Jai seemed determined to get to the bottom of the matter. I looked around at the usual occupants of the lab, divided in their own cliques. The four of us, the senior doctors, the computer specialists; every group seemed intent in their own work. The uniting force was Amit usually but he wasn't there. Gone on one more of his trips. Without him, we didn't exactly flounder but the energy was not there. This was why no one took heed when Jai and I managed to take Archana outside, even though she seemed most reluctant.

'I have work,' she muttered as we sat her down at the dining table.

'It can wait,' Jai said as he sat down beside her. I was on her other side.

'Were you here last night Archana?' I asked her softly. She looked at her hands on the table and I realized she was crying.

'What is it? Were you here?' Jai asked. She merely nodded. I looked over her head to Jai. What could this mean?

'So what happened?' I asked her.

'I...'

'You knew the crashed helicopter had Mohan, right?' Jai asked. I looked at him surprised. She nodded.

'It's obvious. Two minutes before the crash, everything would have gone haywire in his system. The Microbot would have transmitted the information here.'

Archana rubbed her eyes with her palms and sniffed.

'Why didn't you tell us that?' I asked her gently.

'I'm more worried about why there is no report here of the incident,' Jai remarked. He was right. At the end of the day there was a cumulative report that was generated for each of the people who were being monitored.

'So what really happened?' he asked. Archana took a deep breath.

'I don't know,' she said.

'What do you mean you don't know?' Jai asked, harshly and Archana quailed under his stare.

'Hey. Take it easy,' I told him, and put my arm around Archana's shoulder.

'No, Payal. This is not the time to take it easy. We have to know the answers to these questions,' Jai said.

'I saw the report,' Archana finally ventured in a tiny voice.

'Okay, and then what? You recognized it was Mohan's?' I asked her.

She nodded. 'I didn't know what to do. I wanted to alert someone. Anyone. But it was like my body was frozen,' she wept.

Jai was deeply concerned as she said these words. 'But...why didn't you tell us?' he asked. 'Anyhow, you couldn't have done anything to save him, right? The helicopter must have had some sort of mechanical failure and that was why it probably crashed and Mohan's readings right before the crash would have been pretty crazy.'

Archana seemed confused for a moment. But Jai continued talking. 'Listen, these things happen Archana. You must have gone into shock and then, seeing the Microbot switch off when...Mohan died...'

Archana shut her eyes and more tears slipped out.

'But...don't shut yourself from us this way. You should have told us,' he said.

I felt a little impatient with Jai. Even though Archana may have seen only the reports coming in, it must have felt like she was witnessing the crash herself! How could she be rational in the face of something like that?

'What I don't understand is, where is Mohan's report from yesterday? Did you delete it?' he asked.

Archana sighed loudly. 'No, I didn't. In fact I got up from there and just left,' she said.

'But why were you here? Wasn't it our day off? The senior doctors were going to take care of the reports for yesterday, right?' Jai asked.

Archana licked her lips because they were dry. 'Jai, I don't know. All I know is that I was working here yesterday and there was no one with me. I was alone in the lab,' she said.

She excused herself and left. Jai turned to me. 'I think she's lying,' he said.

'What? No! What will she lie about anyway?'

'The report. There's no sign of it. How could it have disappeared completely?'

We were both not sure about what had really happened when the doors opened and the Air Force Chief walked in, followed by his regular coterie. Jai and I got to our feet and greeted him.

'I want to speak to Amit,' he said without any preliminaries.

'He's not in town right now sir,' I replied.

'Well, I want to speak to the person next in charge,' he said. Jai and I looked at each other uncertainly. We were not the Armed Forces to have people next in charge. If we didn't have Amit, we usually managed on our own. I sent Nitin to search for Dr.Sundaram, the senior most doctor at the Lab.

'Why don't you come inside the room, Sir,' Jai suggested. The Air Force Chief looked troubled and he nodded. He and his followers went inside and Jai and I went right after them. Inside, everyone seemed a bit taken aback to see him. He was sitting on one of the chairs, ramrod straight and it made me uncomfortable to just look at him. I saw Archana shooting a few scared glances his way and I thought it was weird.

Finally, he seemed to realize that without Amit, he couldn't figure out who to talk to but he apparently needed some answers badly. He settled for the two of us.

'I'm sure you are aware of the helicopter that crashed yesterday,' he spoke, his voice low and yet commandeering. Archana's face was flushed.

We nodded.

'We lost one of our best men in the crash. Mohan Sivaram. While earlier we thought that the crash occurred because of some fault in the helicopter, I just found out that the helicopter was perfectly fine. There was no mechanical or technical fault in it. This means that the fault was with the pilot and Mohan was too experienced a pilot to make any sort of mistake. So that could only mean that there was something wrong with his health during the flight. And here's where you people come in. Didn't Amit tell me that the Microbot would rule out just such a scenario from happening? Where is he now?'

We listened to him in silence. I knew Jai was thinking the same thing as I was. If there was no fault in the helicopter and something had happened to Mohan, then it would have reflected in the Microbot readings. So why had Archana led us to believe that she had noticed the readings going haywire just minutes before the crash?

'Dr. Amit will speak to you when he gets back,' I said, trying to sound knowledgeable about Amit's whereabouts. The Air Force Chief shook his head.

'No, no. This won't do. I need to look at Mohan's report from yesterday. If he was not well, then I want to know why nobody raised a red flag and alerted us. We would have prevented him from flying the helicopter. The government is after us to find the cause of the crash especially since they lost such an important minister in it.'

I was at a loss for words. Thankfully Jai stepped in. 'We'll get it, Sir. Please wait here for a while,' he said and beckoned me. I walked away with him to a separate part of the lab.

'What are we going to do?' I asked.

'We'll show it to him. What's the harm?' Jai asked.

'But you said you couldn't find Mohan's report from yesterday,' I reminded him.

'Well, even if it's not here, it must be on the central database,' he said. Oh right. I'd forgotten about that completely. All the reports that were collected were synced with the database at the end of every day. So Mohan's last report should be there.

'I'll get them right now,' he said, leaving the lab for the other building where the MBBS students decrypted the data and sorted it out. The central database was located there.

'I'll come with you,' I told him. I was nervous, being in the same room as the Air Force Chief. We quickly apprised him that we would be back and then left. I glanced at Archana and saw that she had the same trapped deer look in her eyes.

CHAPTER - 34

'This doesn't make sense,' Jai repeated for probably the hundredth time. He was sitting before the computer in the other building where he had accessed the central database. I was hovering near his shoulder, trying to read what was there on the screen.

'You mean...'

'Yes. Look at these reports,' he gestured with his hand. Mohan's last report was in the database but what we saw in it completely shocked us. According to the report from the Microbot, Mohan's readings went haywire much before the crash. In fact, just around ten minutes before he boarded the flight. His heart rate had been escalated, his brain activity was all spiky and I realized that there were all the signs of someone who had a nervous breakdown of sorts.

'What the hell happened to him?' I murmured.

Jai looked grim. 'If this report is correct, that means we have not fulfilled our duty to inform the relevant people about this.'

'But we didn't even see it!' I protested.

'Well, I think Archana did,' Jai said. Could that be true? Had Archana known about all of this? Then why had she kept quiet?

'Jai, we'll be in big trouble with the Air Force Chief when he sees this report,' I said as Jai printed it out.

He shrugged. 'We have to live with the consequences because we were responsible for this,' he said. I still couldn't understand it. If Archana who was monitoring the readings had received it, why hadn't she said anything? Why hadn't she raised an alert like how we had done with the Prime Minister?

'Also, I don't understand why she was there in the lab yesterday. Wasn't it the job of the senior doctors to keep track of these reports? How did she get here? Who asked her to come in? More importantly, why did she take control of Mohan's monitoring?' I said as I knew we could shift around the monitoring for some important people whenever we wanted.

'Well, we have to sit down with her and ask her all of this. We have to tell her that we've seen Mohan's report.'

'Do you think she deleted them so we couldn't access them?' I asked doubtfully.

'I don't know how that's possible. You can't delete any report without the right admin password,' Jai said.

We made our way back to the lab, and I was feeling nervous. Jai held the report in his hand and I took it from him, surprised that it showed up only the patient ID number.

'There's no name on it,' I said. 'Why is that?'

'To maintain the privacy of the patients. That's why,' he said as the lift doors opened. To our surprise, the Air Force Chief was leaving the lab.

'Sir...'

'Don't bother. I got the report already,' he said, waving a file. Jai and I looked at each other puzzled.

'But...'

'One of your lab assistants got it for me. I looked through it and everything seems normal. It's going to be a big mystery as to why the chopper crashed,' he said thoughtfully. I tried not to show the shock evident on my face.

'Can I look at that report sir?' Jai asked. I shot a look at him. What was he doing?

'I told your lab assistant that I was taking it and going. Is that a problem?' he asked. I shook my head. At the moment, I didn't know what was right or wrong. Jai took the file from the Air Force Chief who looked impatient and then he handed back the file to him. The Air Force Chief left surrounded by his men and we walked into the lab.

'Well? How come that report said everything was fine?' I whispered to Jai.

'Because that wasn't Mohan's report. It was for patient number MD11079,' Jai whispered back. 79? But Mohan's was 78!

We both looked around for Archana but she wasn't there. She was obviously the 'lab assistant' who had given the wrong file to the Air Force Chief deliberately.

'She better have some answers,' Jai said as he sat down at his workstation and stared at the screen.

I was worried. What had happened to Archana? First she'd made such a big mistake and then she had covered up for it? She was definitely going to get in trouble with Amit. And maybe even fired. Poor Archana, I thought as I sat down at my workstation. What had gotten into her? Why was she behaving like this?

Archana looked red-eyed as she entered the lab. She was surely spending too much time in the rest room today, I thought. I looked towards Jai for some sort of sign. He shook his head. I suppose he thought it would be best to tackle her in the car, on our way back.

Later, Jai asked Nitin to drive and then in the car, he turned and asked Archana, 'Why did you give the wrong file to the Air Force Chief?'

'W-what?' Archana stammered.

'We saw the original file in the database,' I told her gently. 'Mohan's report was there.'

'I d-don't know what you're talking about,' she said, looking out of the window. I caught Nitin's eyes in the rear view mirror and he looked uncomfortable.

'No, enough with the evasion. We saw Mohan's report. He was completely unfit to fly the helicopter and you must have seen his report well before the crash happened. Why didn't you do anything to stop it?' Jai asked, harshly.

Archana looked terrified. I was shocked at the change in her face.

'Archana, what is it? You can tell us!' I urged her. She shook her head and then burst out crying.

Jai looked a bit shamefaced but Nitin looked angry. 'Stop troubling her, both of you,' he said.

'Nitin, you don't know the truth,' I said.

'I don't care. Just don't make her cry anymore!' he said, swerving rashly. I gasped.

'Nitin! Be careful!' I admonished him.

'I saw it,' Archana hiccupped.

'Saw what?'

'M-mohan's readings. I saw it. I wanted to stop him,' she whispered brokenly.

'Why didn't you?' Jai asked.

'I don't know!' she shouted out the words. We were surprised at the vehemence in her tone. Before we could say anything else, she continued in a lower voice. 'I don't know. I just don't know anything. I sat there like I was frozen. I couldn't move, I couldn't do a thing to stop Mohan.'

She started sobbing and the car screeched to a halt. Nitin had applied the brakes too quickly.

'Easy man! Are you trying to get us all killed?' Jai asked angrily.

'I want the two of you to leave her alone,' Nitin said quietly. I knew Nitin had feelings for Archana. But he couldn't protect her from this! She had done something wrong!

'Not happening,' Jai said and turned to Archana.

'What about the report? Why did you delete it and give the wrong one to the Air Force Chief?' he asked.

I saw Nitin's nostrils flare in anger.

'Because she didn't do it! I did!' he shouted.

---❁❁❁---

CHAPTER - 35

The four of us were sitting in the car on a dark road and it was certainly not safe. Whatever this was, we could sort it out once we reached the hospital. I tried to make the guys see sense but they were just not listening.

'Let's go back and discuss this,' I said a couple of times to Nitin and Jai who were squaring off angrily.

'Nitin, I want to go home,' Archana spoke and that was the only thing that seemed to affect Nitin as he started the car and drove in silence. Jai and I didn't bring up the topic again although our minds were buzzing with questions.

When we parked the car in the hospital grounds, Jai stopped Nitin from getting down.

'Tell me why you did this,' he asked curtly.

Nitin took a deep breath. 'She was leaving the lab when I reached and she was a mess. She didn't even talk to me so I went in to see what had happened. I saw that she hadn't raised an alarm for Mohan's reading and the chopper had crashed, so I removed the report from there.'

'Why?' Jai looked bewildered.

'Because I didn't want her to get into trouble,' Nitin replied as if it was the most obvious thing in the world.

'And today? You gave the wrong file to the Air Force Chief. What if you had got caught?' Jai snapped.

'The files contain only patient numbers. How will the Air Force Chief know that it's not Mohan's file?' Nitin asked. I couldn't believe Nitin was saying something like this.

'Nitin, if he reads it carefully, he will know that it is not Mohan's file,' I reminded him.

'There are always indications regarding age, body type and other information in the files,' Jai added.

Nitin looked like he couldn't be bothered. Archana was back to sobbing quietly. God, this was such a mess!

Jai looked at all of us as he spoke, 'For now, we've managed to sidestep the issue of the Air Force Chief finding out that Mohan was unwell before the flight'. Archana flinched every time she heard Mohan's name. 'But this can't go on for long. I can't understand why the two of you would do something like this!'

'Listen dude, just leave it. It's done. It's over,' Nitin said, leaving the car in a huff.

We all got out and I saw Archana walking slowly towards her quarters. I wanted to help her, do something, but I didn't know what. If I told about this to Amit, she would surely get into trouble and so would Nitin.

With a heavy heart, I went back home that night, wondering why things had changed so drastically in my little group of friends. Amit was at home but I didn't feel like talking to him. I was afraid I would end up telling him everything and right now, I wasn't sure if it was a good idea.

I went to sleep, curled up on my side of the bed, not waiting for Amit to come because I was overwhelmed with everything that had happened. Without any warning, I thought of Gautam, where he was and what he was doing. For a moment I was even tempted to send a message to him but then I controlled the temptation and turned around and slept. He had made it clear that he wasn't interested in being friends with me, and I couldn't give him what he wanted from me.

I woke up that night in a cold sweat. I'd had a bizarre dream that Mohan had died in a helicopter crash and that

Archana had seen it happen through the Microbot and yet hadn't prevented it. Then the reality hit me hard. It wasn't a dream. It was absolutely real. I looked at the clock. It was 3 am and Amit's side of the bed was empty. He hadn't come in to sleep at all.

I got up and padded towards the kitchen to get a glass of warm milk to soothe my nerves and wondered if he was outside watching TV. But he wasn't. I turned around and checked the study room and underneath the door, there was no slice of light to indicate that he was inside. Then where was he? Uneasily, I went back to bed, waiting for him to come back but I was tired and anxious about the events of the day and I fell asleep.

In the morning, I asked him where he had gone.

He looked surprised. 'I thought you were asleep,' he said, evading my question.

'Yes, I was but when I woke up, you weren't there. Where were you?' I asked him at the dining table.

'I got a call that there was some problem at the control center. Went to office to check it out,' he said quietly.

So late in the night? I didn't voice my thought, though. I didn't want him to notice that I was behaving strangely because of everything that was happening and it was getting late for the hospital as well. So I left, feeling a tiny little tug of unhappiness in my chest. I hated it when I lied or hid something from Amit. But this wasn't even an option.

In the hospital, I managed to put everything behind so I could focus on my work. Ours was such a divided existence, I thought, as I attended to one of my patients. With our time split between the hospital and the lab, there was little left over for a personal life. And yet, we'd managed. Until now. I hadn't seen Archana all day and I didn't find her in the cafeteria also. I wondered what had transpired between Nitin and Jai, particularly as they shared the same quarters.

When I met everyone at the car park, they all seemed subdued. Jai seemed lost in thought while Nitin looked defensive. Archana however, worried me. She seemed depressed and very quiet. On the way, I tried to engage her in a conversation but she only replied in monosyllables.

At the lab, Jai cornered me and spoke softly. 'I don't know what's wrong with Nitin but he refused to talk about the whole thing last night,' he said, looking uneasily at Nitin who seemed busy.

When I didn't say anything, he continued. 'I can't understand why Archana would botch up when she's normally so efficient.'

I had no answer to that. 'May be, she was too shocked to see what was happening to someone so close to her', I murmured unsure about what to say

What I couldn't understand was, why Nitin would cover up for Archana. Yes, he probably loved her, but even then, this was something too big.

'And the night of the crash, when you and I were at Archana's place, you said Nitin had gone out,' I reminded Jai suddenly.

He nodded. 'He was probably here, trying to cover up for her mistake,' I said.

Jai contemplated this in silence for a few moments. 'Yes, you're probably right. But how did he know that she'd made a mistake?' he asked.

I had no idea.

---●●●---

CHAPTER - 36

Sometimes things come to a head when you're not ready for them at all. Over the next couple of days, our lives changed in ways that I had not even imagined. Jai refused to let the matter of Mohan's death go to rest. I was afraid for Archana, and didn't want her to get into trouble, and yet, I wanted to get to the bottom of everything that had happened.

At home, I was getting frustrated with Amit's increasing tendency to travel. I began to get worried about the state of things between us. The number of things I'd bottled inside kept growing. From the photos of mine I'd found in his study, to the geologist who had been touted as a scamster, to this whole mess with Mohan's death, there was so much that was brewing in our lives and yet, we chose not to talk about it.

Honestly speaking, I was worried the most about Archana. She had changed completely. From being a friendly and outgoing girl who hardly seemed to have any worries, she had become withdrawn and reclusive. Some nights I stayed with her at the quarters but she barely spoke. I tried talking about Mohan to her once but her eyes filled up with tears and I shut up immediately. How could she carry on like this?

Nitin too had changed. He had become like a robot, someone who just came in to do his work without interacting with any of us. I wished for our earlier camaraderie, the banter, the jokes but that seemed like it had happened in another life altogether. One day I saw Archana emerge from the rest room where she spent all her free time crying, no doubt and I came to a decision. I was going to talk to Amit about her. I planned to tell him what Archana had done and that she needed help. I was confident that even though Amit would be shocked and probably angry because we had hidden it from him, he wouldn't be too harsh with her.

Over dinner, I started the conversation. 'I think Archana needs to visit a psychiatrist,' I said.

'Why?' he asked, surprised, as he sipped his water.

'Well, she's been depressed lately,' I replied.

'Over her boyfriend's death, right?'

'Yes, but that's not the whole story Amit,' I said. When he looked at me puzzled, I felt a little nervous as I filled him on what had happened. His expression remained blank as he listened to me. By the time I'd finished, I was getting very anxious because he hadn't said a single word and had grown very still.

'Amit,' I prompted him. 'Say something.'

'When did you find out about all this?' he asked me finally.

'The day after Mohan died,' I replied, realizing my mouth had become dry with nervousness.

'And you kept it from me?' he asked coldly. The tone and the anger in his voice chilled my spine.

'I...I didn't know what had really happened,' I explained lamely.

'And when you did know, then? When you found out that your colleague had done something that amounted to murder, you chose to keep quiet about it?' there was a quiet kind of fury in his voice.

'Murder?' the word tripped over my tongue.

'Yes, murder. If she knew about the signals that his body had sent to us, then she should have done something. She should have stopped it,' he said.

'But...'

'Why do you think I made the Microbot, Payal? To prevent just something like this from happening. And I can't believe that you people conspired to give the wrong file to the Air Force Chief!' he was nearly shouting now. I winced at his loud voice.

'But Amit, we didn't conspire anything. I told you how everything happened,' I protested but Amit wasn't listening. He got up from the table and stalked away in anger.

'Amit!' I called out and went running after him. 'Listen. Please listen!'

'Payal, I'm not thinking straight now. I am absolutely angry now, angry with Archana and all of you for lying, cheating and I think something that amounted nearly to murder. Just leave me alone,' he said, as he went to his study and shut the door.

I was shocked at the way he had reacted. I was getting nervous and worried now. What would he do? Would he fire Archana? Would she get into some sort of trouble with the police? Or would he reveal the truth to the Air Force Chief?

My stomach dipped in worry. What had I done? I thought Amit would be more understanding and would probably come up with a way to help Archana. I looked around, helpless. Poor Archana was surely going to get into a lot of trouble now. I wondered if I should send a text to Jai and tell him what happened but I couldn't bring myself to do it.

I went to sleep feeling miserable, wondering when Amit would talk things over with me. I shut my eyes and tried to think of the happier days of our courtship when Amit had seemed like the perfect man. To be honest, even now in his presence I felt that spark that had brought me close to him. I still felt those reactions and honestly, it was the only thing that kept me going. Even though we barely communicated, even though we hardly spoke, there was that hum of feelings in me whenever I was near him and for now, I thought it was enough.

I fell asleep, worry foremost on my mind. What was going to happen? Sometime in the middle of the night I woke up and saw that Amit hadn't come to bed at all. Anxiously I went through the house looking for him and saw that his study lights were still switched on. I knocked and called out to him.

'Why haven't you come to bed?' I asked. There was such a long silence that I thought maybe he wasn't there inside.

'You go. I'll come later,' he called out finally.

I was on the verge of tears when I crawled back into bed and fell asleep. It seemed like I had slept for just five minutes when my phone rang relentlessly. My eyes felt gritty as I tried to open them and I reached out for my phone blindly. Beside me, Amit was sleeping. I felt a small measure of relief on seeing him.

I answered the call and my world tilted on its axis when I heard Jai speak.

'Archana committed suicide last night.'

---❀❀❀---

CHAPTER - 37

I'm not quite sure how the next few days passed. Everything seemed like a blur. I could only remember it in snatches. I, going to Archana's quarters in a mad rush with Amit. Nitin was crying in the corner while Jai looked grim as the police came. Doctors and colleagues from the hospital expressing their shock. Police questioning us. Her terrible funeral where her parents flew in from Chennai and cried and cried. I wasn't sure if it was real or imagined, but I think I saw Gautam at her funeral too. I just couldn't talk to anyone, look at anyone or function properly at all.

We told the police that she'd been depressed about her boyfriend Mohan's death but we left it at that. Thankfully, Amit didn't say anything but I was worried too. He looked determined for some reason and I didn't understand why.

It was so hard to see her things being taken away and her quarters being emptied out completely. It was like her existence was being completely obliterated. Nitin had taken her death the hardest of all. He had shut himself up in his room and that had got us quite worried. But he emerged after some time and sat quietly without talking. He was depressed for sure. We weren't sure how long it would take him to come out of it.

Nothing was going to be the same again. The three of us missed her chirpy conversations and her laughter and giggling. It was difficult to do anything without thinking of her.

Since I was the one grieving, I hadn't really noticed anyone else other than the three of us. Even Amit. I only remembered him being shocked when I told him of her suicide. For some reason, he'd wanted to know how she had done it.

'Sleeping pills overdose,' I had sobbed as I left the room. Now, four days later, Amit told me he needed me to come somewhere with him. I was mentally fatigued and in no condition to go anywhere.

'Why?' I asked him.

'We're going to meet the Air Force Chief,' he said. I blinked and sat up. Why?

'Why are we meeting him?' I asked through a dry mouth.

'I need to lay the facts before him. If the files were switched, he will find out the truth eventually. I have to protect the Microbot at any cost.'

I stared at him unblinkingly. 'But...'

'Just get ready,' he said curtly.

'Why are you taking me along?' I blurted out.

'Because I need a witness, someone who will affirm that I did the right thing,' he said as he walked away.

I was shaky and nervous when we were taken in to meet the Air Force Chief an hour later in the Vayu Sena Bhawan. I didn't know it was possible to meet someone so important at such short notice but then Amit was now becoming a force to reckon with, at least among the important people. We were led inside the office where we were asked to sit down.

I could sense that the Air Force Chief was not pleased to see us, but there was also some confusion on his face. Amit started talking while I looked on, uneasy and wishing I was anywhere but here.

'You mean this girl Archana knew that Mohan was not feeling well?' he asked, his eyes widened in shock.

'Yes, sir. Unfortunately, no one else was at the lab that day or the tragedy could have been averted,' Amit said.

'But...why? Why would she do that?' he asked, bewildered.

'I don't know. I think she may have had a fight with Mohan before his flight,' Amit suggested. I looked at him surprised.

'So? She decided to let him die?'

Amit shook his head. 'She probably didn't realize that this would happen, Sir.'

'And she gave me the wrong file on purpose? So I wouldn't know the truth?' the Air Force Chief was getting angry now.

Amit nodded. I opened my mouth to protest. It was Nitin who had given the wrong file. Why was Amit letting Archana get all the blame? But I caught a look from Amit and shut my mouth.

'But...where is she now? We need to file a complaint against her!' the Air Force Chief stood up.

'She...she committed suicide last week,' Amit replied and I shut my eyes.

'What?'

'Yes. She probably couldn't handle the guilt of what she'd done. So she took the extreme step,' Amit said.

'This is a very serious matter Amit,' the Air Force Chief said.

'I know Sir. That's why I came to you when I found out the truth. I wanted to assure you that something like this will never happen again,' Amit spoke earnestly.

'I wish I had known that Mohan was in a relationship with this girl,' the Air Force Chief said.

'I wish I'd known too,' Amit said bitterly. I looked down at my knees. Hadn't Amit known about Archana and Mohan? I suddenly wasn't sure any more.

'Well, this is a serious matter. I can't close it so easily,' the Air Force Chief said. Amit looked as though he was trapped.

'But Sir...'

'I need to bring the police into this matter unfortunately Amit,' he said, stroking his moustache.

'Umm...Sir, I hope you will consider the negative publicity that this will get for the Air Force. It will not be a good idea sir,' Amit tried to reason with him.

'But I cannot just close this matter. A senior minister of the government has died, for God's sake! There has to be an investigation,' he insisted.

Amit was silent for a short while and then he spoke. 'Sir, I have an idea. Instead of involving the police at a generic level, we can contact someone senior and ask them to look into this matter.'

'Someone senior? Like who?'

'The ACP of Delhi is a friend of mine. You can initiate this as an inquiry by the police - the lab comes under his jurisdiction. We can ask him to look into this because he will be discreet and no word of this need ever go out,' Amit suggested.

After pondering for a while, the Air Force Chief nodded. Later, in the car, Amit was wiping the sweat off his forehead. 'That was a close call,' he said.

'I don't understand. Why did you go to him in the first place?' I asked.

'Because if we hadn't told it, and if they'd found it later on, we would be in great trouble,' Amit replied.

'But what about the ACP who will investigate? Is he the one who visited us a couple of weeks back at the lab?'

Amit nodded. 'Sure, let him investigate. What will he find out anyhow? Archana's dead,' Amit said.

'Amit, why didn't you tell the truth back there about Nitin? Nitin was the one who had deleted the files,' I told him, flinching slightly at how casually he spoke of Archana's death.

Amit shook his head. 'Nitin made a foolish mistake for the woman he loved. I think we can penalize him internally for that. If I'd got him involved in this, then his whole life would have been ruined and already he's in a bad shape.'

'So you're letting Archana get the blame?'

'Payal, look. I have nothing against Archana. At least not any more. But she's dead. She's not answerable to anyone. This is the only way to save the Microbot project,' Amit insisted.

I stayed silent for the rest of the way home. Amit's insistence to come clean about the helicopter crash had shown that he was still the morally upright man who I had fallen in love with. But transferring all the blame on a girl who couldn't even defend herself, I couldn't quite understand that.

---✿✿✿---

CHAPTER - 38

'Did you see that?' Jai asked, turning halfway in his seat to face me.

'See what, Jai?' I asked, feeling weary. The past few days since Archana's death had taken a very bad toll on me. I was feeling mentally drained and unhappy most of the time.

I had also seen the dignified ACP Aditya Kumar many times since then as he had started questioning all of us regarding Mohan's crash. I had wondered how Nitin would handle the questioning and whether he would break down and tell the truth. What would happen then to Amit's plan to keep the Microbot safe?

'This. I tried to delete this report but the machine asks me for a password. An admin password,' Jai showed. I blinked and tried to concentrate on what he was saying.

'So? What does that mean?' I asked slowly. Jai shook his head a little impatiently.

'See, we can access all the files, but we can't delete them unless we have the admin password,' Jai said.

'So?'

'So how did Nitin delete Mohan's file? File no. 78?' he asked, jogging my memory.

I rubbed my forehead trying to concentrate. Around us, the usual machines hummed and there was a subdued air of people working in the lab. Amit was talking to the ACP in his office.

'Did you ask him?'

Jai looked around warily. 'That's the funny thing. I sat down with him last night and asked him how he had deleted the file. It was almost like he had no memory of doing it. When I prodded him repeatedly, something seemed to have snapped in his head and he remembered. He said he somehow knew the admin password. He says he must have seen the password when one of his friends in IT typed it.'

'Huh?'

'Yeah. He said that he tried a couple of times, and one finally worked,' Jai said, looking serious.

'But...'

'Exactly. How is that even possible? How can such a complicated password with special characters and signs and symbols just appear to him? It makes no sense,' Jai said.

'I guess that will just have to remain another mystery,' I said, turning around to leave.

'Not if I can help it,' Jai said, looking determined. I shook my head. My heart wasn't in it. After Mohan's death, I too had been worried about how Archana had let it happen but after she died, I just couldn't think clearly enough.

Amit was worried about me. I could sense it in his gaze. I think he finally recognized that there was a gap between us, one that was increasing slowly and surely.

'We'll take a short vacation and go somewhere,' he suggested that night.

'Really? What about the lab and the work?' I asked, brightening up for a minute, because the idea to get away from everything was absolutely tempting.

'They can manage without us for a few days,' Amit assured me.

'And what about ACP Aditya Kumar's enquiries?' I asked.

He shrugged. 'Don't worry. He said he will close the case

soon claiming human error and that will be the end of it. We can arrange to fly away tomorrow itself if you want. I want to make sure that we spend some time together and try to get these freak incidents out of our mind,' he said, kissing the back of my neck.

I leaned back into him and shut my eyes. Running away from everything wouldn't solve any problem but it would help me feel better.

'I need to find out about taking leave from the hospital,' I murmured, feeling just the tiniest bit happy for the first time in days.

'I've got that covered. I'll speak with Ahuja, your Head of Department,' Amit said.

I felt a little bit annoyed that he wanted to intervene at my place of work but I brushed it off as Amit was being himself. It felt nice to be taken care of once in a while.

So, Amit and I flew down to Kerala for a few days. It was extremely relaxing although Amit had brought his laptop along and had to spend a few hours working on it, every now and then. I protested but he wouldn't listen. Finally when we were in Kumarakom, staying in the houseboat, Amit finally got into the vacation mood and stopped working.

As we got down near the reception, two hotel staff came running to pick up our luggage. They showed pointed to us the houseboat we were supposed to stay on. That was amazing - parked right on the banks of the backwaters surrounded by the coconut trees. The staff were chatting in Malayalam and laughing. We did not care, nor did we understand a word what they were speaking.

It was one of the nicest times of my life! I don't remember being this happy in a long while. Even if I started slipping into one of my depressed moods, Amit cheered me up. I realized how important it was for us to have this time just for us, without any project or patients.

Even while Amit was working, I would feel happy just being with him. I would sit across watching him and it felt like I was falling in love with him all over again. It was a new feeling for me.

Next day morning, Amit called one of the staff members and started speaking fluent Malayalam to my astonishment. I never knew that he knew Malayalam. He never seizes to amaze me. He was quite flattered when I asked him, saying he had a thing for languages and was learning around 15 odd languages! I remembered him speaking few sentences in Arabic with one of his mysterious visitors some time back as well.

That evening we called and announced our plans to my family. Both of them spoke to Amit. Of course, I made sure that they did not realize that I was away with him on my own!

Somewhere I felt that I had left out another important member of my family, Gautam. Sometimes, the guilt would return. Now, adding to that, Archana's death. It didn't seem to make sense to celebrate life when a young and vibrant person like Archana was dead. But the getaway had indeed unlocked my mind and allowed the stress to float away. I was able to live with the guilt and I finally switched on my phone after nearly three days of bliss.

---✿✿✿---

CHAPTER - 39

Amit had gone out to get us something to eat and I let the November sun soak into me as I sat on the steps of the houseboat with my phone. The moment I switched it on, there was a deluge of messages that made me wince.

I scrolled through them and saw that most were from Jai. He was furious that I'd gone on a vacation. I hadn't told him directly but I'd just texted him before boarding the flight and I had switched off my phone right away.

'How can you go away now?'

'What is wrong with you?'

'Just reply to me'

'I think I may have found something'

'Payal, you need to get back asap'

'What the hell Payal? Just call me when you get my messages'

The messages went on and on in a similar vein. I felt the familiar dread clutching my stomach and I wished I hadn't switched on the phone at all. Nevertheless, I dialed Jai's number, feeling worried about what he would say.

He answered immediately.

'Where are you?' he asked quietly. I was surprised. I'd expected an outburst.

'Kumarakom in Kerala' I replied.

'When are you getting back?'

'Tomorrow.'

'Good. I need to talk to you,' he said, sounding serious.

'So talk,' I said.

'Not on the phone. Is Amit around?' he asked anxiously.

'No he's gone out.'

'Let's keep it to ourselves till we get to details for now. Don't discuss this with anyone including Amit. Yet,' he said stressing on the last word.

'Discuss what, Jai? You haven't told me anything!' He was testing my patience.

'Just come and meet me tomorrow and I'll explain everything to you. I was writing an email to you but now since you called, let's just fix up to meet tomorrow,' he said.

The pit of nervousness inside my stomach grew. What could be wrong? Here I was, in a place that was like paradise and something had obviously been going on back in Delhi.

'I can't talk Payal. Try and understand. I...I'll be talking to Gautam soon,' he said. My ears pricked up.

'Gautam? Why?'

He sighed. 'I'll tell you when we meet up. It's not that important,' he said and then ended the call.

'Okay,' I said, unwilling to hang up but before I could ask him anything more, he had already ended the call.

I looked at my phone, puzzled.

When Amit came back, I debated on whether I should tell him about Jai's call or not. Finally, I decided not to. Jai had after all said not to say anything to anyone.

---❁❁❁---

CHAPTER - 40

Our flight landed in Delhi the following day and although the holiday had done me a world of good, the familiar guilt rushed back when I thought about how I'd just left everything and gone away. Brushing that thought away, I reached home with Amit and unpacked.

Four days of having Amit to myself had been so good. Of course, he'd been distracted and had disappeared for long periods with his phone or he'd been plugged into his laptop but he was there with me and that was all that had mattered.

I texted Jai that I was back in Delhi. He called back immediately.

'Okay, when can I meet you?' he asked.

'Tomorrow? At the lab?'

'No I need to meet you before that. Maybe at the hospital tomorrow morning,' he suggested.

'Jai, what is this about? You're worrying me,' I said.

'I can't talk about it on the phone now. I'm meeting Gautam in half an hour now. We may be able to come up with a plan after that,' he said.

Why was he dragging Gautam into this?

'Why Gautam?' I asked. 'What plan?' The very mention of his name still triggered different feelings in me.

'You'll understand when I explain the whole thing tomorrow,' he assured me.

'Okay.', I said reluctantly. Was he planning to get Gautam back to the hospital? May be, I thought. But why involve me?

Why was Jai dragging me in to it? I was very uncomfortable with the whole situation. Pushing away the guilt whenever I thought of Gautam was not easy and I was just about getting used to it.

The travel had exhausted me. I tried to relax for the rest of the evening but I couldn't focus. Even when I watched TV, my mind kept going back to Jai's words and Gautam's face unnervingly swam before my eyes.

Amit was in his study catching up on some work and I yawned, tired from the journey and decided to call it a night. I stretched out on the bed and shut my eyes when my phone rang.

I picked it up and frowned when I saw that it was Gautam's number. I actually spent a few seconds pondering on whether I should answer it or not.

Finally, I swiped the green icon and said 'Hello'.

'Payal!' Gautam's voice sounded weird for some reason.

'Yes?'

'Jai...Jai's been killed,' Gautam whispered. What? I sat up immediately.

'W...what? Gautam, is this some joke?' I whispered back in shock.

'No! It's not a joke! The police...the police think I killed him,' Gautam said, his voice shaking.

I couldn't speak for a moment. I had just spoken to Jai a while back. How was it even possible? Tears rushed to my eyes when I realized that Jai too, was gone like Archana.

'How? How did it happen?' I asked him, my voice breaking. All I wanted to do was sit down and cry and tears were already flowing down my face.

'Look, I can't talk now. I need to meet you,' Gautam said, urgency in his voice.

'But....'

'Please Payal. I'm in trouble. The police are after me!' he sounded desperate.

'Okay, okay! Tell me where you are now,' I said, wiping the tears from my face. I wanted to break down and cry but I also had to help Gautam. I composed myself and listened to him rattle off an address.

'I'll be waiting for you. Come soon!' he said.

'Okay. I'm leaving now,' I told him not willing to comprehend the reality of the situation.

'Wait!' he said just as I was about to end the call.

'What is it?' I asked.

'Payal, don't tell anyone about this,' he urged. I blinked in confusion.

'What do you mean?' I asked, as I grabbed my purse from the table.

'I mean don't tell anyone I called you. Even Amit. I don't want anyone to inform police, please' he said, sounding strange.

'Okay,' I muttered as I walked outside the house. I quickly hailed an auto and texted Amit, 'There's an emergency at the hospital. I'll talk to you once I am back.'

It slowly started sinking in. Jai was dead.

CHAPTER - 41

'Jai is dead.' The words repeated themselves in my head until I felt like my head would explode. I looked out of the window, trying to make sense of everything that was happening. First Archana and now Jai. How could it be possible? Who would kill Jai and why was Gautam being blamed?

I felt a nervous pit in my stomach as I wondered how things could have gone so colossally wrong for all of us. Just a few months ago we were all so happy and carefree.

We were anxious about how life would turn out but we had no idea that some of those lives would actually be cut short so brutally.

Tears streamed down my face and I couldn't stop. All kind of thoughts were pouring in my mind. Confusion was blurring everything in my head.

Suddenly, I remembered Nitin. Where was he? I picked up my phone and dialed Gautam's number. He answered the phone immediately.

'Where are you?'

'On my way,' I replied, shutting my eyes.

'Okay. I was going to call you now. I...' Gautam paused uncertainly. I didn't know what that pause meant but I opened my eyes.

'What happened?'

'Nothing...I'm going to dump my phone somewhere. I think the police might track me with it,' he said. I winced, thinking how much this had become like a spy movie. He gave me directions to a small restaurant near the Metro Station at Kashmiri Gate and I ended the call, and told the auto driver to change the route. It seemed as though the minutes couldn't move fast enough and to be fair, the distance of nearly 20 kilometers was not easy to traverse.

Amit called but I didn't answer. I couldn't talk to him. I needed to meet Gautam first. But almost instantly panic flooded my head. What if I couldn't meet Gautam? What if he too died suddenly or the police captured him? Call Amit. Call Amit now and tell him! How could Jai be dead? Call Amit right now. The confusion of my thoughts was driving me crazy. I continued sobbing. It was getting too much for me to handle.

I caught the auto driver looking at me in the rear view mirror anxiously. I took a few deep breaths and tried to calm down.

'Jaldi chalana bhaiya, koi dost guzargaya hai' ('Please make it fast, brother. A friend has passed away') I pleaded with the driver. He nodded and the speed picked up almost gradually.

As I tried to calm down, a part of me wondered if it was some kind of elaborate joke. Were Jai, Gautam and Nitin in on it? Would they laugh at me when I got down from the auto? Was Gautam orchestrating this whole thing just to meet me? The absurdity of the situation finally struck home and I realized that this was no joke.

The auto finally stopped before the dingy bar and restaurant and I got down immediately and paid the driver and went inside.

My eyes were seeking out Gautam frantically. What if I'd been too late? What if he'd already been captured by the police? That was when I saw him sitting at a table in the corner. I rushed towards him and he looked at me almost uncomprehendingly. I saw the glass before him and realized he'd been drinking.

'Gautam! Stop drinking!' I urged him fiercely. He kept the glass down and looked at me, his face crumpling before my eyes and I knew it was true. This was no prank.

'How?' I whispered as I sat down opposite him. He shrugged and I could see that he had been crying. Jai had been one of his closest friends. The thought that I'd never see Jai, speak to him again, fight with him as he made patronizing remarks, brought a fresh deluge of tears to my eyes as well.

'He's gone,' Gautam whispered, lifting the glass to his lips once more.

'What happened?' I asked, wiping the tears.

'He called me this evening. Said he had something important to talk to me,' Gautam forced the words out. I nodded. I knew that Jai was going to call Gautam.

'He asked me to meet outside the hospital quarters and I went there at the time he asked me to. But he didn't show up. I was getting annoyed and impatient and I called him. That was when I heard his phone ring nearby,' Gautam recalled, his eyes glazing over.

'Then?'

'I realized he had to be there near me so I called out to him and looked around,' Gautam said. 'I walked around calling out his name and then I found him near a tree.' I shut my eyes.

'He'd been stabbed and there was blood everywhere. I was shocked. I couldn't believe what I was seeing. I looked around for help but there was no one around so I picked him up and carried him to the hospital because he was still breathing,' Gautam explained.

My eyes went round. 'He was still alive?' Gautam nodded. 'Yes, he was alive. I went inside the hospital with him in my arms and he kept muttering something.'

'What?' I asked, leaning forward.

'At first I couldn't make out the words. It just seemed like a random string of letters and numbers,' Gautam said. His eyes were red. I didn't know if it was from the drinking or the crying.

'What letters? What numbers?' I forced myself to ask him.

He shook his head as he tried to recall. And then he looked down at his hands and then started crying. 'His blood was on my hands Payal. It was everywhere. I actually sensed him die,' he sobbed. We had seen so many deaths in the hospital. But this was different.

The picture his words created made me want to cry too. But I took a deep breath.

'Gautam. Tell me what happened?'

Gautam shook his head. 'He kept muttering those numbers and letters to me and I asked him what he was saying but then...his eyes rolled up in his head and he...he passed out. At hospital we tried but he never got back. He just died.'

Suddenly, I felt a huge amount of guilt swamping me. It wasn't the usual guilt I felt when I thought of Gautam. It was something else. Guilt that I hadn't been honest with Amit. I picked up my mobile phone and tapped out Amit's number.

'Who are you calling?' Gautam asked surprised.

'Amit,' I said, looking up.

'What? No. Payal, stop!' Gautam said, and I quickly pressed the home button to stop sending the call.

'What are you doing?' he asked me, looking around nervously.

'I don't know. I just...I just want to talk to Amit. I haven't told him anything. May be, he can help.' I said. Gautam took a deep breath.

'I know you're in love with him,' he said, his eyes looking pained. 'But please try and understand. If you involve anyone else in this, they're just....they're just going to call the police.'

I nodded, understanding his situation. And knowing Amit and how upright he was, I knew that he would want me to call the police too. 'You didn't tell me how the police suspected you,' I said. He winced.

'See, the doctors couldn't save him but they kept looking at me suspiciously. I was the one who got him to the hospital. I was covered in Jai's blood. And these were the people I'd known for so long and even worked with them! But they just kept staring at me and they asked me to wait. I overheard one of them talking to the police that I'd most likely stabbed Jai and I was crazy. I ran from there when I realized what was happening.'

'What do you think Jai was muttering?' I asked Gautam, trying to ignore the part of me that wanted to stop thinking, stop making my mind work. The part of me that wanted to grieve for another young friend, gone too soon from the world.

'I don't know. Random letters and numbers. Something that sounded like JMM0904,' Gautam squinted as he tried to recall them. What could it mean?

But before I could think of what it could be, the feeling of guilt flashed through me once more. I couldn't help but think of Amit who must be wondering why I hadn't answered his call. I should call him and tell him where I was.

'Payal!' the urgency in Gautam's voice made me realize that I was calling Amit once more.

'Are you calling Amit again?' he looked at me disbelievingly.

I put my phone on the table, feeling apologetic. 'I'm just feeling bad about the way I left home. I haven't yet told him about what happened with Jai,' I said. Gautam stared at me, his face blank, and I realized how much it probably hurt him to see how close I was to Amit.

But then I remembered Nitin. 'Gautam, where's Nitin?' I asked, hoping to change the topic. Gautam shook his head. 'I've no idea. I called him up but he didn't answer. I wish he was here too,' he said, shaking his head.

'I'll call him up and see if he answers,' I said and tapped out Nitin's number. It rang for a little while and then he answered. He didn't sound like himself.

'Have you heard? About Jai?' I asked him softly.

'Yes,' he replied. He obviously was crying too.

'Do you know that the police are searching for Gautam?'

'What? Why?' he sounded startled.

'They think...that...that he killed Jai,' I said. There was silence on the other side.

'Where are you now?' he asked me.

'I'm with Gautam,' I said, looking at him as though to confirm whether he wanted me to tell Nitin or not. Gautam looked conflicted for a moment and then nodded. I gave Nitin our address.

'Where is he?' Gautam asked me when I ended the call.

'He didn't say. He heard about Jai. Naturally, he didn't sound like himself, Gautam. He sounded strange. Subdued.'

'What am I going to do now?' Gautam asked, clutching his head. 'This is the worst day of my life. My best friend is dead and I'm being hunted by the police.'

I looked away because it hurt too much to think of Jai. 'Who could have killed him?' I whispered. Gautam shook his head.

Suddenly, the doors to the restaurant were flung open and a number of police men stormed inside. Some of the people in the restaurant shrank away. Gautam got up and tried to run but was caught by the police in front of my eyes.

He struggled a bit but then looked resigned as two of

them pinned him down and led him away. I watched him go, my hand clapped over my mouth in shock.

'Madam, you have to come with us,' one of the policemen said. I looked around in dismay. Was I being arrested too? But then no one had handcuffed me.

'Why?' I asked in a strangled voice.

'The ACP wants to talk to you,' he said.

'ACP?' I repeated and then allowed myself to be led outside.

To my surprise I saw Amit walking towards me, looking worried. I ran towards him.

'Are you okay?' he asked me.

'I'm fine. How did you get here?' I asked him. He pulled me into a tight hug and looked at the police man who had been walking with me.

'I was so worried about you. I heard just now about Jai's murder,' he said. I stepped back and looked at his anxious face.

'Why didn't you tell me?' he asked, framing my face in his hands. I couldn't speak.

'The ACP wants to question me,' I said. Amit frowned. He pulled out his phone from his pocket and dialed a number.

'I'll bring her to the police station tomorrow,' he said without any preliminaries.

'No, she doesn't know anything about Jai's murder. Gautam?' he turned to me and looked questioningly. I took a deep breath and shook my head slowly.

'Believe me, she is not involved in this. I'll bring her in tomorrow myself. She's tired and in shock,' Amit replied curtly. Finally he ended the call and turned to me.

'Let's go home and talk,' he said tightly and we walked away from there.

---❀❀❀---

CHAPTER - 42

On the way back, I shut my eyes because the reality of life had suddenly become harsh. My friends were either dead, or missing, or arrested. How had everything gone downhill so quickly? Amit reached out for my hand and I let him hold it but it felt like I was cold perpetually.

'Payal,' he said softly but I didn't turn to him. I knew he wanted some explanation from me but in my head all I could see was the police taking away Gautam. The look on his face as they arrested him would haunt me for a long time.

Who had tipped them off that he was there? Nitin? I couldn't believe it. Nitin was our friend. He wouldn't do that. Even if he had, how could the police have arrived at the restaurant within minutes of our conversation?

Amit's phone rang and he switched on the hands free to talk. I listened to the one sided conversation with a sense of increasing consternation.

'Aditya, I already told you I'll bring her tomorrow.'

Amit was on first name basis with ACP Aditya Kumar. I shouldn't have been surprised.

'No, I don't know him. He wasn't working with us.'

Gautam.

'Yes. Yes, he used to be Payal's friend.'

I turned in my seat.

'Oh no! How did that happen?'

I felt fear clutch my chest.

'Right now? But we just left that place!'

What had happened? Had something happened to Gautam also? My heart was racing now and I felt a little nauseous.

'Okay, we'll come now. If you insist. Bye.'

Amit ended the call and looked at me.

'What happened?' I asked, almost fearfully.

Amit sighed. 'The police were taking away Gautam when a car crashed into them from the side and in the melee, Gautam escaped. He apparently got into the car that crashed into them may be by threatening the driver, and now they can't track him.'

Amit could read the shock on my face.

'See Payal. I know Gautam used to be your friend. But he's clearly guilty or he wouldn't have escaped like this. If he was innocent, he should have stayed put and helped police to sort this out. This isn't the way,' Amit explained.

My mind was crowded with numerous thoughts. Gautam wasn't guilty! I knew it. But I kept quiet.

'Payal, if Gautam gets in touch with you again, don't go and meet him. Call the police, okay?' he urged me.

I didn't reply so Amit continued talking as he turned the car around. 'The police want to talk to you because you were last seen chatting with him in the restaurant,' Amit said, looking ahead as he drove.

'Are you listening to me Payal?' Amit asked when I was still quiet. I nodded.

'Sometimes....sometimes you don't know what people really are like,' he spoke after a while. 'It takes all kinds of situations to bring out the worst in them. Now...now you've seen what Gautam is capable of. I just...I just want you to be more careful,' he said.

His concern was touching but it was misplaced. I knew Gautam was not responsible for Jai's death. We went back a long way and I knew Gautam better than anyone else. He was definitely innocent.

Amit stopped the car outside the police station where we'd been asked to come. 'Are you sure you can do this?' he asked.

'I have no choice,' I murmured as I got out of the car, thinking that I wasn't even mourning Jai's death! So much was happening that there wasn't even the time.

Inside, we were led to ACP Aditya Kumar's office and Amit and I sat down before him.

'Would you mind if I speak to her alone?' the ACP asked. Amit looked surprised and he pushed his chair back hesitantly and left after a reassuring squeeze to my shoulder.

The ACP looked at me thoughtfully after Amit left and he nodded to one of the constables who shut the door. 'How do you know Gautam?' he asked me.

'We studied together. We were good friends,' I said, feeling uncomfortable about where this was going.

'Were friends? I see. So why did you meet him today?' he asked me.

'He called up and asked to meet me,' I replied.

'Did he say why?'

'Yes. He said that Jai was murdered and he wanted to talk to me.'

'Did he say that he was being considered a suspect?' the ACP leaned forward and asked. I nodded.

'And still you went to meet him? Why?' he asked. I shrugged.

'I didn't....I don't believe he could have killed Jai. After all, they were very close friends,' I pointed out.

'It's not a stretch of imagination though. These things have happened before,' the ACP said.

'But Gautam would never do anything to hurt Jai! Look, he's the one who took Jai to the hospital' I protested.

'So? Maybe they had an argument and Gautam decided to end it with a knife, and realized what he had done. May be then he tried to save him by taking him to the hospital' the ACP suggested. 'If Gautam was innocent, he wouldn't have run from the hospital or escaped from the police van.'

'He...he's being framed for this murder,' I said suddenly. That had to be it. Someone else had murdered Jai and was framing Gautam.

The ACP snorted. Naturally he was skeptical. 'What did Gautam tell you?' he asked me.

'Nothing. We had barely talked when you came and took him away,' I said. I didn't want to tell him what Gautam had said about Jai muttering those letters and numbers. Instead I wanted to know something else.

'How did you know he was there in that restaurant?' I asked him instead. He looked taken aback.

'Why do you want to know that?' he asked me.

'I just want to know if someone tipped you off about his whereabouts,' I said wondering if it was Nitin who had called the police. I found it hard to believe that Nitin would do something so callous. But the ACP shook his head and looked lost in thought. He spoke slowly, as though to himself.

'Actually, I can't share that information, It's confidential.' he said slowly and thoughtfully.

Huh? 'What do you mean?' I asked him.

'It's not important. I knew where he was sitting,' the ACP said. Then, shaking his head as though to clear it, he spoke again.

'Look, I need to know what he told you,' he insisted.

I shook my head. 'We were just talking about Jai and how unbelievable it was that he was dead. Then you guys came and carted him off.'

'Are you telling the truth?' he asked me fiercely. I looked away, a little afraid of him, as though he'd know that I was somehow hiding something from him.

'Yes, of course,' I replied after taking a deep breath.

'But, you were one of the last two people Jai had called before his death. We have noticed a lot of text messages between you two. What was that all about?' he cornered me, glaring at me intensely.

I recovered my composure quickly. 'Yes, that is why I was so shocked when I heard about his death. I can give you all the text messages between us. We were working together, and we were friends. Obviously we kept in touch,' I defended myself.

'But you were friends with Gautam too. Did you talk to him often as well?'

My face turned red. 'No, Gautam was suspended from the college. Since then, we haven't kept in touch.'

'Was he suspended because of Jai?' he asked, narrowing his eyes.

'No! He messed up an operation and hence, he was removed,' I replied. I didn't want to bring up Gautam's drinking binge because that would definitely affect a lot of things and would create another mess in Gautam's life.

'If he contacts you again, please let us know,' he said leaning forward, motioning with his head that the interview was over.

I got up, relieved.

This day seemed like it would never end. In the car, once more I was silent. Then something occurred to me. 'You never told me how you knew I was at that restaurant,' I asked Amit.

He turned to me, smiled shortly and said, 'I spoke to the ACP and found out.'

CHAPTER - 43

One of the things that remained with me was Jai's cryptic dying words. What on earth was JMM0904? It sounded a bit like the registration number for a vehicle but truthfully speaking, it could have been anything.

If Amit noticed my expression, he probably felt it was due to the strain I'd been through that day. But even as I went to sleep, my mind was humming with possibilities. It was probably just a way for my mind to work on something instead of thinking about Jai's death.

The newspapers the following day covered the news of a doctor's murder in the hospital premises and the murderer's daring day time escape from the police. I devoured all the articles in the vague hope that there might be some morsel of information about Gautam. Instead I came to one realization when I read the articles.

JMM stood for Jai M Mehta. It was obvious. May be, he was born on 9th April. But, why would he say that when he was about to die? Why didn't he tell the killer's name? May be, he was attacked from the back. OK, that sounds logical.

I looked up at Amit, wondering if I should reveal all this information to him. But he was engrossed in his laptop and I decided not to disturb him.

My talented friends had their lives cut short tragically. I had to find out why.

Amit got a phone call then and he looked at his phone in irritation. 'Bloody ACP,' he muttered as he answered the call and got up.

I looked up surprised. Why was the ACP calling him?

I heard Amit speaking as he walked away in the direction of his study. I think I heard Archana's name mentioned and then I remembered that Amit had told the Air Force Chief that he would have Mohan's death investigated by the ACP. It was probably about that.

I squirmed uncomfortably. Archana was dead and there was no point in ruining her name. Back then Amit had said that he had wanted to protect Nitin but where was he? Was he missing too? I wondered what the ACP would find once he finished his investigations.

I stared into the distance, wondering where Gautam could have disappeared. Since I couldn't contact him I had to wait till he would contact me and who knew when that would be? Amit came back and sat down, looking worried.

'What happened?' I asked him. He shook his head.

'Nothing,' he said. I looked at him closely. There were worry lines around his eyes. Amit was no doubt getting caught up with everything.

'I can't believe our holiday ended like this,' I said, feeling bad for him, before realization hit me that I was talking about a ruined holiday when my friends were dead. I covered my face with my hands in despair.

What was wrong with me?

Amit put his arm around me and leaned in close. Having him close made me feel a little better and I looked up at him. 'I know. I had wanted you to be free of all this tension and it just seems to be adding up.'

'It will be all right,' I told him, putting my head on his shoulder.

'You think so?' he asked, stroking my cheek gently. I nodded.

'What did the ACP say?' I asked and immediately felt him tense up at my side.

'He says he wants to talk about Mohan's crash and Archana's reports.'

'Oh, so this wasn't about Jai and Gautam?' I asked.

'No, he just mentioned that in passing. Apparently they have set up a manhunt for him and they should be able to capture him soon.' My heart sank. I didn't want Gautam to be 'captured'.

'How are they so sure that he killed Jai?' I asked. Amit shook his head and I straightened up.

'You still want to know? It's the way police do their work. They consider the circumstantial evidence and hold a few people as suspects. They take them into custody and investigate. People who are guilty always try and run away from this. Only a guilty person would run away like Gautam did,' he reasoned. Or someone who was being framed, I thought.

When I didn't say anything, Amit held my face in his hands. 'I know he was your best friend,' he said. 'But obviously things haven't been going well for him since he got kicked out of the hospital.'

I nodded although internally I didn't agree with what he was saying. No matter how bad things went, Gautam was not the type to kill his close friend for anything.

'I don't want you to worry about this. We have a lot to figure out at the lab as it is,' he said.

As he walked away, I had the feeling that somehow, this was not the end of my troubles. I had taken a leave of absence from the hospital for a few days, at Amit's insistence. He said he needed me at the lab to replace Jai, Archana and now, maybe even Nitin. The monitoring of patients who had the Microbot in them had been moved to a large scale set up because there were too many people for us to track now. Even so, Amit told me that he needed people in the lab to actively monitor some important patients and for that, he needed my help.

Also, I wasn't too keen on going back to the hospital any time soon because I didn't want to talk to anyone about what had happened to my friends. I couldn't pretend to be normal when nothing was normal in my life any more.

I got ready and waited for Amit so we could go to the lab together. He was going to drop me off there and head out to meet some people. I didn't mind any more. I had just accepted his being busy as a part of our life now.

As much as I dreaded going back to the hospital, the lab still beckoned me. The sense of purpose there was strangely stronger. I don't know why. At the lab, I felt a little heartbroken when I saw Jai and Archana's workstation. Nitin's place was also empty.

Where are you Nitin, I wondered.

I sat down at my workstation because Amit had emailed me a list of people and their resumes. But my mind was once again drawn to JMM0904. I went back to my email and suddenly, I felt a light go on inside. What if...what if it was the password to Jai's email?

Could it be possible? I looked around at the rest of the team who were immersed in their own work. Amit had said he would be back soon and we could filter the people who would be joining the Microbot team.

I signed out of my email and then, looking around once more, I entered Jai's email address and the letters and numbers. But when I entered them, I got a message that it was the wrong email-password combination.

Disappointed, I logged back in to my email and decided to get back to work. Well, it had been worth a try, I thought. I looked through resumes for some time, my eyes going back again and again to Archana's seat. We had shared so much more than giggles and boy talk. She'd become my friend and close confidante, considering that she had been the one who had identified Amit's growing feelings for me and vice versa. Wishing that she'd left a note at least, I shook my head. It was so difficult to move on when there were still so many unanswered questions.

---❁❁❁---

CHAPTER - 44

Amit had not returned and I had developed a raging headache so I walked upstairs to his room and decided to sleep it off. Even so, I could barely sleep because of all the emotions I had suppressed inside. Images flashed before my eyes - Archana, Archana and Mohan, Jai, Nitin and even Gautam.

I sat up after half an hour, disoriented and disturbed. I rubbed my temples lightly wishing there was a way to clean the slate completely. A new beginning. But even as I wished for it, I knew that I needed my friends and if I couldn't have them, there was no point to a new beginning.

I checked my phone and saw that Amit had left a message - 'ACP called. Stuck in a meeting with him. Will come and pick you up soon.'

I had hoped that Gautam would call me but that hadn't happened. That was when the thought occurred to me. What if Jai's last words were his password and I'd just entered it incorrectly? Almost a little delirious with the thought, I ran back downstairs ignoring the throbbing in my head and blinking furiously.

At the workstation, I entered Jai's email address and then JMM0904 as the password. It didn't work. Refusing to get fazed, I tried different combinations of upper case and lower case letters. The number of tries allowed were running out. Just then finally, one combination worked. I felt my eyes grow round as I realized that Jai's email was opening.

I glanced quickly at his email, wondering if there would be anything of use here and my eyes stopped at the very first item on the list. It was an email from Archana!

Holding my breath, I clicked it open. I checked the date and time stamp. It was on the day she had died and the time was approximately just before she had committed suicide!

My heart pounded as my eyes moved over the lines she had typed out in probably the last half hour of her life.

Dear Jai,

I'm telling this to you because you're the one who has desperately been looking for answers. Actually I can't bear to talk about this at all but I want to put my feelings down in words.

The day Mohan crashed his helicopter, I was monitoring his Microbot readings. To start, I don't remember how I ended up there at the lab that day. All the readings indicated that he was in some sort of big trouble and I knew it. I wanted to raise an alarm and inform someone else so we could help him but...but it felt like I was frozen. I don't know what happened but I couldn't even move.

It felt like my mind was divided.

One part of me wanted to stop him anyhow, to call up someone for help and tell them what was happening. And yet another part of me kept telling me to not do anything. Somehow, this part overcame everything else. I found myself staring at the screen and it was like I was watching him die. And there was nothing I could do about it.

Even as I'm writing this to you, all I know is that I want relief from these thoughts, this confusion in my head. There's so much noise in my head Jai! I want peace. The idea of death is now so tempting. I want to embrace it and never look back. My mind keeps telling me that I should just end it all. How? Is death the answer? Every two minutes, my mind is prompting me that death will relieve my difficulties. I know that it seems like an escape route but I can't fight it any longer.

I'm sorry if my actions or inaction has caused trouble for everyone.

Goodbye.

I read the email over and over again. I knew that Jai too had read it because it had shown up as a 'read email' on the list. What had he deduced from this email? I had thought that reading Archana's suicide note would give me closure but instead it made me imagine how tormented she must have been to take this huge step and I felt like someone had thrown a bucket of ice water over me. Why didn't she tell me about it? Why didn't Jai try and save her? I realized that he may not have read it until after she died. Being doctors, checking emails compulsively was not something we did. It was more of a pastime which we didn't even indulge in that often.

I scanned Jai's inbox for other clues but there was nothing. That was when I spotted an unopened email in his Drafts folder. A memory of Jai's call to me when I was in Kerala surfaced briefly. He had said that he'd been writing an email to me but since I called up he wouldn't be sending it.

Was there a chance that the email he had been composing was still in the Drafts folder?

I clicked it. Jackpot!

My eyes widened when I realized that he had been planning to send it to Gautam and me. I checked the last saved date and it corresponded with the date I'd been in Kerala. I scrolled down quickly and read the email.

Payal/Gautam,

I checked my email the morning after Archana died and I saw that she had sent me an email right before she took those pills that killed her. Her email has raised some disturbing questions in my mind. She claimed that she was there in the lab when Mohan's Microbot readings started coming in and she knew that something was seriously wrong with him. And yet she couldn't do a thing about it. She said that her mind was divided and although she wanted to help Mohan, she just stayed put. She said that even though she didn't want to die, she was going ahead because it was what her mind was telling her to do.

Unfortunately, not being a tech savvy, always online guy, I missed reading it when she sent it. If I had, we might have been able to save her.

After receiving this email from Archana, I decided to investigate properly. I looked up into her Microbot reports on the day of Mohan's crash, to see if I could figure out what she meant when she said her mind was 'divided'.

What I saw was very alarming. Based on the reports, I could tell that she was under a tremendous amount of pressure that day and the brain activity on her reports showed a lot of fluctuations.

Since I knew that Nitin too had been at the lab that day, I checked his reports as well. His Microbot reports also showed a similar level of activity. And there is also the question of how Nitin knew the admin password. How did it just occur to him?

But what really shocked me was that Mohan's reports and Archana's reports are almost of a similar nature and they seem to have started at almost the same time!

There seems to be some sort of pattern here. With all this information in hand, I approached the software engineers who worked on different versions of the Microbot. After picking their brains for days, they finally relented and told me that the communication with the Microbot and the server is not one way but TWO WAY. That means that communication can be sent to the person who has the Microbot.

I asked them what sort of communication can be passed on but they said they were not aware of it. They said that they had developed a messaging protocol but they did not know the details as someone else under Dr.Sundaram had developed it further.

I think there's something very fishy going on here and I need your help Payal. I'm including Gautam in this email because he can be trusted and we need people whom we can trust. Take a look at the attachments in this email. They are copies of the Microbot reports of Archana, Nitin and Mohan

I looked up as the email ended abruptly and Amit was standing in front of me, smiling.

'Shall we leave?' he asked.

My heart was thumping loudly. When had Amit arrived at the lab? I'd been so absorbed in reading Jai's email I had no idea about anything.

I smiled automatically at Amit, nodded and then quickly hit the send button on the email and logged out. My hands were shaking.

What were the implications of Jai's email? How would I ever know?

---❁❁❁---

CHAPTER - 45

Amit's work continued and that also included his social visits and parties. For two days I waited for Gautam to call me. I had hoped he would check his email, read it and then contact me so we could take the next step. But nothing of the sort happened. The email was now in my inbox and I'd read it so many times, trying to make sense of Jai's words. What did two way messaging mean? If the Microbot was sending out messages about our body, was it also receiving them? But why? To what end? And more importantly, from whom? Did Amit know about it?

I knew that the Microbot was Amit's baby and there was no way I could bring this up with him. He'd be devastated if he found out that someone had tinkered with the Microbot and used it for purposes other than what had been intended. On the other hand, I was also worried that maybe Amit knew about it and wasn't doing anything.

That evening, Amit asked me to get ready for one of those routine parties. I had begun to hate them, because I wasn't sure if I was there as merely eye-candy. But at least this time, it was one of the high society parties just a few houses away from ours. 'At least I can walk back home, if I feel bored,' I thought. Reluctantly, I got ready.

A lot of important folks whom Amit had met because of his work with the Microbot had been invited to this same party as well. I had a smile pasted on my face and after sometime my face started aching. But Amit seemed happy, basking in the glory of his success amongst all these important people and I kept up the façade for his sake.

That is when we bumped in to the ACP. We both were surprised and taken aback to see him.

'Amit, I need to talk to you,' he said urgently. Amit looked uncomfortable and he smiled tightly.

'Look, let's talk shop later. This is a party after all,' he said, throwing his arm around my shoulder and walking away from there.

'But I never seem to be able to catch hold of you,' the ACP called out. Amit made a face but only I could see it. He turned around to face the ACP.

'I'll come and meet you tomorrow in your office. I promise,' Amit smiled and he was almost immediately pulled into another group of people. I had managed to step away from him and now I realized that the group of people had separated us as well. Amit waved to me and nodded, saying he would catch up with me soon and he walked away. The ACP shook his head and walked up to me and I looked down at the carpet, remembering the last conversation we had, over Jai's death. It had not gone well and I still felt resentful towards him for pursuing Gautam although he was just following the leads he had. The ACP seemed to have forgotten about that though.

He held a drink in his hand and sipped it, his eyes still focused on the door through which Amit had left.

'He's been that way all these days. Keeps making appointments and then calling them off,' he said.

I kept quiet because I didn't know what to say. 'Can we at least talk?' he asked, looking worried.

What? Why? I didn't want to talk with him. I looked around the room and saw that Amit had returned but was busy talking with someone else. He glanced at the two of us for the merest of seconds. I quickly tried to communicate with him through my expression, my irritation with him at having been left alone with the ACP. Amit had already turned away.

He clearly didn't care.

The ACP had already launched into a monologue. 'See, that day after you asked me how I knew about Gautam's location, I realized I had no idea how I knew. It made me think. How was it possible to exactly pin point the location where Gautam was hiding, without any tip off?'

I turned to him, interested although there was the familiar nervousness churning in the pit of my stomach.

'So, what are you trying to say?' I asked.

'I'm saying that the answer presented itself to me on its own. And I want to know how,' he said.

His words echoed with something that I had read in Jai's email about Nitin. How had Nitin known the admin password? How was it possible for either of them to gain knowledge about something that they had no idea about earlier?

'Also, the case that the Air Force has entrusted me with, the crash of their helicopter in which they lost a pilot and a minister; there are some things that are not adding up,' he said. I frowned.

'What do you mean?' I asked.

'There was no mechanical fault with the helicopter,' he said. The Air Force had already told us that.

'And even though the pilot was supposed to be in excellent health, the correct Microbot reports that we got from the lab showed that he was under a huge amount of mental strain. So why let him fly? Why let him crash the helicopter?'

I chose to remain silent. I couldn't possibly tell him what Archana had written in her email.

'I had actually been quite complacent when I started the investigation and I almost considered shutting down the case and moving on. But after you questioned me about how I knew Gautam's whereabouts, I began to wonder. So I started talking to people at your lab and I've spoken to Amit but not as much as I need to.'

'And?' I asked, unable to stop myself.

'I still need answers from Amit,' he shrugged. 'And as for Jai's murder, I keep thinking that it's Gautam who killed him. Over the years I have learnt not to rely on just my instinct but evidence. In this case, I am trying very hard to override my own instinct and get to the truth,' he said. 'It's giving me splitting headaches but I don't care. I will find the truth!' he said vehemently, looking distressed. He sighed deeply.

'There is so much pressure from Air Force to finish the investigation. This murder of your friend on top of that is just adding to it. Sometimes, Payal, it feels like my thoughts are not my own. Not to mention all the stress in my personal life! I want to finish this investigation and go for a vacation with my family. I'm really messing up things in my family at the moment. All I know is that for the past few days I've wanted to shut down this investigation and move on. It seems like the best thing to do but then I also know it's not the right thing. That's why I haven't been able to let go of the investigation. With my mind divided like this, I just can't think straight.'

Mind divided? I remembered reading those words in Archana's email as well. For some reason, that phrase had got stuck in my head. But how could two different people use the same words to describe what they were feeling?

'Maybe we can go outside and talk,' I suggested. Maybe I should tell him about Jai's email and all the other things that were just piling up in my mind. The ACP nodded and we were about to step out when the lady hosting the party bumped into us and smiled. It was one of the many new friends Amit had made, someone whose name too, I didn't know. Some party this was, I thought, annoyed. To my surprise, she touched my forearm lightly, indicating that she wanted to talk to me.

I smiled automatically, nodded and told the ACP to carry on and I'd join him soon. The lady whispered to me that she had heard Amit and I were engaged. 'Aren't you two throwing an engagement party?' she asked. I smiled automatically.

'Yes, soon!' I assured her and tried to leave when someone else started talking to us congratulating me for Amit's success. I nodded politely and couldn't leave for the next five minutes. I realized I wanted to talk to the ACP about all the things in my mind right now. If he was beginning to think that Gautam might be innocent, I needed to help him out.

The hostess however announced that dinner was being served and there was a rush of people towards the dining room. I looked around for Amit, wondering if I would spot him somewhere when I heard a loud scream outside.

Most people rushed towards the source of sound, and I followed them as well. I was shocked on seeing the ACP standing near the entrance, holding a revolver in his hands. People around him stumbled and bumped into each other to get away from him.

I couldn't believe my eyes. What was he doing? I immediately thought of Amit. Where was he? Was he okay? But my eyes were immersed on the scene before me.

I stepped forward and the ACP shook his head. He spoke softly but I could still hear him clearly enough.

'I'm sorry,' he said and placed the revolver calmly at his temple and pulled the trigger.

---❀❀❀---

CHAPTER - 46

What happened after that was like a blur. The blood spatter, the screams, ACP crumbling into a heap, the running of feet - I just sat down on the floor where I'd been standing, unable to believe what I'd just seen. Amit came rushing out towards me, and he stopped short when he saw what had happened.

I felt numb. I had just seen someone take their own life. And this wasn't someone who had seemed remotely suicidal. What on earth had just happened? He had been perfectly fine just minutes ago. He did mention about pressures at home but in the same breath he also spoke about his plans for vacations and other things. What made him take such a horrific step so soon?

Police and medical services had arrived and one by one, eye witnesses recorded their statements. People left using the back door because the front door was blocked by the ACP's body and all the blood. Amit and I were too shocked to talk to anyone or even each other. What on earth had made him take such a step? Why did he do this in a party, of all places? Why were people just dying like this?

I couldn't understand the fact that he'd been perfectly fine just minutes before. In fact, I was going to go and join him outside. What had happened between then and now? The police came and took away his body.

Amit was asked to go to the police station along with the hosts to complete the reporting formalities and eventually, I slowly walked back to our home. I was feeling numb and cold.

Goosebumps had broken out on my skin. I reached home and mechanically washed up. I sat in the living room, trying to process what had happened but at the same time, I felt claustrophobic. The metallic smell of blood was still in my senses and I wanted fresh air and someone to talk. At the same time, I felt exhausted and I wanted to curl up and sleep and not get up for a long, long time.

I brushed away the rapidly falling tears and walked out determinedly when I stopped at Amit's study. The door was open and Amit, usually never let the door remain open. I wanted to step out into the fresh air but for some reason, my feet were frozen on the spot. I peeped into Amit's study, remembering the time I'd found my photos in his desk. I'd never managed to ask him about that. Putting away all the events of the previous hour at the back of my mind, I stepped inside the study and shut the door.

Inside, it was cool and dark. I sat down on a chair and looked around, wishing for anything that would take my mind away from recent events. How long would it take for Amit with the police? I didn't want to stay here alone any longer. I got up and walked around the study in circles, this place where Amit spent so much of his time. What did he do here? I wondered. The desk was empty but dusty. Like no one had used it for a while. That made me frown and I walked up to it. There was no other notable furniture in here except the desk. Amit's laptop also wasn't here. Puzzled, I rummaged in the drawers, wondering if I would find those photos. They were still there under a couple of notebooks.

I curled my fingers around them and pulled them out, feeling the same tug of unease when I'd found them earlier. What had Amit meant by taking these photos when I was still officially Gautam's girlfriend? It seemed too trivial a thing to ask now, in the face of all that was happening, and I knew I would have to let it go once again.

Sighing I put the photos back where I'd picked them up

from. A gust of wind blew inside from the open window and I shivered. I walked up to the window and pulled it to shut it and that's when I spotted something I hadn't seen before.

There was another door on the side of the room.

It was almost concealed by the book shelves surrounding it. Puzzled, I let the window be and walked up towards the door and pushed it because it wasn't fully closed. How come I had never seen this when I came here before?

I stepped inside and my eyes widened when I saw that there was a full-fledged lab, a replica of our regular lab but on a much smaller scale!

I walked inside in amazement, looking around at the three computer stations and the massive screen that occupied a huge part of the wall on one side. Why hadn't Amit told me about this? What was he doing in here that he didn't want anyone else to see?

I couldn't believe this. I looked around at the computers and wondered what I would find there. But first I walked over to the lit up screen on the wall and saw that it was populated by a huge number of constantly moving dots. It was like the Microbot monitoring screen that we had back at the lab but this one was different. There were names of people above the dots and on one side of the screen there was a list of names.

I moved closer and tapped one of the dots and a small information header opened up above it. Surprised, I read what was on it. It had a few personal details of the person who represented the dot. Eyes widening, I tapped on it again, and the health information that was processed by the Microbot came up. Out of curiosity, I tapped it a third time and the information was replaced by coordinates that provided the GPS location of the person.

I stepped back in shock. Did this mean that anyone who

had a Microbot in them could be tracked by GPS? Why had Amit hidden this from all of us? I stumbled back further as thoughts raced through my head.

If Amit had access to the GPS location of the Microbot-enabled person, then this changed everything. He would know where everyone was. Was this how he'd known where to find me when I had met Gautam after Jai's murder? He simply had to look up my address here. My eyes widened when I remembered how Amit had known that I was at the mall when I had met Gautam. I'd always wondered about it, but I couldn't figure out and I'd forgotten about it eventually. But now it made sense.

What was Amit using this information for and why was it a secret? I was positive no one else knew about it or someone would have mentioned it at some point of time. Like that messaging protocol that Jai had mentioned in his email. Some of the developers had told him that the Microbot could be used to send messages to the person with the Microbot but they hadn't given him details because they didn't know themselves. And yet, that too was a secret because none of us had known about it. Why had Amit hidden two such important details about the Microbot?

I was very confused. I sat down for a moment, trying to process my thoughts. Both these details were important. The Microbot was GPS enabled and it could be used to send messages.

Hesitantly I looked at the massive screen to see where Amit's dot was. I tapped on it thrice to see his location. He was on his way back.

---✿✿✿---

CHAPTER - 47

Who could possibly help me now? All my friends were gone. But then I realized that it wasn't true entirely.

I scrambled back to the screen and looked up the dot that represented Nitin. I was nervous and worried and I couldn't find it quickly enough. Then, shaking my head, I went to the left hand side of the screen with the list of names and saw Nitin's name finally. I tapped on it and the information bar on the right hand side opened up. I perused it quickly, hoping to find something that would help me. Since I was seeing Nitin's current medical condition which was all haywire at the moment, I saw that there was a tab on top which said 'Location'.

I tapped that and the location history for Nitin for last 3 days along with his current location populated the screen.

Was Gautam with Nitin? The only way to confirm that would be to check where he was yesterday around the time Gautam was being taken away by the police. Nitin had been on his way to meet us anyway.

I was right. The location history pinned Nitin to a spot not too far from where I had met Gautam.

I stepped back and tapped on Amit's dot and saw that he was now twenty minutes away from home. Taking a deep breath, I tapped Nitin's name on the left hand side once more and the information side bar disappeared. The screen looked just like it had been when I came in.

Shakily, I walked out from the hidden lab that I had stumbled upon purely by chance. I went to my room and picked up my phone and taking a deep breath I dialed Nitin's number.

'Please let Gautam be with him,' I prayed, closing my eyes.

Finally, the phone stopped ringing as someone answered it. It was Nitin.

'Hi Payal,' Nitin said, his voice so low I could barely hear him speak.

'Nitin, is Gautam with you?' I asked him, hoping against hope that I was right.

'Yes,' he replied, his voice sounding lifeless and dull. I knew he'd been disturbed by Archana's suicide but now he sounded like someone else altogether.

'Can I talk to him?' I asked, glad that my hunch had been proved right.

'Okay,' he said and then I sensed some shuffling as Gautam took the phone.

'Payal! How did you know I'd be with Nitin?' Gautam asked in a whisper.

'I…I...first I want to know why Nitin helped you escape from the police,' I said quickly, glancing at the clock. I had to tell Gautam whatever I had learnt before Amit came back home.

'Payal, we're in deep trouble,' he said.

'I know...'

'No, no you don't. Nitin...Nitin is not himself. He's a mess,' Gautam said.

'But why?'

'He...he says he killed Jai,' Gautam whispered.

'What?' I was shocked. I couldn't believe it. 'But Jai was his friend, his room-mate! Why would he kill Jai?'

'He says he doesn't know why. All he knows is that the moment the thought came to his head that he had to kill Jai, he couldn't stop himself. He hates himself now for what he did and...he's become very unstable now Payal. I'm scared to leave him alone for too long,' Gautam said.

Oh god. What was happening? Sweet natured, lovable, goofy Nitin had killed Jai!

Or had he been made to do it? My eyes widened in shock when it all finally clicked together. I took a deep breath. Suddenly I remembered that day at the seminar where I met Amit for the first time. Amit had used my mind's signal to make Nitin's hands move!

The enormity of the situation was just sinking in. If my theory was correct, Amit was indeed a mastermind. He had the means to find out a person's location, their health situation and he could send messages to their brain, whether it was information in the form of passwords or instructions to do something they would never do ordinarily.

If I was right, then...my head reeled with the possibilities. Just thinking about the things that Amit could have possibly done, made me stagger. I took a deep breath to tell Gautam about my theory but he was speaking to me in a rush of words.

'I don't know what to do now. We're both in trouble. The police are looking for me and I can't leave Nitin and go anywhere because I'm scared he might do something to himself,' Gautam spoke in a rush.

'Gautam, you have to tell Nitin that it wasn't his fault,' I said slowly.

'What?'

'Yes. I think that he didn't kill Jai of his own volition. I think he was 'made' to do it. By the Microbot,' I whispered.

'But...'

'Gautam, don't interrupt. Just listen. I don't have much time,' I said. 'Remember those letters that Jai was repeating right before he died? It was the password to his email. I opened his email and saw that he had got an email from Archana before she committed suicide. The urge to kill herself was too strong she said. Then I saw that Jai had an email in his drafts folder and it was addressed to the two of us. Jai had found out that Archana's and Nitin's Microbot reports showed a lot of unusual brain activity at the same time that Mohan's crash happened. He had even attached the reports in the email. I forwarded it to you.'

'Wait, wait, and slow down a bit. Go back a little. What are you talking about?' Gautam sounded thoroughly muddled. I bit back an impatient retort.

'Gautam, I think Amit can control the Microbot-enabled people,' I said finally. The words hung in the air in silence.

'What?' Gautam seemed to have finally found his voice.

'Yes, Gautam,' I said, calmly, even though I wasn't feeling that way inside.

'But...how do you know all this?'

'I just discovered a hidden lab inside his study. He's got a monitoring screen that also shows the GPS positioning of the person who has the Microbot,' I said.

'And that means...?'

'That means I can't leave him and go anywhere right now or he will get suspicious. I have to behave as though everything is all right. And anyway he would know how to track me wherever I go,' I said bitterly.

'But Payal, shouldn't we take this matter to the police?' Gautam asked.

'Well, most of the senior police force is under his control now,' I said, remembering the ACP who was also dead now, for no apparent reason. Was that one more Microbot fatality?

But…how? Why? Was the ACP getting too close to the truth? Had Amit induced him to kill himself today? I recalled that I couldn't spot Amit around the time the ACP shot himself.

'What if we contacted the Government? Or some ministers?' Gautam asked. My eyes widened when I realized the extent to which Amit had spread his net.

'OH MY GOD! That's just it, Gautam. They all have the Microbot in them! Which means that they are all puppets in Amit's hands,' I said.

'You mean to say that there's no one we can turn to?' he asked, sounding desperate.

'No, I don't think we can.' I said slowly, realizing this was even bigger that I could imagine!

It wasn't just about us four. I realized that it was about the whole nation!

'Virtually, the whole nation is in his hands; he did a coup without an army!' I muttered slowly. I wasn't sure if Gautam even heard me. Anyway it didn't matter. The words were cementing the reality in my head.

My mind reeled when I thought about how Amit now had control over every single person who had the Microbot in them. That included most powerful men in the country, including the Prime Minister! I sat down on the bed with a thump.

'Meet me tomorrow at the hospital at 10 am,' I told Gautam quickly.

'The hospital? But...'

'Listen to me. It will be fine. Come behind the cafeteria or something. Make sure that no one sees you. Usually by eleven, hardly anyone is there.'

'But...'

'I'll try and figure out something and maybe...maybe we can find someone who will help us. At the same time, you have to make sure that Nitin doesn't do anything stupid, like suicide,' I said. I heard the front gate open.

'How?' he asked, sounding baffled.

'I don't know! Tie him up if that's what it takes,' I told him. I had to end the call now.

'Payal. It's our last chance to fix this,' he said.

'No, it's our only chance,' I said, ending the call just as I heard Amit open the main door and walk inside.

That night was one of the most difficult nights of my life! If 'Sleeping with the enemy' were to be remade, they should use my story!

My hands were trembling when Amit came in. I couldn't control it. I was worried that he would notice it and become suspicious. He frowned when he saw my trembling hands and he walked towards me slowly. I was on the verge of a breakdown myself, wondering if I should run or shout or just cry.

But there was no suspicion in his eyes. There was compassion and sympathy as he drew me close to him and patted the back of my head. 'Ssshhh… it's okay, Payal! I know it was shocking for you. It was for all of us,' he said and held me tightly.

'All of us? Are you sure?' I thought. But I had to stay calm.

He had assumed that I was in this state because of the death of the ACP. In fact, I had almost forgotten about him because of all these discoveries I had made. Amit held the future of our nation in his hands and he looked absolutely nonchalant as he patted my back and consoled me, over the death of an innocent man.

A death he'd most likely caused himself.

---✿✿✿---

CHAPTER - 48

'How did you manage to come away without Amit suspecting?' Gautam asked as I sat down beside him. If things weren't messed up, I might have laughed at how he looked. He'd tried to disguise himself by wearing a cap on his head whose visor was pushed down to hide his face. He'd also done something to his face, making it look brown. Make up! I shook my head as I remembered the crazy guy he always was.

'I told him that I was getting nervous sitting at home and I wanted to be in a different environment. Hospital was the best place, he said. I made it sound like his suggestion!' I said with a grim smile.

We were sitting inside one of the empty consultation rooms and I had quickly brought Gautam up to speed on what I'd learnt. The expression on his face spoke volumes.

'He made them do all this?' Gautam repeated when I fell silent.

'That's what I think. It's the only explanation that makes sense,' I said.

Gautam contemplated this in silence and then something seemed to have occurred to him. He turned to me, his eyes darkening. 'Do you realize that he could have made you fall in love with him too?' he asked.

I blinked. What?

'I was there for only his first lecture but I remember it clearly. He asked us what love is and then he explained that love could be broken down into biological factors. What if he tried to do the same thing with you? Remember the little magic trick he played on us, transferring your thoughts to Nitin and making his arm move?' he said, looking at me intensely.

Gautam's words were like a sucker punch. Could it be true? I couldn't think clearly. I shut my eyes and my mind raced back to the moment I started having feelings for Amit. It seemed like a blur now but I knew that things had intensified only after I had injected the Microbot into my body. Gautam could be right, I thought with an increasing sense of shock.

'Payal! Are you okay?' Gautam asked when I didn't say anything. My thoughts were clearly on my face though and I couldn't speak. All these days, I had thought I was in love with him when...

I took a deep breath. I couldn't talk about this now. 'Listen, let's worry about this later,' I said quickly to change the subject. I didn't want to dissect my feelings at the moment. Not with Gautam sitting opposite me, anyhow.

'Gautam, this isn't just a personal issue anymore. It's bigger than all of us. Do you realize that? The whole country is virtually under him now!' I said shakily. The sheer enormity of the matter was too much to handle. It put us on par with fighting with the whole establishment!

'What do you mean?' Gautam asked.

I turned to him, my eyes wide with apprehension. 'Do you know that it's not just the Home Minister and other important ministers who are under his control? Even the Prime Minister has the Microbot in his body!' I whispered. Gautam's face paled.

Just then, my phone beeped. It was a message from Amit, 'All well?' My hands started trembling. Gautam put his hand on mine and firmly squeezed it.

'Is it from Amit?' he asked. I nodded.

'Reply to him!' he urged. I looked up dismayed. He

continued speaking, 'If you don't, he'll get suspicious. You can't even lie because he knows where you are.' He lifted his hand from mine and indicated towards my phone.

He was right. I took a deep breath, picked up the phone and quickly typed, 'Yes, sitting in Hospital Cafeteria. You ok?'

Within seconds, he replied, 'Yes, back at lab'. I put the phone away and turned back to Gautam.

'Okay, what's the plan now?' Gautam asked.

I took a deep breath. 'The Army is our only hope,' I said.

Gautam looked surprised. 'What do you mean?'

I recalled how skeptical the Army chief had been when Amit demonstrated the Microbot. 'The Army unit refused to get the Microbot injected. We should contact them and ask for help.'

Gautam looked thoughtful. Finally, he nodded. 'Let's do it. I hope it works!'

The morning passed by in a surreal manner. The two of us tried to get in touch with the Army Chief but it was not easy. After all, one couldn't just look up for his number in the telephone directory!

Finally, I had to use Amit's name to cut through various channels, hoping the Army Chief would talk to Amit out of curiosity, if nothing else.

Just as the call got connected, Gautam whispered, 'Remember, he will have a very small window to understand what you're saying. You have to explain everything fast'.

The General was surprised when he heard me speaking.

'This is Amit's fiancée, Payal, Sir,' I said, looking away from Gautam, who stiffened imperceptibly. I had to focus on the matter at hand and figure out everything else later.

'What is it? I thought Amit wanted to talk to me,' the Army Chief said gruffly.

'Sir, we have discovered a huge problem with the Microbot,' I said, my eyes focused on Gautam's back as he stared out of a window. He turned just then and smiled at me reassuringly. Feeling a bit fortified, I continued. 'At the moment, we cannot ask anyone else for help. You are our only hope.'

'What do you mean? And why are you telling that to me?' he asked, taken aback.

'I cannot explain it on the phone sir. We will have to meet.'

'Look, I'm busy...' he said but I cut him off.

'Sir, the fate of the entire nation rests in your hands,' I said, hoping he would understand the seriousness of the situation.

'What?' he asked.

'I'm not making this up, Sir. I'm serious. There's a huge problem with the Microbot and we need your help to get rid of it. There's no one else I can turn to,' I explained quickly.

'But why can't Amit do anything?' he sounded puzzled.

'He's part of the problem. Please meet me so I can explain it to you,' I entreated.

'Okay, you can drop in to our headquarters now. I'll instruct the staff to let you in.' he said finally.

But that wouldn't work. If Amit tracked my movements and found out that I was at the Army Headquarters, he'd know something was wrong.

'Actually Sir, you would have to come and meet me,' I said, realizing how absurd that sounded.

'What? Do you realize what you're asking young lady?' he boomed. I gulped and then finally said, 'It's to do with GPS.' That caught his attention.

'What GPS?' he asked. I took a deep breath.

'The Microbot is GPS enabled, which means that anyone

who has implanted the Microbot can be found, right down to their exact coordinates. And I have one in me,' I said, feeling sick at the thought. There was silence on the other end.

'Sir?' I asked him after a while.

'Okay, I'll meet you there,' he said. We sent him our coordinates.

Half an hour later, we were sitting down with the Army Chief, General AK Singh. He stroked his moustache and listened to me in silence.

Finally, he spoke. 'So you're saying that he can control people through the Microbot?' he asked. His eyes didn't reveal what he was thinking. Had he believed us or did he think this was some fantastical story I had come up with.

'We don't have proof but I know he's been doing this,' I said, telling him about Jai's email where he spoke about the two way communication between the Microbot and the server.

'And you're saying that he can track anyone who has the Microbot in their body?' he asked again. I nodded. I went over the incidents with him, quickly, counting them off on my fingers.

'Mohan, the air force pilot, Archana, Jai and now the ACP, are all people who have been victims of his machinations, Sir,' I said, wincing at how I had thought he was the love of my life.

'But again, you have no proof,' the General reminded me. I nodded.

'Sir, the President, the supreme commander of the armed forces, the Prime Minister and many more have the Microbot in them now. The risk for the nation is too high to ignore the Microbot,' Gautam urged the Army Chief. He wouldn't want to let this opportunity go. His fate was hanging in there. Our fate was hanging in there. Well, the Nation's fate as well!

When the Army Chief looked thoughtful, Gautam looked

at me and then addressed the Army Chief. 'Can't you take him into custody Sir?' he asked. The Army Chief shook his head.

'We cannot do that. Only the police can, and anyhow, we don't have any evidence of his crimes. All this is supposition and hearsay,' he said.

'Then what do you suggest?' I asked, feeling crestfallen, knowing that the police were under Amit's thumb.

'Where is Amit now?' he asked.

'He told he's at the lab,' I replied.

'What if we take him in and occupy this lab? We'll do it in such manner that no one will come to know till it is controlled' he asked.

I gasped. 'But there are people working there sir!'

'We will remove them first, don't worry. But do you think it will work?'

I shrugged. 'Honestly, I don't know. Amit had been talking about some control centers when he was setting up the Microbot. They were like mobile towers apparently, so that the Microbot could connect to the server no matter where the person went.'

'Look, if we can't find those control centers, the least we can do is demolish his power. Let's start with the lab,' he said. 'Maybe it is connected to the control center and we might get some results.'

'Who else is involved in this? He must be having a good number of people working for him,' he asked.

Dr. Sundaram's name crossed my mind. I wasn't sure if he was involved or to what extent. But, in my current state, I had no faith in myself.

I was doubtful about it but we had no recourse.

--- ✿✿✿ ---

CHAPTER - 49

Over the next couple of hours, Gautam and I watched the Army get into action. I decided that if Amit got wind about my whereabouts, it was too late for him to stop me now. Gautam went and got Nitin with him. I went along with the Army personnel towards the lab.

On our way, I noticed how quiet Nitin had become. If Amit was tracking us, he'd probably be surprised to learn that our locations were the same. I wondered if Amit would put two and two together and do something to instigate Nitin further. Or me. While that thought was scary, we continued hoping that Amit wouldn't suspect anything until the lab had been destroyed.

When I left this morning, he'd been sleeping. I had looked in on him and felt so sad when I walked away. But now, I didn't even trust my feelings. They were all probably fake. Like him.

'One good thing about this lab is that it's so far from the city,' the General commented. 'This way no one will suspect anything and we can hopefully get control of it without making a noise.'

We reached the lab and the Army personnel surrounded the lab comprehensively before we were instructed to move in.

Being employees, Nitin and I went inside first, followed by the General and few other armed men. There was no one at the reception. I quickly pressed my thumb at the fingerprint scanner and the door opened up. The armed men quickly spread inside the lab across.

Dr.Sundaram quickly moved towards us from his desk. He was visibly shaken by this sudden movement.

'What is going on here?' he asked with authority.

'We cannot tell you anything right now. We are just following our orders. We have been asked to vacate this place with immediate effect,' they replied.

'I'm not coming anywhere. I'm very busy at the moment,' the doctor said, trying to pull back his arm. His glasses were askew and his mouth was open in shock and dismay as he saw the Army take out others, similarly.

'What are you busy with?' the General asked, stepping in because the extraction procedure was taking so long.

'I work on the Microbot, like all these people here,' Dr. Sundaram said, looking around, and then his eyes widened in recognition when he spotted me.

'Payal! Tell them! What are they doing? What evacuation are they talking about?' he asked, looking dazed.

'Dr. Sundaram, I will explain everything to you. But first we need to know if Amit is here,' I said, walking up to the senior doctor who kept shaking his head as more and more of his colleagues were led outside.

'Amit is not here, he has not been in since morning' he said and my heart sank.

'We'll check his room anyway,' the General said and he sent up a couple of his men to search.

'Payal, what's happening?' Dr. Sundaram asked me again, struggling to get away from the Army men.

I signaled to them to let him go but they obviously weren't going to take orders from me. I quickly explained to the General that Dr. Sundaram might prove to be valuable for us in locating Amit. At a nod of his head, the Army men let him go and he walked towards us.

We sat down and I explained everything to him. After he had heard everything, he fell back in his chair, his eyes closed in despair.

He was one of our most respected seniors here, easily in his late fifties to early sixties. Today he looked every bit his age. Gone was the man who would banter with Amit and make jokes about us indulgently.

He opened his eyes and I could see that he was terribly disturbed. His eyes were filled with pain. He had spent precious years of his life working for the Microbot project, only for Amit to ruin everything. He looked betrayed and upset and I could perfectly feel what he was going through. It was what I was going through as well, just on a different level.

He kept shaking his head.

'Amit, what have you done? This project was one of the most important for the whole mankind! Ah! We have screwed it up this way!' he kept whispering. The General made place for himself beside the doctor and sat down.

'What do you mean by that Doctor?' he asked him.

Dr. Sundaram looked defeated as he turned to me.

'Remember the day when Amit answered all those questions that Jai and you asked?'

Of course I remembered. I'd been really impressed by Amit then. How anyone could have such an awesome memory, I had wondered.

'Well, that was not because Amit knew all the answers in all the textbooks,' he admitted.

'Then?' I asked surprised.

'During that time, we were in the initial stages of the development of the two way communication for the Microbot. The version of the Microbot that he injected in himself, along with all the ministers had the latest update of this software.

Ideally, we wanted to use this technology for psychosomatic diseases, to reduce pain by masking the brain's responses to pain. So we developed a messaging protocol with the help of engineers which would send messages to the brain through this system.'

Gautam and I shared a look. Dr. Sundaram's words just confirmed what I had feared. 'But what does this have to do with Amit answering those questions?' I asked.

Dr. Sundaram shrugged. 'He used to upload entire books through the messaging protocol into his brain as he felt that it took too long to read a book physically. Of course, reading and understanding are two different things. But he could do both. He is a genius, you know.'

'This was path breaking!' he continued in a trance, mostly talking to himself. 'It was supposed to mean that you don't need to learn a language to talk to others. Just upload the entire language pack. He tried that too, uploaded few language packs himself to test it'.

I looked down at my feet. Everything had been a sham then.

'What about GPS then? Did you know that?' I asked.

'Yes, Microbot was always GPS enabled. Especially since it was connected to Mobile towers, they were always traceable. We had developed it to help people if they were stuck under a rubble or lost somewhere or even if during some medical emergencies to locate them', he rattled out.

Wow.

I had a sudden thought and I looked up again.

'So, when you said about masking pain for psychosomatic diseases, do you think the Microbot could be used to influence someone to do something that went against their natural beliefs?' I asked.

'You mean...all those people dying...' Dr. Sundaram trailed away. He looked troubled.

'I wish I had an inkling of this. I wish I could have stopped him from such gross misuse,' he murmured. 'He had such grand dreams, such big ideas and to think that he let it all go for...'

But the General was getting impatient with Dr. Sundaram's words. He spoke curtly. 'Doctor, we have very less time on our hands. Can you tell us how to disable this system?'

'No, I don't know that. After it went live, we were not aware of how it was done. We were busy with our usual work and I think some operations team took care of it,' Dr. Sundaram, said. He kept shaking his head as though he couldn't believe what was happening.

'Where's the ops team? Who are they?' the General asked and Dr. Sundaram kept shaking his head.

'I don't know. I don't know,' he said, looking in despair.

'Can we disable or shut Microbot's power in the body ? Asked Gautham.

Dr. Sundaram, with a disappointed look, said, 'No, Microbot gets charged internally with body heat and blood flow. It cannot be shutdown till a person dies'.

'So what do you suggest? Do we blow this place up to stop this menace?' General asked. He clearly losing the patience and wanted it to end fast.

'I am not sure if this is the control center for the whole of the live Microbot. But I can see if this whole thing can be shut-down through the power source along with it's back up power.' Dr.Sundaram said.

General nodded as the Dr.Sundaram called couple of his engineers to go along with some of the army personnel to get it turned off completely.

In the meantime, the personnel who had gone in search of Amit returned empty handed and said there was no trace of him anywhere.

It was time for us to move out.

'Does anyone know who or where the ops team is?' the General shouted once, to get some response from the scientists and doctors who were vacating the building. There was no answer. Dr. Sundaram was led out and he turned to look at the building where he had spent so many years of his life, making the Microbot.

'It's all gone,' he said, his face crumpling. 'Why did he do this? Why?'

The Army Chief's face was red with exertion. He looked angry and impatient as we seemed to be running out of all options. I felt that way too. Actually, I couldn't quite describe what I was feeling. There was too much going on in my head at the moment.

'Where will they all go now?' I asked the General as we vacated the building ourselves.

The main grid was turned off. The entire building now was dark. No trace of any kind of life.

Just then we heard a thunderous noise of a helicopter over our head. All the dust and the dry leaves around us started forming a dust storm of sorts. And then it happened.

There was heavy bombardment from the top. Continuous firing was on as we all started running all scattered across the building. Gautam just grabbed my arm and started running towards the denser part of the forest.

As I turned and saw Nitin lying on the floor. He was hit by one of the bullets.

--- ❁ ❁ ❁ ---

CHAPTER - 50

It lasted for almost 15-20 minutes. We did not know what was happening.

However, we had Army on our side. Initially shaken up with this unexpected attack within our own territory, they quickly recouped and started firing back at the Chopper that was raining bullets.

I was worried for Nitin. I had clearly seen him getting hit.

I noticed him move a little. Gautam saw that too. He signaled me to stand right there and swiftly moved to the place where Nitin was lying. He quickly grabbed his shoulders and pulled him under the shade of some trees away from all this.

I was still anxious to know how he was. Gautam signaled to me that he was breathing. That was a relief. I did not want to lose one more of my friends to this madness today.

There were many others hit by the continuous machine gun bombardment. This was something out of movies for us. I could see the same fear in Dr.Sundaram and other scientists' eyes.

After few minutes, we saw some of the shots by army hitting the chopper. That must have triggered panic. The helicopter just disappeared as it had come.

Slowly, everyone started regrouping. The army personnel were now on the move to evaluate the impact of this sudden ambush. The entire lab was almost looked like a rubble. It was destroyed.

Since army personnel had surrounded the place, they were the first ones to take the hit from this ambush. We saw couple of army men hit and severely hurt.

I ran towards Nitin and Gautam. Nitin was breathing slowly. He was hit in his abdomen. He was bleeding profusely. He needed to be rushed to the hospital just as few of the others seriously injured. We had to act fast and stop the bleed.

General, who till that time was leading the forces from the front came towards us and said, 'I am sure this is not it. I am sure this is a concrete proof of what you were mentioning, Payal!' then took a pause and uttered slowly and chillingly,

'The country is in grave danger'.

--- ✿✿✿ ---

CHAPTER - 51

The General had ordered for a Chopper to take the injured to Army Hospital. Nitin was moved in there too. We assured him that he would alright as Gautam and I along with other Doctors in the team attended to as many as possible to stop the bleeding.

Now, we were there again - just stranded and not knowing what to do.

'Who was it?' everyone seemed to have the same question. But Gautam asked General.

'Don't know yet. But looks like heavily armed already. Only armed forces have such kind of ammunition in India.' Said the General, looking worried.

'Must be another one or two of Air Force pilots under his spell', he slowly made the point I was scared of. This was scary, if it was true.

General then turned to Dr.Sundaram, 'Doctor, do you think the chopper went back since it destroyed the lab hence lost out on its own signal?'

Dr.Sundaram was unsure. He said, 'If he was controlling them through this lab, why would he destroy the same lab? This may not be his main station.'

How can we find out if he still had us under his control, I thought.

There were still many from the Lab standing there confused about what they had witnessed. I turned to General asking what do we do with them.

'We will be taking them somewhere safe. I just hope they all don't have the Microbot in them or Amit might cause them to kill each other,' the General joked. I paled at his words when I realized the seriousness of the situation. It was a possibility that I hadn't considered.

'Don't keep them together!' I said suddenly.

'Don't worry. I was just joking. We are taking them to the Army Head Quarters and they will be safe there,' he assured me.

'Now we need to wait and see what the effect of this destruction of the lab has. Whether it worked.' I looked away towards the lake, hoping against hope that it had worked and the Microbot had stopped working.

'Where do we go now?' I asked, looking at Gautam.

'You can come with us. You will be out of Amit's reach,' the General said. I doubted that. If Amit could make someone attack us, Mohan crash the helicopter, or make any of the others do whatever he had wanted, he could do it from anywhere. I was never going to be out of his reach.

I felt the slightest tinge of pain near my temples. Blinking, I looked around as Gautam came up to us.

'Did it work?' he asked hopefully. The pain had morphed into tiny hammers pounding at my temples. What was happening! I shut my eyes and opened them again. I felt dizzy with pain.

'We have to wait and see,' the General responded. Both of them were unaware of what I was going through.

'Wait for what?' Gautam asked. I clutched my head as pain shot through it and words flashed inside my head. Go to Amit. You love him. He loves you. Amit. Go to Amit, the words kept repeating.

'Payal!' Gautam shouted in concern as I collapsed on the ground, convulsing in pain.

'Make it stop! Make it stop!' I shouted as I clutched my head. I could barely see what Gautam and the General were doing. I couldn't even open my eyes. I was fighting hard. Fighting an internal battle with myself.

'What's happening to her?' I could hear Gautam's scared voice as he lifted me in his arms and carried me. I wanted to crumple up somewhere and die. Maybe the pain would stop then.

'I have no idea,' the General said as they put me in the back seat of the car.

'It's Amit,' I managed to get the words out amid the red haze of pain.

'What?' Gautam asked, shock and anger evident in his voice.

'He wants me to go to him,' I murmured weakly before passing out.

---✿✿✿---

CHAPTER - 52

When I woke up, I realized we were in the car and now close to the Army headquarters. Gautam was tenderly pushing away the strands of hair that had fallen on my forehead and I smiled weakly. I sat up and touched my temples tentatively. The remnants of the pain was still there.

'I'm going to kill him when I find him!' Gautam said softly but menacingly.

'How are you now?' he asked. I nodded, unsure of saying anything.

'This is rubbish!' the General blustered as he turned around in his seat to look at me. 'If he's using the Microbot to send messages to you then obviously the lab wasn't the control center!'

Tears pooled in my eyes when I thought of the pain that I'd felt sometime back. Gautam squeezed my hand gently and then let go. I think, the General noticed it.

'Payal, have you seen the fighter pilots playing this daredevilry? The act where their jets are spinning and heading towards the earth and just before it hits the ground, this daredevil takes off once again. Have you seen any of them?' the General asked me.

I was totally surprised at this totally out of context question at this hour where the tension was gripping us. I nodded awkwardly at the question.

'You know what happens there? Since you are doctors, you sure know that there is this type of liquid in the inner ears that gives the sense of stability and balance to a human being', he continued.

'Endolymph', Gautam said almost disinterestingly, not knowing where this was heading to.

'Yes, that stuff.' The General said with a smile. 'Being a liquid, when the plane is falling and spiraling, after couple of spins, the liquid inside the ear also starts spinning. Once the liquid and the plane's spirals are in sync, the mind starts giving you a message that everything is alright.'

Now, he had all our attention.

'We train the pilots to ignore the inner messages, which they always knew to listen to since childhood and start believing the machine that tells you that you are falling. The machine tells you to pull up, while your brain tells you that you are okay!'

'Now, Payal, that is one of the things you have to quickly adapt and learn not to listen to your brain's instructions. Take the right decision even though your mind is divided right now. You have to focus and select the right one. That is the only way you can beat him at it.'

I was mesmerized listening to him. I knew I had to fight. This was something different.

Gautam then intervened to bring us back on track.

'You said that Amit has another lab in his house? Maybe the control center is there,' Gautam suggested. The General's eyes lit up momentarily.

'But we can't blast that lab! It's in a primary residential area,' I protested. It was my house. The home I had set up with him. Physical pain was one thing. This was something else altogether.

'What if we go to the house and confine Amit inside another room so he cannot use the control center? Or use Dr.Sundaram's people to get the lab off the grid?' the General suggested.

I looked at Gautam. It seemed like a really long shot but it was the only option we had left. So instead of heading towards the Army Headquarters, the car moved towards Janakpuri and I settled back in my seat, worried of how I would face the pain if Amit decided to use it again. The General quickly made some calls instructing all to move to different coordinates.

When the huge group of the Army personnel descended on the house that had been my own until this morning, I realized immediately that Amit wasn't there. I just knew it. Couple of servants at home were completely scared and they froze looking at the armed men moving inside the house. I asked them to go back to their rooms in the out-house.

I ran in and went straight to Amit's study and saw that his laptop wasn't there. I pushed open the door to the lab and saw that it was pretty much intact. The entire team was running behind me.

'He's not here,' I called out. The General came inside and stood beside me as I looked at the screen that showed the active Microbots out there. The dots were moving around constantly.

Gautam was looking around at the equipment with a great deal of interest. If things had been different, I'd have been embarrassed to have Gautam here in this house, where I'd lived with Amit for months. But now, there was nothing to feel.

'Why do the brilliant ones choose the wrong path?' he wondered loudly.

I wish I knew. What Amit had achieved with the Microbot had been magnificent but when had he turned to the other side? When had he allowed dark thoughts to claim who he was? And more importantly, why?

'I know how we can locate Amit,' I said, looking at the left-hand side of the screen where I'd looked up Nitin's location last night.

'Are you sure you can do this?' Gautam asked, coming to stand behind me. I turned around to him. What did he mean?

'I mean...' he saw the question in my eyes. 'You are in love with him and...'

I shook my head firmly.

'Not are. Was. I was in love with him and even that may not be real,' I said bitterly and turned away. I moved up closer to the screen and tapped on Amit's name. The right hand side of the screen lit up with Amit's coordinates.

The General moved closer to me, shaking his head in amazement.

'Thank God I didn't allow him to inject the Microbot in my people. Imagine how dangerous it would be for the soldiers if their locations could be so easily pin pointed. If this information is sold to the wrong hands? Disaster!' he said.

'Bloody hell,' he muttered when the name of the location popped up seconds after the coordinates were displayed. 'He's in the Air Force headquarters'

---❁❁❁---

CHAPTER - 53

The General smiled at us reassuringly. 'I'll talk to Rocky and get it sorted out'.

Rocky? Both Gautam and I looked at each other in confusion.

The General smiled slightly. 'The Air Chief Marshal. Back in our NDA days, we used to call him Rocky because he looked like Rock Hudson, the famous Hollywood star. He even used to dress like that.' Then, shaking his head, he snapped back into business mode. He picked up the phone to call up the Air Chief Marshal.

'Rocky! It's been a while!' the General started. 'I know, yes. Okay, you probably know why I've called. I need you to hand over Amit,' he exhaled. The General fell silent as the Air Chief Marshal spoke but going by the General's reactions, it wasn't good news.

'Listen to me, Rocky! He is evil. You don't know what he has done. I have just witnessed it myself. This is snowballing in to a major crisis for the nation,' he pleaded. It wasn't just his contemporary he was talking to now. It was also his friend.

The room fell silent and we could hear the muffled voice of the Air Force Chief but we couldn't make out what was being said.

'What do you mean I have no proof?' the General bellowed. Gautam and I looked at each other apprehensively. 'That man has done much harm already! Looks like we were attacked by one your Choppers. The lab now is destroyed. He tried to kill all of us through manipulation.'

There was a pause.

'No!' he shouted, 'We did not shoot your chopper down! They shot us! We fired in defense and they just took off after destroying the lab! A lot of people are injured - a couple very grievously. We did not even know that it was an Airforce chopper!'

There was an awkward pause, and the General slowly asked, 'Did you know about the attack? Did you order that?'

This was getting catastrophic. It was getting snowballed in to something massive!

We watched the General pace around in the room angrily as he listened to the arguments from the other side. 'Amit is an honest and upright man? What nonsense! He's controlling you. You're not in the right frame of mind!' The Air Chief Marshall said something again.

'You can't let him hide out there!' the General shouted.

'No, you listen. If you continue to harbor him, there will be consequences,' the General threatened. Gautam and I looked at each other in panic. What could he mean?

'Yes. I mean it. We're in Amit's house right now, sitting in his lab where he has been accessing your location and everyone else who has the Microbot in them. Not only that, he's been messing with your minds as well!' the General explained with an increasing sense of impatience in his voice.

I looked down at the floor, wishing I'd been a little more alert.

'You have to hand over Amit or there will be a conflict situation the likes of which you have never seen in your entire life,' the General spat out and ended the call.

He looked at the two of us, his eyes flashing in anger.

'That Amit has Rocky firmly wrapped around his little finger!' he said, expelling a breath loudly.

'What did you mean by conflict situation, Sir?' Gautam asked cautiously.

'What do you think?' the General snapped at him, pacing back and forth. 'They think it is us who have shot down their chopper. He does not believe that his Chopper attacked us!'

'This is unprecedented. Conflict between two services will generally never happen given the hard core ethos built into the basic character of the armed forces. But the situation here calls for it,' he said, as though he was trying to convince himself to assure he was on the right path.

'I have to fight them to save them from all this', he exclaimed.

I wasn't sure that he had been serious but the look on his face meant that he had no qualms about carrying out his threat. This was getting worse than what I'd imagined!

Amit had actually caused a rift between the Army and the Air Force, I thought, panic clenching inside me.

To add to our troubles, one of the Army personnel came and informed us that a police team was waiting for us outside. We walked outside to the hall and a grim faced inspector waited near the sofa.

'Sir, you will have to vacate this house immediately,' he said. The General bristled at this.

'What do you mean?' he asked importantly. Anyone else would have quailed at his tone but the inspector looked unfazed.

'Sir, this house belongs to Dr. Amit Deshpande and you are occupying it unlawfully. You need to vacate it,' he said.

The General turned to us and addressed me. 'This Amit chap works fast, doesn't he?'. I nodded unhappily.

'This is my house too,' I said suddenly, uncomfortable in the silence that had fallen when I spoke. I sensed Gautam stiffening beside me.

'What do you mean, madam?' the inspector asked.

I took a deep breath. 'I am Dr. Amit's fiancée,' I forced the words out.

'I'm sorry. That won't work. Unless you're married to him or the house is in your name as well, you're all trespassing on private property,' the inspector said stiffly.

'Now you wait here a second,' the General interrupted. 'You go back and tell that Amit to do what he wants. We're not leaving until we have him in our control. You are supposed to be arresting him instead of harboring him!'

I noticed that he hadn't come alone. There was a group of policemen with him who stared at us aggressively. I looked at them nervously as they walked towards the door.

General then pointed to his heavily armed men and said in a menacing voice, 'How do you plan to fight us, Inspector? You with your army?'

'Sir, we're leaving now but it would be in your best interest if you vacate immediately,' he said.

'Otherwise?' the General pointed to the army men with him who had enough armory to blow up half the city.

'Otherwise I'm afraid we will have to forcibly remove you and we won't hesitate to take the help of the Air Force if required,' he pronounced coolly.

He left, leaving us speechless.

CHAPTER - 54

I understood what the General meant by conflict situation now. Amit had brought the nation to its knees by antagonizing the Air Force and Police against the Army. He had done what had been inconceivable!

While the General was still coming to terms with how Amit had managed to net both the Police and the Air Force, his mobile phone rang. It was the Home Minister. He answered the call with a frown on his face.

The Army Chief's face reddened as he continued speaking to him. 'Absolutely not! Can't you see what's happening?' The Home Minister spoke again and the Army Chief listened in silence for a little while.

'No, we're not going to let you do this. No,' he said and ended the call. His face was thunderous as he held his mobile phone in his hand, looking like he wanted nothing better than to fling the phone at the wall.

Obviously, the Home Minister too was on Amit's side. I quailed to think of the number of people who were under Amit's influence now. The Police, Air Force and so many ministers.

He shook his head and turned around to us and spoke forcefully.

'Team, we are in a grave situation. One that our country has never witnessed. We cannot let go now. We are at a point of no return. We may have just an hour or so, before the entire situation escalates. And by that I meant, it could reach the President and the Prime Minister, who we know are also under Amit's control. I have no idea what it could lead to.

Prepare yourself for the worst. They might dishonor me and discharge me from duty or who knows, they could resort to severe action, and they may even bomb this place.'

WHAT!

We looked at each other dazed. I couldn't believe Amit would actually bomb this place, his house! But once again, the doorbell rang. The General shot a look at one of his people who ran and opened the door.

'Post someone near the gates. Get some tanks as well if we need reinforcements. Get some anti-aircraft guns as well. I don't want anyone coming in,' the General called out to someone else. I peered to see who was at the door. The Army cadet who had gone to open the door shut it forcefully and returned to us.

'Who was it?' the General asked him.

The cadet looked nervous. 'Sir, there are many journalists and media vans outside,' he said.

'Journalists?' the General asked, puzzled. 'What do they want?'

The cadet looked uncomfortable. 'They wanted to know if the Army was moving in to Delhi with the intention of occupying the city,' he said. The General growled in anger.

'What? Tell them that it is routine exercise to counter internal threats such as terrorists' he snarled out.

Amit was using every trick in the book to get us to vacate his house. First he sent the police and now he was sending in media, to pressure the Army into leaving. I was finding it hard to fathom that the man who had meant the world to me was responsible for the world crumbling under my feet.

---❁❁❁---

CHAPTER - 55

When he had controlled his anger to an extent, the General turned to me. 'It's obvious the control center is not here. Or how would he be able to manipulate everyone like this? We need to find a solution NOW,' he said.

'Sir, is it possible to bring a few of the software engineers here? Those whom we removed from the lab before the blast?' I asked suddenly. Gautam looked at me surprised.

'Yes, but why?' he asked.

'They may be able to try and hack into the system if we provide them with the right kind of tools and the lab might have everything we need,' I suggested. The General nodded and spoke to someone over the phone.

It took flat 15 minutes for the software engineers to reach the house. Army vehicles might have done the wonders. By then, we were all very tense and wound up. Anything could happen, now that Amit had shown just how powerful he was.

Predictably, they were all uneasy about the situation. They were wary and upset because the lab where they had spent years doing research and collecting the Microbot data and analyzing it was gone. But they were not aware of all the details.

Dr. Sundaram too was with them. He was looking around the house with a great deal of interest, probably wondering how Amit had managed to make so much money to buy such a huge house.

'How many of you have the Microbot?' I asked them. A few of them raised their hands.

Thankfully, those were just a few and surprisingly, Dr. Sundaram was not one of them. My face contorted in pain suddenly as the headache began once more. Amit had probably seen that we were not letting go of the house and he was just increasing the pressure from his side. Literally.

I clutched my head with my hands and collapsed to the ground. Gautam caught me before I fell and he managed to get me into a sitting position. I was still clutching my head.

'The pain!' I cried and shut my eyes tightly. Amit had renewed his assault on my mind, telling me that he needed me and he wanted me to join him. I realized that his attack was two-fold. Messages interspersed with pain.

'What happened to her?' Dr. Sundaram asked, shocked, as Gautam massaged my temples slowly.

'It's Amit,' said Gautam.

I managed to point to my medical kit. Gautam ran towards it and took out heavy dosage of pain-killer injections. Usually, we used these in case of severe burn victims or accidents. I had them in bag as I usually attended most of the neuro accident cases.

Finally, the pain subsided. Breathing heavily, I turned to the group of people who were looking at me with a great deal of interest.

'Have you been getting any ideas to do certain things that you would normally never do?' I spoke slowly, addressing those who had the Microbot. Some of them frowned but they all shook their head. I wasn't taking any chances though. Amit was desperate and if he found out that the software engineers with the Microbot were in the lab at this house, he might try to induce them to do something violent.

'Sir, send these people somewhere safe, ' I told the Army Chief. He looked bemused.

'Make up your mind, young woman. You wanted them to come and now you want them to go?' he asked.

'No, I want these people, without the Microbot, to remain.' He nodded, understanding what I wanted and then gruffly gave orders for the rest of them to be taken away.

I heard one of them muttering about 'noises in his head' as he was led outside and I knew I'd been right to send them away. Amit would get to them the moment he knew they were with us.

I led them to the mini lab inside the study and quickly apprised them of the current situation, especially regarding the people who had the Microbot in them. The team looked shocked. It took Dr.Sundaram to convince them of what was happening.

'I knew about the messaging protocol. I even told that other chap, Jai, about it. But I didn't know that Amit was actually using it to do something like this!' one of them said loudly, disbelievingly.

'Well he's certainly using it, and he's making a pretty good mess of things. He's got the Army and the Air Force at loggerheads with each other, the Police are in his pocket and the media at his beck and call. Unless we do something to stop him, we might see a civil war of the kind that has never been seen before,' I said, impassioned.

Gautam slid his hand into mine and tightened his grip in a show of support. I pulled my hand out, still feeling sick about how I had treated him and had fallen for Amit. Now was certainly not the time to dwell on that but the thoughts came on their own, and these were not Microbot influenced, for sure.

'So can you guys hack into the system?' I asked. They looked thoughtful and mostly doubtful.

One of them spoke up finally. 'Look, we can try and hack into it. But it will take us days,' he said.

'Days!' the General exploded. 'We have mere hours. Not even that. Minutes. Who knows what that fellow is up to right now?'

I looked at him fearfully. He was right. I was afraid of even myself. If Amit could make Nitin kill Jai, who knew what he might get me to do? No one was safe with me around as well.

'I'm sorry but we don't have the admin password or we'd have easily got into the system,' the software engineer spoke.

'Think of something,' the General urged looking at all of us. The urgency of the situation was not lost on me. That was when something snapped inside my head and I turned to Gautam.

'Nitin!' I said.

---✿✿✿---

CHAPTER - 56

'What about Nitin?' Gautam asked me in surprise.

'He knows the admin password! Remember?' I said in a rush.

Only then I recalled that Gautam hadn't been around for all of this and he'd probably forgotten Nitin's role in the whole story. I quickly updated them about how the password had just appeared to Nitin, and he had used it to delete Mohan's report.

'Can we get Nitin here?', I said excitedly.

Gautam wasn't convinced, 'Payal, he is gravely injured. I am not sure if he can make it, if he is not already in some kind of operation to remove any kind of bullets from his abdomen.'

'Are you sure about this Nitin chap, Payal? I can arrange to get him as this situation is more important than each one of our lives, but we need to be sure.' the General asked me. I nodded my head vigorously.

'What if Amit changed the password after that?' he asked and my face fell. I hadn't thought of that.

'No harm in trying,' I responded. 'After all Amit may not have thought much of Nitin other than being a temporary pawn in his game.'

'Well, let's hope you're right,' he said.

'Okay, here is what we'll do. Let me try and organize our own rescue choppers to move him out of hospital along with all the doctors and get him here.' Said the General.

'No, it's not practical. I'll go there instead', offered Gautam.

'If he is conscious, I can make him talk', he opined. It sounded reasonable.

Next few minutes, we heard a chopper on top of the house. Our first reaction though, having just survived a chopper attack, was if Air Force chopper was back.

Thankfully, it was that of the army, came to fly Gautam to the Hospital where Nitin was admitted.

While leaving, he just pressed my hand and said, 'Payal, you are the one to do this. I know you can.'

There was an element of pride, grit and faith in his eyes.

---❁❁❁---

CHAPTER - 57

Gautam called on my mobile. I quickly picked it up and kept on speaker phone so that everyone could hear.

'Payal, I just got in on time. They were planning to take him in to the operation theatre now. We don't have a lot of time. He is still awake but very unstable. In any case, I'll go to his room now and put him on as well.'

Nitin was not sounding himself. Amit had messed around in his mind quite a bit and made him commit murder. Obviously he was a changed person. Adding to that this attack and getting hit must have driven him to the brink.

It took a lot of cajoling to ask him if he remembered the password. I was nervous now because if this didn't work out, then we could do nothing. The thought of what would result was terrifying to me - a faceoff between the Army and the Air Force. There was no way the country could survive that.

'Nitin, do you remember the password you used, to delete Mohan's reports?' I asked him.

'Who's Mohan?' he asked. Oh God! Had Amit erased all memories from Nitin's head? Was that even possible? I looked at Dr. Sundaram, the query clearly on my face.

'Well, he can't completely remove the memory,' Dr. Sundaram said. 'At best, he can suppress it. But to be honest, I don't think this is Amit's work. This poor boy here has suppressed the memory himself because it is connected to something painful, I think.'

'So Amit may not have accessed Nitin yet?' I asked, even though I had no hopes now. If Nitin couldn't remember

Mohan, then how would he remember deleting the report?

Gautam then softly spoke to Nitin 'Nitin, remember Archana?'

Nitin's voice changed as if to weep. 'Archana's dead,' he said painfully slowly.

'Do you know why she died?' Gautam asked him gently.

'No. But I couldn't save her', he said in a low voice.

'Because Amit made her do it. He made her stand by and watch Mohan die. He made you delete the reports from the server. He made you kill Jai,' Gautam said, his voice breaking off.

Nitin started crying.

'He's having a mental breakdown,' Dr. Sundaram said. The General looked impatient.

'Can he remember the password?' he asked.

'Nitin, you told Jai you got the password to access the server, into your head, just like that. Do you still remember the password?' I asked in very soft voice as if I was talking to a small kid.

I could sense Gautam's anger towards Amit and I shared it too. The love that I had felt for him had disintegrated completely.

'I...I think I remember it,' Nitin said, finally.

Gautam said he handed him a paper and pen and he wrote down the password in a shaky hand, crossed it out a few times, threw the sheet of paper away and then wrote it down on a new sheet of paper, as we all waited patiently in complete silence. He handed the paper to Gautam.

Gautam spelled each character one by one slowly over the phone. The connection was bad. We had to hear every single character twice.

Gautam said then, 'Guys, if delay any further, Nitin won't make it. So I am sending him in to the OT'. And he cut the phone

I gave the password to the software engineer who typed it in the computer. And we all waited with bated breath.

Would it work? Would we be able to access the control center ourselves?

It worked! Amit's conceit had made him think he was above all forms of reproach. It would be his costliest mistake, I thought.

'Now that you're in the system, what did you hope to achieve?' the General asked, stroking his chin, looking troubled.

'The first thing to do,' Dr.Sundaram said angrily, 'is to change the admin password and every other damn password out there! That'll stop the monster from accessing the system'. I nodded. The engineers proceeded to change the passwords and then looked at me expectantly. That was when a thought occurred to me.

'Sir, once the engineers figure out the messaging protocol that Amit uses to control people, then we can use it to control him. After all, he too has the Microbot embedded in him!' I said excitedly.

'Message him for what?' he looked lost.

'To send us the control center's location!'

'Does that mean the control center isn't located here?' he asked doubtfully.

One of the engineers looked up. 'Chances for that are less. You need commercial grade power connection, equipment and backup. We don't see any of that around.'

'Oh! Well then, let's hope that it works. If it's within the country, we may need thirty minutes at the most to reach and destroy it. I'll get all my long range missiles ready if we need one,' he said.

We watched as the software engineers worked on the system, tapping away at keys and finally one of them lifted his head.

'We're in. We can send his Microbot a message,' he said.

I wanted to clap my hands but I realized that I wasn't feeling any glee. It was more a case of 'getting this over with'.

'Let's go full throttle, boys! Well done!' an excited Dr.Sundaram exclaimed.

---❁❁❁---

CHAPTER - 58

Amit must have relished the sense of power there was in controlling another person's actions. But I didn't feel it when we finally sent him the message. I felt sick. I felt used and desperate enough to try his own tactics back on him. We had asked him to give up the location of the control center. Once the message had gone, we waited.

'Do it again,' I said when nothing happened after five minutes. I had controlled my urge to go to Amit despite his constant efforts, and he had responded to my 'disobedience' by unleashing pain upon me. Even though this was the first time he was on the receiving end, where he was being asked to do something he didn't want to do, I knew that Amit was resisting it. After all, by now he would have wised up and he probably knew that we had access to the messaging system now.

Just then Gautam came back. The chopper that brought him back was kept there for any kind of emergencies.

Because of all these activities, along with media a lot of people gathered around the house, just curious to know what was going on! That was even dangerous.

I glanced at Gautam as he walked in. He was looking around in the study. He had come across the photographs that Amit had stashed in his desk and he looked up at me, questions in his eyes. I shrugged and looked away. I didn't know what I was going to do when all this was over but I was glad Gautam was back to being my friend.

I turned to the engineers. 'Try once more,' I ted my words to the engineers. They looked at me doubtfully. 'Just do it,' I urged them. The only way to stop this madness would be to give Amit a taste of his own medicine.

My phone started ringing and I saw that it was a call from Amit. I looked up and whispered his name and everyone looked at me expectantly.

'Answer it!' the General said. I nodded and swiped across the screen, switched on the speaker phone and kept the phone on the table.

'Payal,' Amit's disembodied voice floated up. I shut my eyes momentarily.

'The game is over Amit. Send in the control center location,' I opened my eyes and spoke briskly.

'Just listen to me,' he said.

'No. There's no time. We need the location of the control center now,' I replied and nodded towards the software engineer sitting at the computer. He understood my signal and sent another message to Amit.

'Look. I need to talk to you,' he said, his voice wavering because he was trying to fight his own mind.

I folded my arms across my chest.

'I never meant for any of this to happen. I didn't want all these people dying but once it started, it snowballed out of control,' he said, trying to explain.

'You were always in control Amit. You controlled others as well,' I said firmly.

'I...I just wanted things to work in my favor. What is wrong with that?' he asked. I looked at the phone in disbelief.

'What is wrong? You have caused so much suffering and pain to so many people!' I shouted at him.

'I never wanted all this, remember? I just wanted to help people!' he protested. I shook my head.

'If you really wanted to help people, then you wouldn't have killed them!' I replied angrily.

'I'm not a murderer! The minister had to die as he was not cooperating but Mohan, Archana, Jai were all collateral damages.' his voice crackled through the speaker phone.

'Look, you're wasting our time. Just tell us the location of the control center and let's be done with this,' I told him.

'Don't let me down now, Payal! I did it all for you and you initiated it. Remember? You were the one who told me to accept the Home Minister's offer. You know I love you more than anything else! I fell in love with you the moment I saw you. I remember every single moment from that day, Payal! Please don't let me down today!' he continued to plead.

'You remember the day you saw me in the parking lot? I knew you were looking at me. I knew you wanted to escape from the clutches of that loser. I had to liberate you from him. And this is how you repay me for all the love I gave you?' he asked.

Gautam looked angry on hearing these words but I shook my head, indicating him to keep quiet.

'So you admit you made me fall in love with you,' I said, wincing when I thought of all that had happened.

'Well, I had to do something. I couldn't let you slip away,' he replied. The General pointed to his wrist watch and shook his head. We were wasting time.

'Amit, this is enough. You know you've been cornered. It's better to cut your losses now and surrender yourself to the police,' I said.

'That, is NEVER going to happen,' he said and ended the call. I stared at the phone in surprise and then, angrily turned to the software engineers.

'Just bombard him with messages until he goes mad!' I said. 'And if that doesn't work, Dr. Sundaram, can you tell them how to give him a massive headache like how he gave me?'

Dr. Sundaram sighed and nodded.

'Do it. He'll give up the coordinates once he knows we're not going to stop for even a second,' I urged him.

The anger inside me refused to lessen. He had actually admitted to making me fall in love with him. But that was just one aspect. When I thought of the innocent lives that were lost, I was afraid I wanted to give him more than headaches. But I realized that Gautam was watching me carefully. I couldn't become like Amit, just to make him give up the co-ordinates. So getting revenge was out of the question.

The General let out a huge breath. 'Look, I have the Army helicopters on standby waiting for my word to come through. But they are slow. I would have loved to have the Air Force help us out here. But nevertheless, once we know the location, as long as it's in India, we will destroy it in minutes.'

'Once we get the location, we could even use BrahMos. Due to the onboard inertial navigation system with three gyroscopes and three accelerometers, BrahMos is a 'fire and forget' weapon, requiring no further guidance once the target has been assigned and it is launched. That'll do the job wherever it is within the country!'

It sounded like he was convincing himself rather than instructing his subordinates. Two of his officers took the cue and ran out, phones glued to their ears, may be to organize the weapon and keep it ready.

'Okay sir,' I said, covering my eyes with my hands. I was tired. I wanted my life back. Even the anger against Amit had exhausted me. I didn't realize when Gautam had come to my side so I was surprised when he picked up my hand once again. This time I did not pull it out. I wondered how long it would take for Amit to relent.

When there was still no response after ten minutes, I asked them to change the tone of the message.

'Threaten him. Tell him if he doesn't give up the location in five minutes, we will make his head explode with pain,' I told them. They tapped away the message swiftly.

'And give him a dose of the pain as well.' I was screaming now.

Within minutes, I heard a beeping sound from my phone.

---•••---

CHAPTER - 59

It was a text message from Amit.

'He's sent the location,' I called out, unable to believe it.

Reading out loud the coordinates of a secluded spot in Western Ghats near Pune, I started jumping in joy. The General nodded and took the phone from me and passed on the coordinates to his pilots who were waiting to destroy the control center.

'It's over?' I asked him and he nodded and said, 'In a few minutes'.

He had used BrahMos and to back it up, he had used choppers from his Pune base to reconfirm the destruction of the control center. He did not want to leave any stone unturned now.

Just as we were waiting, he got the confirmations from a couple of his sources.

'I think everyone, will start behaving normally once again. So let me call up the Air Force Marshal and see if he will give up Amit now,' he said. He dialed the number and spoke.

'I see. You didn't know what was happening? Yes. I know. That's what I tried to tell you. He's not a savior of people. He's a killer. Block him right now and pin him down before he does something more drastic', he said and then loudly exclaimed,

'What?'

Gautam and I looked at each other. What had Amit done now?

'Goddammit! I should have known this would happen,' we should have sent massage to Airforce chief to arrest Amit first" the General shut his eyes wearily as he ended the call.

'What happened sir?' I asked.

'He's gone. Escaped,' he said.

'But this happened just now. How could he have escaped so quickly?' I asked surprised.

'Well he must have given up the coordinates to stop the relentless messaging and the pain. And he must have left immediately because he knew that the Microbots would stop acting once the control towers were destroyed,' the General said.

I walked up to the screen where the dots had been moving and saw that all the dots were stationary now. I tapped on Amit's dot and the message flashed up -'Inactive'. I checked all our dots. The message was the same.

The Microbot had stopped working.

A part of me was relieved that destroying the control center had worked finally and none of us were under Amit's insidious control. A part of me was sad that so many people, my friends particularly, had lost their lives to Amit's nefarious schemes. But a greater part of me was angry that he had got away.

'Let's go Payal,' Gautam said.

I had no idea what would happen to me now, where I would go, what I would do. I didn't glance around even once at the house that had been my home for so many days now. It had all been a sham and I'd fallen for it. The amount of disappointment and anger in me, almost made me feel dizzy. Then I realized it was because I hadn't eaten anything for a long time.

'Gautam let's go the hospital cafeteria and get something to eat,' I told him. He nodded and we left together.

As we stepped out on the street, people brushed past us as we walked on the road and I realized they had no idea that Gautam and I, with the help of the Army, had just saved the country. We had prevented a civil war and stopped so many more lives from being wasted.

No one knew that the nation had been on the brink of such horror.

No one ever would.

---✿✿✿---

EPILOGUE

Payal looked at us and I shook my head in amazement.

'That was some story!' I exclaimed.

They looked at each other and smiled. They knew the impact they had made on me. For last five days of the cruise, I had just been living Payal's life.

'That was simply amazing, General! To think that it was your 'biggest war' as well! I would love to write about this. Can I? What do you think?' I asked, looking at the two of them.

The General smiled and asked, 'Would anyone believe you?'

'Of course not! I will make sure that I keep this as fiction. I still can't believe it myself. It is going to take some time to sink in.'

In the meanwhile, Dr. Gautam walked up to the table and announced that the cruise was docking and people were getting down, hinting we should move on as well.

As we were exchanging pleasantries, the staff of the cruise wished us well but just as we were making our way towards the bridge, I noticed that Payal's face had paled all of a sudden. Gautam too had noticed the change in her face.

'What is it?' he asked, putting a hand over her shoulder.

Payal was breathing heavily and dots of perspiration had broken out on her forehead, and she looked around a little frantically. We all followed her gaze, wondering what was going on.

'Payal, what is it?' Gautam asked, shaking her shoulder gently.

'Amit. He spoke just now,' she said, looking around almost fearfully.

'What?' we all looked at her shocked. For me, the story became all the more real just then.

'You can hear him? In your head?' Gautam asked, his voice low and angry. Payal nodded.

'He said: You look lovely in this blue saree, but I miss my Payal ki Jhankar the most!'

---✿✿✿---

ACKNOWLEDGEMENTS

A novel, as they say, is born through multiple births - from the day a story was conceived in the author's mind to the days that the story starts taking shape on a paper (say, MS Word now), or an editor picks it up, or the day reviewers give their critical comments to change the course of the novel.

Divided Minds had a similar fate.

At first, it was a concept that was born out of multiple independent news articles I read on different things.

Then, it was my family, Nalini and Suresh Koppikar - my parents; Varsha, my wife; Yash, my son; Savita and Sujata - my sisters; Ameya - my nephew and Shree (Shreenatha Narayana), my friend and colleague, were the first one's to hear and appreciate the story and encouraged me to write this up. (In fact, they asked me to make a movie out of it!)

Once story took its birth, it was Andaleeb Wajid, a well-known author and a wordsmith, who nourished and polished it. In fact, it was Andaleeb who suggested the name 'Divided Minds'. It was the first time that I was writing with the protagonist and the story-teller being a woman. It was very important for me as no other character would have shown the sense of betrayal, courage mixed with amazement of things happening around. It was Andaleeb helped me with subtle nuances that a girl of mid-twenties would go through. I couldn't be more thankful.

Once it was written and edited, I was still in doubt if I had treated the novel well-enough. Hence, I sent it to few of my family and friends cutting across different generations and geographies. I received absolutely brilliant feedback and review comments that resulted in changing at least 30-40% of the novel once again!

A big thank you to Arun Hiremath, Col.R.N.Ghosh, Naintara Aralimarad, Manasi Baindur, Aarathi Varadachar, Savita Koppikar, Sreevidya Tharakaram and my Dad, Suresh Koppikar for those great feedback and detailed reviews. You helped me make the novel stronger.

Thanks Shreenatha Narayana & Varsha Koppikar for multiple re-reads and feedback.

Thanks Sapna Ink, Darshit Shah and Paresh Shah for the publishing.

Thanks NotionPress team for marketing and distribution.

There are many people who support me in this madness regardless of the situations. Thanks for standing by me and supporting me - my in-laws, Sheela and Sharad Shirali, Mallikarjun Hiremani, Rotarians of Indiranagar Friends in PickleJar and FTGMP and many friends and family. You are my strength!

Thanks to all readers for your valuable time. I hope you found it enjoyable.

--- ✿✿✿ ---